"Flesh demands sacrifice for its existence."

– Cālix Leigh-Reign

Contents

"Never confuse lust for anything other than what it is. There isn't a man alive that wouldn't gladly take what you are so willing to offer."

— Pawn of Innocence,
Chameleon

Chapter

ONE

ZIA FANCIFULLY INDULGES in imagined rehearsal as her five-inch stilettos click against the pavement outside of Fargo Tower, with layers of her former self beneath her dainty feet, making each new step more delightful than the last.

Danish pastry, smog, and budding tuberose tickle the back of her throat with mounting resolve that not one more rebellious day will escape where she'll allow herself to come up empty-handed.

There are tons of polished gems buried beneath the daunting heap of amateur first drafts. She just needs to dig her hands into the muddy slush pile and pull them out. She envisions the gleeful moment of discovery several more times before pushing through the revolving glass door.

After the writer's conferences in New York, she's surprisingly relieved to be back in Los Angeles. She ponders the irony of how she'd loathed the setting one minute, only to crave it the next. When she'd left a few weeks ago, she'd become so exasperated with her lackluster career she'd absentmindedly passed up a juicy manuscript, which eventually landed on her colleague's desk. A colleague who has since been promoted to senior agent.

Since she'd impatiently skimmed through the query and sample pages that launched an obnoxious colleague's career and is now battling regret with a sword of tenacity, there are certain distractions she's forfeited. The first being her last ounce of socialism.

She steps into the elevator and presses the button for the corresponding floor to Spark Worldwide Literary while trying not to drop her double-shot, caramel-pumpkin spice latte in the process. She needs the coffee more than life itself right now.

She barely notices the shuffling bodies entering and exiting as she prioritizes the day in her head.

"Slush," she sighs while visualizing the never-ending nuisance of grammatical errors that slow down her reading.

"I take it that you don't like slush," a deep voice vibrates, startling her. Her heart thumps.

"Oh! I'm so sorry. I didn't realize that…I…"

"It's quite alright. Happens to me all the time." The tall handsome stranger's voice rumbles in a deep, resonating, southern twang.

She glances over her shoulder as he switches his iPhone from his right hand into his left. She sighs once more while nervously tucking the wayward strands of her wavy brown hair behind her right ear.

"I've never seen you here before." She inadvertently reveals both curiosity and wariness.

"Yeah, I just transferred to Banks & Filmore. My name is Bryce. Bryce Fink." His penetrating eyes simmer as he extends his right hand towards her.

Zia glances at his hand as it hangs ambivalently in the air before quickly reminding herself that a greeting isn't a commitment or a date.

"Zia. Nice to meet you and welcome to the building." When she places her tiny hand inside of his, her anxiety stirs, so she courteously withdraws her hand.

"Thank you kindly, Miss…"

"Just Zia."

"Well, just Zia, thank you for the warm welcome."

His grip isn't as strong as one would expect, considering the muscular biceps bulging through his blazer. His hands are soft, so she assumes he couldn't be anything more than a paper-pusher at the law firm. Possibly an intern. He looks much too young to be an attorney.

His black tailored suit screams of a maxed-out credit card to exude a level of wealth he likely doesn't possess.

"Are you a Banks & Filmore employee?"

"No." Just when she considers elaborating further, the elevator announces they've arrived on the 6th floor; neither her stop nor his since B&F is on the top floor and Spark is on the 11th.

The door opens and Lillia White from TransMedia joins them for the ride, cradling a stack of manila envelopes in her left arm.

"Hi, Zia! You're back! How was New York?"

Lillia embraces her friend, who quickly decides not to discuss anything about herself in front of the total stranger who calls himself Bryce. She can easily avoid this conversation by asking Lillia the right question since Lillia's one of those people who doesn't really listen. She just waits for her turn to talk.

"It was nice, Lillia. How are you and the family?"

As Lillia chatters on incessantly about her two toddler sons and husband, Zia smiles politely while ignoring the hole the stranger is burning into the back of her head. For every word Lillia speaks, more oxygen is sucked from the small space and Zia's skin tingles from the moist warmth. When the elevator finally announces their arrival on the 11th floor, relief washes over her.

"Well, Lillia. I'm sure I'll be seeing you later today for lunch."

"Great! See you then and welcome back!"

She hastily exits the seemingly cramped elevator and nearly falls on her face. She balances herself while waving at Lillia, noticing the stranger is staring directly at her.

"It was nice meeting you, just Zia." He winks as the elevator door closes.

She blushes but marches forward, pushing the frosted glass doors open. Jazmine, Spark's administrative assistant extraordinaire, greets her as she enters.

"Welcome back, Zia!"

"Thanks, Jazz."

Jazz smiles warmly while hugging Zia from across the desk. Jazz is preoccupied with receptionist trainee, Jennifer. Jazz monitors the protégé as she takes calls but still simultaneously brings Zia up to speed.

"I'm sure you wanna get right to it. So, for starters, your recent snails have been arranged chronologically on your desk, courtesy of yours truly. No one has touched your digital slush. HR hasn't sent us any assistants or interns, so all associate and junior agents are still on their own for the moment. A fresh pot of coffee is brewing and here are your messages."

Jazz is an administrative ninja and Zia honestly doesn't know what their sector would do without her. The switchboard lights up as Zia grabs the yellow slips of paper from her grasp.

"Thanks, Jazz. We'll talk later."

Jazz nods, smiles, and returns her focus to Jenn.

Spark's senior agents have more clientele than they can handle, while associate and junior agents are still frantically building their lists.

Zia is twenty-three years old, has been at Spark for two uneventful years, and she's barely a junior agent. She's heard the tales of others rapidly climbing the ranks on the fragile wings of one or two authors they'd signed whose books have sold millions. That's the breakthrough she's working toward. Profitable fragility.

She slams her bottom into the leather chair and immediately powers up her MacBook. She gulps down a few more swigs of her latte while browsing messages. Editors, follow ups, invitations to host and judge writing contests. She sets those messages aside because her carnivorous appetite salivates for meat.

She keys in her password and opens a snail while the operating system loads. There are about thirty of them and the stack will just bury her if she doesn't dwindle it. Her eyes twinkle, knowing her 'one' will eventually find its way to her lap, and it could be anywhere.

Her submission guidelines are pretty simple—a strong query with a clear synopsis, a brief bio, accompanied by five sample pages. She's overly eager for her envisioned moment of success, so she decides not to pass simply because someone doesn't precisely adhere to the guidelines.

What matters is the story.

The first query is from Katherine Van Zant of Rhode Island. She tears the envelope open and digs in. Katherine holds a graduate degree and is a published poet. She's subbed a young adult fantasy about a vampire who falls madly in love…and Zia loses interest almost immediately.

Pass.

Query number two attempts to straddle too many genres and the entire synopsis is written from the main character's point of view. She sighs but chooses to chance it by reading the first few pages. It's wrought with grammatical errors and the writing is scattered. She should have surmised that from the query.

Pass.

On to the third. It has decent structure, but it's dystopian, and she's not a huge fan of that. She gives the attached pages a go, but nothing is happening.

Pass.

Query four contains too much back story. Decent writing, but pass.

After she breezes through about seven more queries, she tags the stack for form rejections, then digs into her digital slush. Hopefully some of her requests for partials have arrived.

INBOX: 1,322 unread messages.

She takes a sip of her golden liquefied drug and cracks her knuckles. "Okie dokie, Zia. Let's do it."

She's admittedly not brave in her personal and social life, so she balances her cowardice by slowly morphing into a beast in her professional life.

Three hours into her excavation, a new email arrives with a different title in the subject line than the traditional 'Query'.

"Subject: Fire Pages Conference"

She'd met several dozen new writers at that particular conference, all of whom were invited to query unless their work fell into a genre she doesn't represent. She'd specifically instructed them to check her submission guidelines before querying. It's only fair that any author who subs her after attending the Fire Pages event authors get priority. She clicks on the email and opens her mind.

> *Dear Ms. Zia Lennox:*
>
> *It was an honor and pleasure to hear you speak at the Fire Pages Conference in New York last week. Your informative speeches inspired me to query you exclusively regarding my manuscript titled Chiseled Bone. It's an 85,000-word crime/thriller/mystery that follows psychopathic murderer, Julius Kelp, as he preys on young women via the internet by disguising himself as various people.*

Aside from the unusually long run-on sentence, it captures her attention. This genre stopped selling years ago because the market was too heavily saturated.

She recalls the corporate memo detailing how editors had *requested* Spark agents shift their gears and mysteries involving crime simply became dormant. Now agents may see one mystery/crime/thriller submission for every thousand others.

As she continues reading the intriguing query synopsis, her hands become grabby for the sample pages, so she skips right over the author's bio and closing signature to see they've included more than the standard five pages. Just as her translucent eyes settle on the first sentence, Jazz enters.

"It's lunch time. You need the break."

"Actually, I'm thinking about skipping lunch today."

"No, Zee. You told me not to let you slip back into old ways when you returned. Whatever it is, print it, and bring it to the cafeteria. But you're having lunch downstairs. It's called socializing."

Zia sighs because she'd specifically begged Jazz to drag her along, forcefully if required, to spend time socializing with others in Fargo Tower instead of shutting herself away from everyone. She chose Spark because of the social location and ability to separate work from home. The company's base salary, size, and reputation were the icing.

There are twenty-five floors in Fargo Tower and all of them are full of employees from different powerful corporations. Zia decided she needed to start networking at some point. She just has a very hard time smiling when she doesn't feel like it, listening to repetitive stories from people who refuse to change, and laughing at jokes that aren't funny.

She prints out the 25 sample pages of Chiseled Bone, grabs her purse, and heads down to the cafeteria with Jazz, annoyed the entire descent. Her mind is focused on the pages she's clutching against her chest.

Jazz shakes her head at her obsessive best friend.

"Zee, some of the employees are really cool. Just give them a chance. Besides, you never know who you might meet."

Jazz winks her eye while delicately elbowing her because she believes her anxiety-ridden friend will not only form a financially successful bond with a co-worker, but also meet Mr. Right over a cheeseburger and fries.

Zia's not interested. Instead, she's focused on finding the right author. Mr. Right is a fairy tale fantasy she reads about in books, and even *he* sucks. So, technically she's already met and married him many times over.

Spending time with Jazz is sufficient because she's a great friend. Besides her, Zia has none. Her family insists she's anti-social, though she isn't. She's an impatient ambivert and that's easily misconstrued as many things.

They grab their trays and select their dishes. Zia snatches a slice of pepperoni pizza, a garden salad, and a bottle of sweet tea. Before she's able to remove her debit card from her wallet, Jazz pays for their lunches.

She begins to protest, but Jazz stops her.

"Don't."

"I'll get us next time."

They sit in the corner of the cafeteria overlooking Wilshire Boulevard. She outwits Jazz by selecting a booth that only seats two, sticking her tongue out to gloat. Jazz rolls her eyes.

As Zia bites into the greasy cheesy slice, her eyes wander down to the sample pages.

Jazz giggles and pulls out her cell phone.

"Go ahead, Zombie Zee. I know your mind will just drift off if I attempt conversation before you've read it. Satisfy your craving and we'll talk in a minute."

"Love you, Jazz."

"Yeah, yeah."

While Jazz texts, Zia loses herself in the captivating sample pages. The Julius Kelp character is sly, cunning, intriguing, and possesses the traits that typically cause women to swoon out of sensible thought. He's handsome, wealthy, powerful, well-mannered, debonair, and a cultured gentleman; the embodiment many women complain to have gotten catfished by because catfishers lie about the holy trinity—pictures, finances, and relationship status.

Based on the brief synopsis, Kelp will obviously take his deception far beyond the holy trinity, but she wonders how. The way the author crafts their words, she's swiftly becoming attached to Julius Kelp, rooting for him to be the good guy, though the synopsis casts him in a negative light.

Before realizing it, she's finished the sample pages, and desperately desires more.

"You read through that one mighty fast."

"Yeah, it's amazing. Like, so amazing."

"That's a word you rarely use."

"Very true indeed." Zia's shoveling salad into her mouth when she notices Bryce exit the lunch line with his tray. She ducks her head behind Jazz. "Shit."

Jazz turns her head in Bryce's direction.

"Don't!" Zia's embarrassed by her own loud whisper.

"Who the hell are you hiding from?" Jazz frowns.

"Just some creepy guy I bumped into on the elevator this morning."

"And what exactly makes him creepy?"

"He just...I don't know, but I don't want him to see me right now. That's all."

"Okay, Zee...really? Stop being dramatic and tell me what happened."

"Nothing happened exactly." She remains slouched in her seat while keeping her head hidden behind Jazz's. "Well, he was flirting with me. Kind of…I don't know okay."

Jazz eyes her friend incredulously.

"Flirting how?" She doesn't believe a word Zia says about the stranger because her anxiety compels her to exaggerate situations involving attractive men.

"He was umm, like, just giving me the eye." She carefully keeps her head concealed

"So, he *looked* at you?"

"Never mind, Jazz. Can we just get out of here please?"

"Uh, not until I have coffee. After I have *my* cup of coffee, then we can leave. I'll be right back."

"Jazz!"

Finding this situation comical, Jazz snickers. When she rises to leave, Zia attempts to grab her arm. She jerks backwards, leaving Zia with a fist full of air.

"Jazmine, no! Don't leave me!" Her loud whispering turns a few heads in the immediate area, so she reluctantly sits back and braces herself.

After Jazz goes to get her coffee, Zia accepts the fact that she's exposed with absolutely no cover. Bryce is sitting three empty tables directly ahead of her. If he glances up, he'll be looking right at her, so she prays he continues doing whatever it is he's doing on his cell phone.

She fidgets in her seat and fiddles with the grease-stained sample pages, shuffling and reshuffling, before neatly stacking them. Feeling quite ridiculous, she grabs the typical human barrier…her cell phone. Deciding she may as well go back to that email to find out the author's name, she scrolls incessantly, all the way down to the end of query to read the brief bio and closing signature.

It's signed, Baxter Leopold.

She doesn't immediately recall his name or even his face, but she stars the query as important to ensure none of his emails are spammed and appear first in her inbox.

Her impatience compels her to reply, requesting the full manuscript. She hits the send button before realizing how rude her coldness will come across. She didn't compliment his work nor converse in any way. She'd simply made the impersonal request.

She bites down on her bottom lip in regret. If he decided to query a different agent after receiving her boorish response, she'll wallow in disappointment for longer than she can afford. With those sample pages, any agent in their right mind will jump as fast as she had.

Piercing thoughts fill her head, reminding her she can't afford to mess this opportunity up. She angrily wonders why the geniuses of the world haven't invented a way to zap sent emails by now.

In the middle of her mental whipping, she notices shiny black leather shoes near her own feet.

"Just Zia."

She reluctantly lifts her head. Bryce's smile is shining down on her like a million suns. His jet-black hair, soft eyes, long lashes, perfect teeth, muscular build, and six-foot-three frame summon parts of her she'd hexed into dormancy.

She smiles uncomfortably while acknowledging she cannot escape the situation, so she decides to speak and endure in order to maintain a professional image.

"Hi."

In the distance, Jazz is grinning and clapping her hands together in an idiotic cheerleader fashion. Zia's at a total loss for words, so she redirects her gaze to the ground in quintessential teenage fashion.

There's a thick uncomfortable silence until Bryce shatters it.

"Well, just Zia, I didn't mean to disturb you. Just thought I'd say hello." He disposes of his empty tray on top of the trash bin located a few feet away and exits the cafeteria.

She releases the mother of deep sighs once he's out of sight. Jazz slams back down in her seat and pummels her friend with a barrage of questions.

"That is the so-called creepy guy? Superman? Please, tell me my hearing and vision are impaired, and that you said more to him than just *hi*?"

A headache forms and annoyance swell inside of Zia's chest. She's not interested in dating anyone, and she's terribly uncomfortable when approached by strangers. Jazz knows this.

"Jazz, not now okay. I'm going back up."

She grabs her purse and sample pages before exiting the cafeteria, neglecting to dump her tray. She's in desperate need of fresh air.

She glances at the elevator but decides to sneak out on the enclosed employee terrace instead. After inserting her Fargo Tower badge into the slot, followed by a thermal scan of her palm, the door unlocks. She eagerly bursts through it.

A few others are taking smoke breaks, so she searches for an area where she can inhale untainted oxygen. She frantically lunges to the farthest east end of the patio, then leans over the railing.

She inhales a few times, allowing her tensed nerves to unravel. No one but Jazz and her parents know she suffers from anxiety, and that's the way she wants to keep it.

Working at Spark allows her to reintroduce herself to the world on a daily basis but at her own pace, instead of staying caged inside of her modest condo. She tries to gradually allow herself to become comfortable being around others, but strangers trigger her attacks. Well, certain strangers. Those she's physically attracted to, which is the real reason why she's single.

She's resolved that no man will ever understand her. Her pessimism has her convinced that potentials will simply categorize her as a headcase, and accordingly waste her time while enjoying the pleasure of her body before moving on. She prefers to skip to the end where she just moves on.

Every woman she knows, even in passing, has admitted to intentionally or inadvertently changing themselves to fit whatever environment they're in. Specifically, intimate relationships. If he likes sports, she does. He disagrees with her spending habits, she becomes the queen of frugality. He's timid about menstrual cycles, she becomes Batgirl three days out of every month. He maintains his identity, while she slowly reduces herself into no more than a reflection of him.

When the breakup happens, the lost are left with nothing but regret, running back to the same family and friends they'd forsaken for that man, claiming to have learned so much, only to meet the next Mr. Wrong and start the tiring cycle all over again.

One tremendous breakup is all she's ever needed to save her camouflaging for professional settings only, where failure is much safer, since sex and time are non-refundable.

Though most are guilty of slipping into corporate costumes Monday through Friday to reach the top, few rarely succeed, but their failures are still successes because they've gained the knowledge and that's where she's shifted her efforts; on win-win situations. Not a new relationship, no social charm schools, no dating, no strangers, and no fairytales. Just her career.

She's had enough air and her composure has rebounded. She makes her way to the elevator, returning her focus to a happier place.

Chiseled Bone.

She must have it.

Chapter
TWO

Z IA SIGHS, SLAMS herself into the office chair, and flails her arms while gazing up at the ceiling.

"First day back, God. Please, meet me halfway," she thinks.

"Please?"

She yanks her purse open and snatches out the Xan. She often tells herself she should've stayed with the generic brand because this one makes her feel zombie-ish for a while, but Xan's a fast-acting drug and that's usually what she needs.

She shoves the bottle back and angrily throws her purse onto the sofa chair in defiance. Her frustration builds, accompanied by heightened defenses. She refuses to be enslaved by this condition, confident she can make it through a work day without those damned pills.

She pivots her chair around, draws her shoulders back, wakes her MacBook from hibernation, and resumes her work. She responds to emails from editors and current clients at rapid speed, typing over 80 words per minute. She definitely wants them on her team, so she needs to act like it at all times.

Deciding her windowless office could use some brightening, she selects a playlist. Allowing the sounds of Prince to fill the small room, she dances around in her seat to the Purple Rain soundtrack while simultaneously searching her inbox for partials, locating three. She prints them out and sets them aside.

Then, she digs even further into her slush and gloriously loses track of time. After every twenty or so queries, she refreshes her inbox, still hopeful that Baxter Leopold will respond with his full manuscript. She is entirely too obsessed about it already.

She gyrates her bottom in a circular motion and throws her hands up in the air while singing along to the lyrics of "Let's Go Crazy." She's feeling herself and whipping her full head of unkempt, natural tresses around when Jazz walks in.

"Are you okay?"

Zia pauses the music and regains her composure. Jazz laughs while handing her the day's mail.

"I think that dance comes *after* you get the goodies."

"Shut up, Jazz. I'm just setting the mood for my first day back okay. Is that all right with you?"

"Mm, well, it's 5:30 and I'm clocking out. Do you need anything before I leave?" A wry grin spreads across her porcelain-perfect face.

"No, I'm okay. I'll be leaving in a few. Call me when you make it home."

"Uh huh. I will." Jazz shoots Zia a goofy glance before exiting.

Laughing out loud at herself, Zia thumbs through the mail before tossing it on her desk, deciding to have a closer look tomorrow. For now, she opts to go through another twenty in her digital slush before getting the hell out of there.

First, she needs to use the restroom and could use a little snack. She grabs some cash and heads downstairs to the cafeteria. It's closed, but there are vending machines.

The building is a bit creepy after everyone has left. It's so large and quiet you can hear a pin drop. She exits the elevator and walks swiftly down the dimly lit hallway. She inserts her badge into the slot for the ladies' restroom and quickly relieves herself.

She washes her hands but avoids the mirror because she already knows why Bryce looked at her the way he did earlier in the cafeteria. She's a self-proclaimed sad mess, wearing boring gray slacks and a white col-lared shirt. No flair or color whatsoever.

At least she wore her stilettos, though she hadn't taken the time to style her rebellious mane. She'd just brushed through it a few times this morning and let it be—and it has *been*, all day. Untucking her shirt, she relaxes her posture a bit because the day is done.

She rubs her face and finds that her hazelnut skin to be bit on the dry side today.

"Whatever. Who was I supposed to impress? The four walls inside of my coffin of an office?"

She dries her hands on the white terry cloth hand towel and tosses it into the wicker basket before flouncing her soft legs down the hallway, toward the vending machines.

The sound of her heels clicks loudly against the linoleum and the feminine sway of her curvy hips energizes her with each step. She needs all the juice she can get to finish out the evening.

She carefully views each window of treats. While weighing her options, she angles her petite five-foot-two and a half frame to gain a better view of the goodies at the bottom. Licking her lips, she salivates over the chocolate donuts she knows she shouldn't have.

"Mmmmm."

She inserts her money into the slot and makes her first selection. Now for something with a crunch. She moves to the next machine and tilts her head indecisively.

"Can't decide?"

The brute grumbling voice startles her. She jerks and clumsily bangs the crown of her head against the glass.

"What the hell?" She clutches her chest as her nerves twist into knots.

Bryce ceases his approach, shoving his palms into the air.

"Whoa. I'm sorry. Didn't mean to startle you."

"Well you did!" She tries to catch her breath and rubs the crown of her head, feeling quite the fool.

"I just came down for a snack to help me stay awake. I didn't imagine anyone else would be here."

"Try to make your presence known next time instead of creeping up on me like that." She recognizes how harsh her tone is, but she's frazzled and upset that she's alone with a stranger, yet again. The same damn one, in fact.

"Again, my apologies. Are you okay?" He steps forward and reaches out to touch her.

She recoils, slamming her back into the vending machine, trembling uncontrollably.

"I'm not going to hurt you."

Her back is pinned against the glass and her breathing is so loud she makes a conscious effort to calm down. She commands her breathing into normalcy, so he won't go around telling everyone in the building she's some wacko freak.

"Oh, um no. It's not that. I—I just didn't expect anyone else to still be here." She manages a feeble smirk while peeling her back from the reinforced glass. She turns to resume making her selection as if nothing happened when her head spins. She stumbles, and he wraps his arms around her waist.

"You should probably sit down and let the dizziness pass."

She's uncomfortable, but no longer afraid. He guides her over to the bench against the wall, where she sits. He kneels in front of her and lifts her face to his. His eyes are kind, sultry, and inviting.

He holds her gaze for too long and creases his brow infinitesimally. Catching the perplexity in his eyes, she turns her head away, extremely self-conscious about her eye condition. Most people rudely gawk at her and it makes her feel like a freak of nature.

"Stay here. I'll be right back." He walks in the direction of the restrooms in a pair of white sneakers; the culprit of his silent approach. He's also switched his blazer for a black t-shirt.

She admires his exquisite form and bites down on her bite lip, salivating over his taught buns.

"Oh my God, Zia. You didn't hit your head that hard, did you?" She leans forward when her head spins again. She glances down at the donuts in her left hand, squeezed into a melty mess. She's grateful it's at least contained inside the wrapping.

He comes rushing back with a white towel and fills it with cubes from the ice machine. As he walks toward her, his heart tremors at the sight of her. Never has he seen a woman more exquisite or beautiful. He vibes to her powerful frequency as he's never experienced with another human before.

She's admiring his body while he's admiring all of her. Both of their movements seem to appear in slow motion to the other. His muscular legs move gracefully, in consideration of his generous package. Her eyes inadvertently bulge at the sight. Her skin tingles and her eyes make love to his chest.

Her vaginal muscles retract, so she squeezes her thighs together, attempting to douse the flames. His olive skin is so gloriously lustrous she believes it dulls her honey cocoa. His features are reminiscent of Christopher Reeve, adding dimpled lips. He blushes in response to her gazing, so she quickly averts her eyes but inhales his cologne when he kneels before her.

"I'm going to place this compress on top of your head okay?"

She nods, appreciative of the warning. The coolness slowly numbs her throbbing scalp. The instant relief relaxes her but now she's a bit queasy. He eyes her so intently she wishes she could teleport back to the safety of her office.

He, on the other hand, is purposefully prolonging the moment, anything to remain in her presence. He gazes into her eyes again, revealing the question burning inside him.

She hopes he doesn't ask. She despises when men ask her '*The Question*'.

"I need to get back upstairs."

His heart plummets into his stomach. She stands on her wobbly legs. He grabs her. A fit gal, attending the gym six days a week, she stands erect instead of leaning against him; ever defiant.

"I'm fine, really. Thank you, but I need to get back to work."

He reluctantly releases her and she walks toward the elevator. When she pauses, he's instantly beside her. His warm palm radiates heat through her blouse, near the small of her back. She uses him to steady herself to remove her stilettos. He holds her arm as she rests her hand on his shoulder.

He wants to kiss her more than he desires oxygen to sustain his life.

"Better not chance it," she whispers. Her words come out more playfully than she intends.

When he smiles, the depth of his smoldering eyes steal a part of her. He delicately touches her cheek with his thumb. Concern adorns his impossibly gorgeous face.

"Are you sure you're okay? At least allow me to escort you upstairs."

Moments like these sweep women off their feet and her indignation won't allow such a thing, so she hardens unnecessarily.

"I'm fine." She removes her hand from his shoulder and pinches the counters of her shoes between her fingers, feeling his eyes on her as she walks away.

As soon as Zia stumbles through the front door of her condo, her dog, Bugs, greets her by jumping on her legs. She disarms the alarm, locks the door, and quickly resets it. She bends down and scoops him into her arms.

Bugs is the beagle her parents had given her when she'd graduated from college. They didn't want her to be completely alone and with Bugs around, she never truly is.

He's her best friend and she loves him to pieces. His gold and white floppy ears are the best. He licks her cheeks and barks. When she puts him down, he excitedly and impatiently runs around in circles.

"Missed you too, buddy."

She drops her purse and partials onto the sofa before grabbing his leash. She takes him for a quick walk around the gated community. He bounces from patch to patch until her head swirls.

"Time to reel it in, buddy."

When they make it back inside, Bugs runs into the kitchen, taps his empty bowl with his paw, and barks.

"Alright already."

She sets the alarm and drops her keys on the table. Before she's done refilling his dog bowl, he shoves his head into it. She just continues pouring around it. She smiles and laughs at him because he enjoys his food the way everyone should. Cake, especially.

She turns on the shower water, returns to the bedroom, and opens her laptop. She hastily undresses, dropping her clothes everywhere. When she sits naked on the bed, her thoughts return to Bryce and his warm eyes. She's never seen eyes so full of kindness. She defiantly dismisses the thought, instead redirecting her focus to work, hoping Baxter Leopold emails her that manuscript soon. Her obsession deepens.

She's come across authors who focuses more on stellar first pages because they learn how important they are, and then let the rest of their story fall flat. That's one of the reasons why she volunteers for writer's conferences. She enjoys attending and meeting authors from around the world.

While there will generally be mostly writers who create stories that remain drawn inside the lines, there will be those few minds that cannot conform to the boring established rules no matter how hard they try. Those few tend to create the most vivid worlds. She believes she met one while in New York.

She's optimistic of a few things. First and foremost, that Chiseled Bone is wholly as great as she truly feels it will be, and her rude email doesn't deter the author from pursuing her.

She's more than a tad bit curious about Baxter Leopold. She can't recall his face or even having heard his name at the Fire Pages event. She makes a mental note to Garble Search him.

HE BREWS HIMSELF a fresh pot of coffee and presses a button on a nearby remote control. The closed black-out drapes electronically part ways to allow the view of the New York sunrise to vanquish the darkness.

Perched in front of the window, he gazes out, and sighs deeply; content, yet anxious, and excited. There's a world bursting with women who are vying for a chance to be his next muse. Why keep them waiting any longer than necessary?

He paces 'cross the Down-White-Oak hardwood floors in his tri-level condominium located in Megladon Tower, in the elite Flatiron District of Manhattan while contemplating who he'll follow up with today.

"Hmmmm, who shall it be? Rebecca or Emmalee? It's tough to decide."

These things take time, so it's imperative to stay on track. Otherwise, his domestic lady companions feel rushed, and he faces failure. That's one thing he can never accept. Deciding Rebecca and Emmalee are equally ripe with ignorance, naivety, and beauty—he chooses Rebecca.

With exotic beauty hidden beneath ordinary flaws, she's the more dangerous of the two because her beauty is layered and imperceptible. Therefore, so she must go first.

No man of consequence openly desires her because she's reached that magical age of twenty-six. This has made her desperate and clingy. He likes that.

The thought of subtle manipulation stiffens his rod and he gently strokes it through his boxers. That familiar itch has begun sending electrifying chills through his body. His eyes roll to the back of his head.

"There is no aphrodisiac more powerful than the moment of anticipation."

Rebecca's family has written her off as someone who is stupid and refuses to learn from her mistakes.

"Even women despise women so they're aware of their own inferiority."

He finds himself ever so grateful society views women just as he views them, disdainfully, and placed here only for the pleasure of whomever desires to occupy their orifices. Be it man, woman, or beast. The only unfortunate portion of their existence lies within their ability to reproduce. *Someone ought to fix that*, he thinks.

He removes his favorite ceramic mug from the cupboard and strategically decorates the countertop with a spoon, two packets of raw Stevia, and Silk caramel-flavored creamer. Before pouring the coffee, he aligns, then realigns every item perfectly, taking care in the tiniest of details. Any one item out of place sets his teeth on edge and when that happens, there's pure-fire hell to pay.

He gently stirs until his coffee is well blended and gives it a taste.

"Ahhhh, perfect."

Next, he contacts his assistant, who promptly answers on the first ring.

"Please, have Douglas pick me up in exactly two hours. I need to do some shopping today. Also, cancel my meeting and reschedule it for Tuesday. Yes dear, thank you."

He glides over to his desk and anxiously hovers his fingers over the keys.

"Good morning, Rebecca love. I dreamt of you last night and felt the time has come for us to meet. Join me for lunch in the City."

Chapter
THREE

As Zia types and sends personalized rejections for the partials she'd received, she rolls her eyes and sighs in annoyance. Today she's having lunch with Jazz, Jenn, and the newest senior agent, Makayla Souza. Makayla's one of the few senior agents who make it a point to regularly visit the office. The rest work from home, as is their prerogative. She's also the agent who was promoted after she'd lucked up on the same manuscript Zia had passed on.

Lunch with Jazz is great, and sometimes even with Lillia, but she has zero interest in listening to Makayla brag about her clientele and newfound wealth. Zia's certainly not hating on her success, though there is a tinge of bitterness behind her agitation. She's always happy for the humble and modest. Never for the braggadocios.

If others plead for a success story, then by all means, respond, but that's not Makayla. She'll introduce her accomplishments into any conversation and carry on until someone changes the subject. Zia sighs in annoyance at the thought.

She had surely wished the partials she'd read this past week were as promising as their first pages were, but they all seemed to fall flat. She'd spoken about this at the Fire Pages event. In the three weeks since she's returned from New York, her slush pile has been a huge disappointment. Except for Chiseled Bone, that is. But then again, she won't know until she receives the full manuscript.

She damns Baxter Leopold for torturing her this way, then damns her own non-elite agent status. Regret intrudes. While agents like Makayla usually only lay their precious eyes on top notch material because corporate assigns them human filters, here she sits, bombarded with unedited first drafts.

Once agents land one or more successful clients, aspiring authors tend to polish their manuscripts more carefully before subbing. She certainly looks forward to that day becoming a reality.

Th e sound of her fingers tapping against the keys hypnotizes her and she falls into the responses, taking care with those manuscripts she'd like to revisit once major revisions have been made. She always recommends resourceful information, useful tips, and suggestions. She's never conde-scending to an aspiring author.

She wants to encourage them to keep writing, not give up. She's always careful to include the many things she liked about their story. Th e only drawback is the open door it leaves. Some take that as an invitation to email her incessantly when she only wants to hear back when new material is being subbed.

Zia's been thinking ahead lately. Mostly of what she'll do if Chiseled Bone is as great as she believes it will be. In her heart of hearts, she knows she won't sit around on her hands waiting for corporate to tell her the market is ready.

She's already decided to bypass in-house editorial and sub directly to Sasha Leoneé; the acquisitions editor at Reaping Willow Publishing. Sasha loves to get the inside track on cutting edge material and they have a great professional relationship. Zia's not waiting for a door to open. She plans to kick the damn thing down.

Jazz sticks her head in.

"Hey, you ready?"

"Yeah, let me finish this email and I'll meet you out front."

She smiles and closes the door. Zia completes the last sentence, spell checks, and sends. When she enters the lobby, Makayla and Jenn are waiting by the front desk with Jazz. She suppresses her sigh before marching forward, while repeating in her head she can do this.

"Hi, Zia! Glad to have you back," Makayla squeaks while smirking snobbishly.

Her fake enthusiasm rubs Zia the wrong way because she's been back for weeks now.

"Thanks. It's good to be back. Hey, Jenn."

"I'm so super hungry," Jenn groans while patting her stomach.

"Yeah, me too. Let's go," Jazz agrees.

Zia knows Jazz is anxious to get them away from prying ears, so they can *network*. Zia mentally rolls her eyes but fights the facial expression.

They make their way down the buffet line of Fargo Tower's cafeteria. Zia takes her time with her selections, lingering and procrastinating. Jazz notices and nudges her. Zia nervously tosses her a smirk while Jenn and Makayla secure their table.

"It's just lunch, Zee. Don't overthink this, okay?"

"I know. I'm okay," Zia forces with a smile.

They pay for their food and join the others. Zia reluctantly sits next to Makayla. Jazz sits across from her bestie, next to Jenn. Since Makayla and Jenn are already chatting amongst themselves, Zia takes advantage of that by biting into her chicken burrito. It's so yummy that as far as she's concerned, they can talk their heads off about anything, as long as she can shove her face quietly. Of course, Jazz won't let that happen.

"So, Zee. Why don't you tell Makayla about the new manuscript you just came across?"

Zia squints her eyes with a mouth full of food. The look on Makayla's face transmits her disinterest in anything *anyone* could possibly have to say. Zia swallows her food, wipes her mouth, and takes a gulp of sweet tea before responding.

"Well, it's uh...it's crime...fiction."

"Crime? That genre is as dead as its title," Makayla spits.

Zia despises agents like Makayla, who're so puffed up with knowledge and following trends, they completely lose their people skills.

"I thought that Spark sent a memo last year reminding agents not to sub material from that genre until further notice," Jenn inquires in a mild and friendly tone, while nervously tucking the strands of her honey-blonde curls behind her left ear.

"Uh, yes they did. For good reason," Makayla huffs before Zia's able to respond. "They don't sell. People don't want stories that make them think. They want the kind that are relatable and entertaining. Basically, reality TV on a page."

Makayla tosses her professionally styled hair over her shoulder and snorts arrogantly. Physically, she's a cross between Jessica Biel and Jennifer Lopez, but she has a Tomi Lahren personality. That may go over well with men, but not with women. No one likes her. They just tolerate her.

"What people want changes like the weather," Jazz rebuts. "Whatever genre is heavily saturated today, won't always be and it'll be a gold mine for a brave agent."

Jazz isn't the type to follow anyone else and her tone reveals it. She eyes Zia for confirmation.

"That may very well be, but we work for the largest lit agency in the country," Makayla snaps back. "If they invest millions of dollars to research market trends, it would only be wise if we trusted the information they provide. Anything else is career suicide."

She and Jazz lock eyes, but Jazz isn't the first to look away.

"Makayla," Zia sighs, "I completely understand where you're coming from. I'm just reading it right now for fun. Maybe someday when the market changes, it'd be a good fit."

"Why waste valuable time even reading it right now when you could be reading something else within the guidelines? Do you think I'd be where I am right now if I wasted my time reading junk I knew couldn't go anywhere?" Makayla continues.

Aaaannnd cue. The door has been opened by no one other than the puffy twit. Makayla found a crack to ooze through all by her snotty self.

Zia stops Makayla before she starts because Zia's face may not be able to maintain its current shape much longer.

"Instead of purchasing a carefully crafted book, sometimes I prefer to read something raw. Like I said, it's just for fun. Not every bit of my time is professional. We all gotta take a break some time."

"You're right about that," Jenn adds. "I could use a vacation but corporate denied my request."

Zia and Jazz are thankful Jenn changed the subject. Having the least seniority at the office, Jenn's stepped on quite a bit.

"What time block did you request?" Zia asks.

"December 11th-20th."

That's off-peak. Everyone is winding down for the holidays and most calls trail off by then. Zia wonders why they would deny her.

"Oh, that really sucks," Jazz mumbles between bites. "I'll email Vanessa and ask her what's up with it."

Though Jenn had intentionally stepped into the conversation to prevent Makayla from hogging it, she steps right back in without missing a beat.

"Well, I broke up with Mike last week," she sighs in an over-exaggerated fashion that lacks emotion.

Jazz and Jenn simultaneously gasp.

"Oh my gosh, I'm so sorry. Are you okay?" Jenn asks, placing her hand on Makayla's forearm.

"Yeah, I'm absolutely fine. He just couldn't handle my recent success. I mean, not many men can handle the pressure of being with an intelligent woman who makes more money than he does."

Zia rolls her eyes and continues chewing her food. Makayla drones on with her self-worship, disguised as self-pity.

"After I bought the house and new car, his attitude completely changed for the worse. He started cancelling dates and making pitiful excuses for everything. Ultimately, I just couldn't keep fighting for someone who wasn't fighting for me."

"You make some valid points," Jazz concurs.

Luckily for Makayla, Jazz is a compromising person. Zia, on the other hand would never have admitted that she had anything solid in that so-called breakup. After all, she likely boasted and bragged about her success ad nauseam with him as well. That would run anyone off. Makayla's almost thirty and seems quite miserable. Zia resolves she will never be like her.

"All it took was a little bit of money to reveal who he was. When I was a struggling damsel in distress, I guess it made him feel like Superman to the rescue."

Makayla sips her lemonade and looks up across the room. "Speaking of Superman."

The others follow her line of sight to Bryce, standing in the buffet line. Unable to duck or hide because Makayla and Jenn will ask her why, Zia sits up straight and continues eating her food. She chews nervously while reciting *"please, don't come over here"* in her head, trying desperately to ignore reality.

"Oh my God! Who is *that*?" Makayla asks as her cheeks rise and flush a pathetic strawberry.

Jazz and Jenn both turn their bodies. Makayla kicks them underneath the table.

"Don't look!"

"Well, how the hell are we supposed to know who you're talking about?" Jazz blurts.

Jazz is utterly annoyed, so she glances over her shoulder anyway, then she looks directly at Zia before quickly averting her eyes.

"I've never seen him before. He's gorgeous," Jenn concurs while blushing.

"Yes. Yes, he is, and he's headed this way," Makayla warns, whipping her hair and preparing herself.

Zia, on the other hand, attempts to swallow a mouth full of food and starts choking. Jazz hands her a bottle of water, but Makayla jumps away like there's an outbreak of tuberculosis.

"Oh my God, ewww. Gross!" she screeches like the ass she is.

"Okay, you should stand up," Jenn advises, reaching for Zia's arm.

Bryce beats her to it by grabbing Zia from her seat.

"Hold your arms above your head and try not to panic," he instructs her.

His soothing voice and close proximity summons Zia's goosebumps. His eyes are so full of concern and she can't understand why. He doesn't know her.

She's humiliated by the loud coughing, but her throat tickles, and she can't stop. Very little oxygen is coming in and it's making her nervous.

"It's okay. You need to cough. Coughing forces the food to move from wherever it's lodged," he soothes.

He rubs her back and the heat from his skin nearly scorches her. She flinches, but doubles over. He grabs the bottle of water from Jazz's outstretched hand.

"Here. Try to take a sip."

She swallows a miniscule amount and coughs a few more times. Out of her right peripheral, she spots Makayla lustfully eyeing him, batting her eyelashes, and flipping her hair.

"I—I need to use the restroom," Zia croaks.

She dashes into the nearest restroom and leans over the sink. She turns on the faucet and splashes cool water on her face. She coughs a few more times when Jazz enters.

"Are you okay?" she asks while rubbing Zia's back.

"Yeah, I'm good. I just tried to swallow too much food at once. So stupid of me."

"I saw your facial expression change when Makayla spotted him. That skank doesn't need another man to ruin. You clearly like him, so why not just talk to him instead of having these embarrassing moments?"

"Jazz, no." Zia turns off the faucet and grabs a towel.

"Why the hell not? From what I saw, you were jealous."

"I'm not interested, that's why. If I were, it'd be different, but I'm not. The more I ignore him, the harder he tries to get my attention. What kind of psychopath is going to do that?"

"It's called persistence. Like you chasing after a manuscript you shouldn't."

Zia squints her eyes and juts her lips in trademark fashion, grateful that Jazz opened the door to another topic.

"Corporate doesn't know everything. Besides, I've had an epiphany."

She intentionally springs this on Jazz now, so she won't rush to leave the restroom. "What's this epiphany?"

"Well, I think that corporate knows the crime fiction genre is primed and ready for a grand resurrection. I just think they're saving it for select senior and partner agents. Basically, someone who doesn't need it. I'm already thinking ahead."

"What do you mean thinking ahead?" Jazz inquires as she folds her arms across her chest.

"You know exactly what I mean. I'm bypassing editorial and going straight to Sasha. There's no policy that expressly enforces subbing to in-house editorial first. It's simply an expectation all agents take advantage of to protect their own reputation with the publishing houses. Not to mention, it's corporate's way of monitoring material so they can control who succeeds and who fails."

"I'll ignore that last part because you're reaching, but you're not an editor Zee, and this is a crazy idea."

"Overthinking things has gotten me nowhere. Besides, I do have a bachelor's degree in English. I'm fully capable of proofreading and editing a manuscript. If I weren't, Spark wouldn't have hired me."

"You've got a point there. Just be careful. Spark is the only lit agency paying a base salary. Don't give them a reason to fire you. Or worse, embarrass you in front of the likes of Makayla."

"She doesn't count and I'm sure she was *chosen* as their golden girl. There's always one. We don't know all of the dynamics of her so-called success."

"I really, really don't like her," Jazz confesses.

"Then why did you insist we have lunch with her?"

"Because," she barks while snatching the towel from Zia's hands, tossing it into the wicker basket.

"Because what, Jazmine?" Zia puts her hands on her hips and glares.

"Because I want the senior agents to start talking about you. That's why."

"What? Why?"

"That's how golden girls are chosen here." She winks her eye before opening the door.

"I don't want to be chosen. I want to work for it."

"Oh, and you will. Come on, let's go."

"We're gonna have a little talk—you and I. Very soon." Zia smirks as they return to the cafeteria.

They slow their approach when they reach the entrance of the cafeteria to witness Makayla hanging on Bryce's shoulder. Disgust fills Zia's stomach. Makayla's actions are desperate and ridiculous, flipping her hair repetitively, and laughing obnoxiously loud.

Bryce isn't interested in the least, but he's a southern gentleman with the finest manners. He dare not be rude to a lady, no matter how insufferable she is. He glances around, hoping for an escape or rescue.

Jenn's back is to everyone and she's preoccupied, texting. All he can think of is Zia. Her face, her eyes, her lips, her scent. His interest left the cafeteria when she did.

The clicking of heels against the tile captures his attention. He anxiously turns their way. His facial expression changes completely. He fixes his eyes so intently on Zia she glances over at Jazz to break the contact. He abandons Makayla mid-sentence and walks toward Zia. The look on Makayla's face is one of pure astonishment.

"Are you all right?" he asks, cupping Zia's face in his hands.

Her heart pounds, knowing everyone is staring at them. She lowers her head to free herself from his grasp.

"Yes, thank you. I guess I need to chew more thoroughly in the future," she giggles nervously.

Jazz clears her throat.

"Oh—this is my friend, Jazz—Jazmine. Jazmine, this is Bryce."

"It's a pleasure to meet you, Bryce," she beams.

"The pleasure is all mine." His genuine gleaming smile brightens the room as he kisses her hand.

Zia smirks at her blushing best friend.

"Do you guys, like, know each other?" Makayla interrupts in an irate tone.

Everyone wonders where the hell she'd come from when she was across the room just a second ago.

"I mean because you're all, like, staring at each other. Have you met before?"

Her nasally nosiness causes them to answer synchronously.

"No."

"Yes."

He shoots a glance Zia's way, slightly taken aback by her "no" answer.

"Well, kind of," Zia nervously explains. "We've run into each other a few times. Here…at work." Zia wonders why she's attempting to clear up any misconceptions when she doesn't care what Makayla thinks.

Makayla suspiciously darts her eyes back and forth between the two of them.

"Zia was the first person to welcome me to the building. She's been an angel," Bryce offers.

"Oh, well here's my card. B&F does a lot of business with Spark. You should have a contact," Makayla shamelessly proposes, shoving her card into his face.

"Thank you, but uh—I already have a contact," he declines while staring at Zia.

Makayla's mouth is trapped in an open position.

"I should be getting back to work," he adds, while stepping closer and eyeing Zia intently. "I'm glad you're okay. We'll catch up later."

Zia dry gulps as he walks away. The three of them return to the table. Jenn glances up.

"Hey, are you okay?" she probes.

"Yeah. Something just went down wrong."

Zia smiles while Makayla sulks awkwardly in the corner. She's not the center of attention, so she's lost interest. Plus, her ego is bruised. Glamorous and recently rich Makayla couldn't bag a newbie employee and it's eating her up. Well, hell. Zia and Jazz are doing everything they can to prevent laughing out loud.

They've finished their food and are ready for coffee, but both decide on an espresso. Not the weak watered-down cafeteria brand.

"Hey, Jazz. Wanna walk with me to Starbucks up the street really quick?"

"Oh my gosh, yes! I need one so bad. Do you guys wanna join us?"

Zia disguises her disappointment in Jazz for extending them an invitation.

"No, thanks. I've been here too long," Makayla replies. "I don't even *need* to be. I just came for a meeting. I can actually go *home* now." She stands on her Popsicle legs, and tosses her hair while buttoning her last season, cherry-red blazer.

"I can't," Jenn apologizes. "I have to get back to the phones or they'll make a big deal."

Jenn isn't salaried like agents. She's hourly and they give her the hardest time for petty things. Before anyone can say goodbye to Makayla, she walks away.

Zia's anxious to get out of the building.

"We'll see you in a bit Jenn," Zia offers while grabbing Jazz's hand and dragging her toward the staircase.

The two of them jog up one flight, then dash out of the revolving glass door entrance. As soon as the fresh air hits their face, they burst out into laughter.

"Did you see the look on her face?"

"It was freaking priceless! Zee, oh my God." Jazz doubles over laughing.

"I never would've thought today would be the best day I've ever had at Spark. She nearly died of humiliation and I'm the one who almost choked to death. It doesn't get any better than that."

They order their coffees and chat about the cafeteria incident until their stomachs hurt from laughter.

"So anyway, seriously Zee, let's talk about this plan you have. I want in."

"What? Why?"

"I started working for Spark as a receptionist when I was sixteen. That was nine years ago."

"Wow. Nearly a decade. You're intelligent, resourceful, and you know everyone. You should be president by now."

They chuckle, but Jazz clears her throat the way someone does when they're holding something back.

"We'll save that little story for another time. For now, let's dot our i's and cross our t's."

Zia ponders how she ever lucked up on a wonderful friend like Jazz.

On the way back to Fargo Tower, they chat away about the plan and intermittently venture back to Makayla's rejection.

Jazz attempts to convince Zia to initiate contact with Bryce, but her mind is made up that she will not approach him. Even still, she can no longer deny the connection. She's inexplicably drawn to him.

Chapter
FOUR

PREPARING HERSELF FOR an ordinary Friday, Zia opens her office door, then freezes. Red roses blanket her desk. She gazes around to see tons of them everywhere, in crystal vases, completely filling the room. The sweet scent swirls into her nostrils as she stoically inches around the desk to her chair. She's too stunned to sit, so she gawks.

She wonders who could've sent them. After dropping her purse onto the floor, she searches for a card. Locating it, she eagerly rips open the tiny envelope, and removes the white linen parchment.

> *"Have dinner with me. Tonight at seven. I'll be waiting down-stairs—Bryce."*

"Wow," is all she can manage before plopping down and smiling.

A warm blush floats to her cheeks.

"Oh my goodness, Zia!" Jazz exclaims as she enters. "When Jenn called to tell me that the florist was delivering tons of roses to the office, I never imagined that they'd be—"

"For me?"

"Sorry, I didn't mean it that way. I…"

"It's okay, Jazz. I'm just as surprised as you are."

"Who are they from?" she begs, with her eyes wide with excitement.

Zia shoots her a guilty look.

"No way! Superman?" Jazz gasps.

"Yup. Christopher Reeve himself."

"Well, was there a card?" she inquires while flailing her arms around like a crazy person.

Zia chuckles while holding the card up in the air, still in disbelief.

"What does it say?"

Zia doesn't respond fast enough, so Jazz snatches it.

"Hey!" Zia squeaks, leaping forward to retrieve it.

Jazz jerks and turns away. After reading it, she turns back around with the largest grin Zia has ever seen.

"You're going!"

"No, I'm not."

"Yes, the hell you are and don't give me any crap about work or anxiety. At some point in your life, you need to overcome it because this—" she holds up the card, "is likely never going to happen again."

"Thanks for the vote of confidence, Jazmine." Zia snatches the card and slams her body in the chair.

"You know damn well what I mean so don't start with me."

"Jazz, I…"

"…save it. We're taking an extended lunch to go shopping. No excuses."

Jazz closes the door and Zia hunches her shoulders. She's slowly deciding to go, but resistance has her in a chokehold. She can't just sit and drown in thought or her anxiety will take her prisoner. She carefully arranges the roses on the desk and opens her laptop. She eyes her smiling reflection on the dark screen.

She's definitely going.

After Zia's matched a few manuscripts with the appropriate editors, she pushes herself into overdrive and time escapes her. Another two hours quickly pass when Jazz bursts into her office.

"Zee, come to the front desk. Now!"

She's smiling, so Zia knows that it couldn't be bad.

When Zia approaches the front desk, there's a gentleman holding a box and a clipboard.

"Miss Lennox?"

"Yes." Wariness oozes from her every pore.

"I have a delivery for you. I just need you to sign here, please."

She slowly signs her name on the clipboard and returns it to him.

"What is it?" Jazz and Zia ask simultaneously.

"I have no idea…just that I couldn't accept a third-party signature. Have a nice day, ma'am."

Zia removes the large white box from his hands and carries it into her office, with Jazz on her heels. They close the door and begin moving the roses aside to make room on the sofa. Zia tugs on the gold ribbon. Her hands tremble as she removes the lid. Shoving the delicate golden tissue paper aside, she unveils a shimmery black gown.

"Holy shit! Is that a…"

"…yes, Marchesa. Jazz, this dress easily cost over a thousand dollars!"

Jazz covers her mouth with her hands because she knows that it likely cost over twenty thousand but won't rattle her friend's nerves even more.

"Oh my God, Zee. What did you do to that man?"

"Nothing!"

Zia hasn't done anything but avoid him. Jenn knocks on the door, calling for Jazz.

"Jazmine, you're needed at the desk."

"Okay," she replies. "Zee, I'll be right back."

Zia stands frozen like an idiot, staring at the dress. This is exciting and scary at the same time. She drowns herself in thoughts of what Bryce is trying to prove by likely charging his credit cards to the limit to impress her.

She traces her fingers along the expensive fabric, conceding that she is, indeed, impressed. Jazz flings the door open and rushes inside with two more packages.

"Here! These just came."

She shoves the packages at Zia, but Zia just stares at them.

"Fine. I'll open them if you won't."

Jazz is like a kid in a candy store, and it makes Zia smile, so she joins her. They tear the first box open and remove a pair of Louboutin, Ombré, Crystal, Leather pumps. Size seven and a half.

Zia's more perplexed about how he knows her shoe size.

"Zee! These shoes retail for $4,000! I should know, I was ogling the yellow-purple ones a few weeks ago in Saks."

Zia's confused about why her friend is breathing so heavily. They're just shoes. Expensive shoes, but still just objects. No man is going to buy her off. Now she's afraid to open the last box, but she picks it up anyway.

"Zee, I swear if you don't open that box."

Zia flips open the top, removes a black velvet box, and gulps as she opens it. Inside, are Cartier diamond, heart-motif earrings that sparkle in her eyes.

"Jesus!" they both exclaim.

Zia drops them on the desk like they're hot coals.

"You don't think this is a bit extreme, Jazz?"

"No. It's a lot romantic. There you go, overthinking again. We're definitely going to get something done to that head of yours."

She continues talking while Zia glares at the diamond earrings.

"The office is buzzing, so I'm going to act as your publicity agent, go make a statement, and then we're leaving."

Zia doesn't respond, so she gently nudges her.

"Did you hear me?"

"Yeah," Zia stutters, breaking free from her trance. "Yeah, I'm ready."

"Great! Makayla will DIE when she finds out!" She wickedly rubs her hands together.

"Jazmine!"

"Just kidding."

The door closes and Zia's thoughts sprint. What will he expect from her after buying her all this stuff? Her cell phone jingles. She sits in the chair and pulls it from her purse. It's an email. She decides to check it from her laptop while she's near a printer, just in case. She swivels around and clicks on her inbox.

> "Hello Ms. Lennox and thank you for your direct response. I'm very excited to hear back from you. I have attached the full manuscript of Chiseled Bone to this email in a Word document. If you should have any questions, please don't hesitate to email or text me. 212-555-8818. Thank you for taking an interest in my work."

Zia shoves her hands into the air, thanking God. She's been waiting. Two exciting events in one day? She's on a roll. She sends Baxter a more personal response to make up for the previous one. She clicks the print button then pushes away from the desk with a huge smile on her face.

Zia and Jazz completely forego nutritional sustenance and head for Rodeo Drive. They enter Selena's Elite Salon and approach the counter. Jazz sashays, Naomi Campbell style, in her stilettos, with her head held high. She confidently tosses her glossy raven tresses over her shoulder.

A stick-figured young woman with blue eyes, blonde hair, and an orange tint greets them. Jazz takes charge of the conversation.

"We need an emergency appointment, please. For like, right now."

She eyes the receptionist through her Caribbean amber green eyes and waits for the unnecessary dance to begin.

"I'm sorry, we're booked six months out. Everyone knows that."

"Come on Jazz, you know better," Zia reminds her.

These salons will have tons of available time but pretend to be booked up so others will find their services more appealing. Marketing Strategy 101. Jazz pats her friend on the hand, unmoved and determined.

"What's your name, hon?"

"Amanda."

"Amanda, listen to me…she has a date tonight. A last-minute date with a high-profile attorney. He delivered over $30,000 worth of merchandise to her desk this morning for this date. No way can she wear Cartier, Marchesa, and Louboutin with her head looking like this. No way. Please, help us!"

"$30,000 for one date? Marchesa?"

"Yes!"

Amanda doesn't believe it either, but she's clearly intrigued. Judging Zia's appearance, Amanda wonders what level blaze just walked through her salon doors. She takes another look at Zia and crinkles her nose. Zia frowns right back.

Amanda looks back at Jazmine's perfectly tanned-golden skin. The resolve in her judgmental blue eyes forms as she determines if the ladies can afford the ridiculous prices.

"Listen, we work in the Fargo Tower on Wilshire. Every elite corporation you can think of has offices there and we're all friends. If you do us this favor, we'll just owe you one. How about that?"

Jazz hands Amanda a business card and smiles. She's a very convincing negotiator.

"She would need the works, so we'd have to charge double," Amanda snaps, lifting her head in a snotty manner.

Jazz boldly produces her American Express card. Zia snatches her by the arm and tugs her away from the reception desk.

"Jazmine, have you lost your damn mind?" she whispers.

"I'll be just fine. You can pay me back in the distant future. You are *not* missing out on this date. Not on my damn watch."

She shoves Zia back towards the counter, slams her card down, and bulges her eyes.

"Fix her!"

Zia sarcastically juts her lips, wanting nothing more than to shove the inflated price up Amanda's behind. Then she remembers that her hair isn't date ready and surrenders.

Amanda snatches Jazmine's credit card, swipes it, and then guides Zia towards the back. She returns to hand Jazz her receipt. Zia notices Jazz showing Amanda something on her cellphone. They converse for a minute and Jazz begins making her way out of the salon.

"I'll be back at two, okay?" she yells to her friend.

"Where are you going?"

She doesn't respond and disappears. Amanda rudely shoves Zia into the stylist's chair. Zia despises visiting Rodeo for this very reason. The people are snobby when they're living paycheck to paycheck just like most others.

Acclaimed hair stylist, Reyna Zimmer, washes, blow dries, trims, and curls until Zia's eyes cross. Reyna primps and plays with her hair a little more before calling to Amanda.

"Look at this miracle," Reyna announces to Amanda.

"Oh my God! You are a genius!" Amanda exclaims.

"I am," Reyna beams in agreement.

Reyna swivels Zia's chair around towards the mirror. Zia stares at the stranger in the reflection.

"Wow," is all Zia can manage.

She moves her head from side to side, admiring how Reyna trimmed her once long tresses to shoulder-length. Bold curls adorn her face. They bounce every time she moves her head. She never knew her hair was alive until now. The wavy bob partially covers her left eye. That's easily Zia's favorite part.

Reyna proudly and patiently watches.

"Thank you!"

"You're welcome. Your friend is waiting for you in the lobby," Reyna says while removing the black vinyl cape from around Zia's neck.

Her attitude is far more tolerable than Amanda's.

"By the way," Amanda adds, "I've been dying to ask you—what color are your eyes?"

Now her attitude improves because she's nosy.

"Medically, they're classified as colorless. Legally, they're gray," Zia answers flatly.

Jazz gasps when she sees Zia's transformation. They squeal and giggle like kids all the way down Rodeo, and back to Fargo Tower.

They enter Spark's lobby to find Makayla gossiping with others. White hot jealously hurls from her eyes like a flame thrower. Zia smiles as she passes her. With all the money and success, Makayla finds time to come to Fargo Tower just to be nosy. It's official, she's miserable.

Zia finishes out the day trying her best not to move her head too much. She doesn't want her curls to fall before she's had a chance to show them off. When everyone else clocks out at 5:30, Jazz comes in with her arsenal and they get started.

They play music and chat while Zia prepares for something she'd sworn off a year ago. Jazz gives her eyes a smoky, smoldering look, and extends her lashes with some miracle mascara. Zia's excitement grows as the time passes. Until it's almost seven, that is. Then panic sets in.

Jazz looks her over, satisfied that she's done the best she could in the time they had. Fatigue takes its toll and she slumps into the chair. Zia's taken enough of her time. She can handle it from here.

"You look absolutely stunning, Zee! Wow! He is going to lose his mind," she beams.

Zia hugs her tightly. Since she'd independently selected M.A.C. Ruby Woo lipstick, she's careful not to stain Jazz' white work shirt.

"Thank you so much, Jazz. You are truly the very best friend in the world. You're wonderful."

"I agree with this."

They laugh, and Jazz grabs her purse.

"Oh, don't forget the clutch. Not that clunker," she points disgustingly at Zia's old purse.

"Right. Thanks."

"Well, I'm outta here. Text me all night. Take pictures. I need all of the details."

"But of course."

Zia escorts Jazz downstairs to the parking structure and watches her drive off. After she's out of sight, Zia unlocks her car door, and tosses the pages of Chiseled Bone and her everyday purse into the backseat. She then scurries back up to the lobby and out of the front door.

She doesn't see anyone right away, but then a cream BMW pulls up to the curb. Bryce exits, wearing a dark gray tailored suit that fits him magnificently.

He stops midstride. His eyes sparkle.

"Wow! Just wow. You look amazing!"

"Thank you."

She lowers her head to conceal her flushing cheeks. He takes her hand and kisses it. He opens the passenger door and she gracefully slides inside. Her eyes scan the interior. It doesn't have the new car smell, but it definitely looks brand new. It's equipped with leather seats and automation.

He gets behind the wheel and beams ten suns worth of sunshine at her. "Ready?"

She nods, and he takes off.

They arrive at Skyline Restaurant. He exits first. She nearly opens her own door but snatches her hand away from the handle.

He takes her by the hand and guides her inside. The ambience is breathtaking. Soft lights, white linen, candles lit all over, and the waiters are dressed in all black suits.

They approach the host, who eyes Zia oddly, as though she's out of place. This causes her to nervously look around, only to notice the absence of diversity. She's instantly uncomfortable.

"Reservation for Fink."

"Ahh yes, Mr. Fink. Right this way."

Zia assumes that they're heading somewhere towards the back of the restaurant, near the restrooms or the kitchen, when they enter an elevator that exits rooftop. There's a table waiting for them. The only table. Bryce proudly smiles at the astonished look on her face. He pulls out her chair and she sits.

"I'm at a loss for words, Bryce. This is all so wonderful. But you didn't…"

"I'm a grown man. I do as I please."

Their server opens a pre-selected bottle of wine and they enjoy a romantic dinner with subtle conversation between bites. As lovely as it all is, Zia just doesn't believe this is who Bryce truly is. These theatrics seem forced; as if he's doing all of this because he assumes it's what she wants or expects.

She's relieved when they exit the restaurant. While waiting for valet, Bryce places his finger beneath her chin, lifting her face to meet his.

"I'm not ready for this night to be over," he whispers. "Would you like to go back to my place for some conversation?"

"Yes, I'd like that."

She finds herself desperately wanting to get to know the real him; not this facade.

They arrive at a gated community in the city of Malibu, right on the water. It comforts her to see that he lives in a townhouse and not a mansion. When they walk through his front door, he guides her towards the sofa, where she sits.

She absorbs her surroundings while he starts a fire before exiting the room. The furnishings are simple and elegant. She makes herself comfortable while watching the fire grow. Music begins playing softly. She smiles because his selection makes it clear that he's still trying to impress her.

There's a question that's just burning her up inside. She decides to ask him to get it out of the way. He comes back into the room without his tie or jacket and a bottle of wine in hand.

"I figured we may as well keep the shivoo going since it's Friday. Would you like a glass?"

"Yes," she promptly answers.

He chuckles while handing her a glass of sweet red. He anxiously sits beside her on the sofa. The fire crackles and burns in anticipation of their heat.

"Bryce, how did you know my shoe size?"

"Oh, that's easy. The night you smashed your head into the vending machine, I caught a glance at your size when you removed your heels."

She'd totally forgotten about that part. She thanks her lucky stars that he's not stalker crazy. That was a concern she can now dismiss. She sighs and relaxes more. He refills her glass.

"You are the most beautiful and exotic woman I have ever met. From your aggressive, defiant personality, to your bowed-legs and transparent eyes."

"Thank you. You're a rare gem also. Plus, you've never asked me 'The Question'."

"What question is that?" he giggles.

"The 'are you mixed' question.'"

"Why would you think I'd ask you something like that?"

He takes a sip of his wine and places the glass on the mahogany coffee table.

"Because I've never met a man who hasn't asked. Very few women either."

As the wine takes its toll, she lowers her head. He grabs her hand.

"Zia, whatever it is, I will never judge you." His eyes grow intense.

"I'm a black woman, Bryce."

"Yes, I have noticed that."

They laugh. She places her glass next to his.

"No, that's not what I meant. It's just that men always ask me about my heritage because they're interested in genetic components that may dilute the part of me that society doesn't accept as equal. But I'm not biracial. I'm a woman of color. That's it. My eyes are this way because I suffer from a rare condition that slowly destroyed the melanin in my irises. By the time I turned fifteen, the color had nearly disappeared. After that, the worst kind of men began approaching me because I exhibited a European trait. They were literally obsessed over it. So stupid."

Disgust churns like acid in the bottom of her stomach as she reminisces on a past that she had blocked out. Not the right conversation to have on a first date. She shakes her head. His thumb wipes away a tear that she hadn't realized had escaped. He moves closer and imprisons her eyes.

"I never asked you because I don't care about that. I care about getting to know the person you are. Sure, we all look at each other and the physical is appealing to our eyes. Sure. But if it stops there, that's by choice and that choice is a reflection of who we've chosen to be as people. I'm sorry that those morons scorched your mind. Sometimes life brings us the worst to prepare us for the best."

He places the palm of his large, but gentle, hand against her cheek and inches closer to her face until she's inhaling his breath.

"You are, by far, the most beautiful person I have ever met. I've thought about you every second of every day since I first saw you." His voice lowers to a huskier level.

His lips delicately graze hers as he speaks. She can't tear her eyes away from his. Her heart disobeys, and she relents, devouring his mouth. He runs his fingers delicately through her bold curls. She trembles.

He opens his eyes every couple of seconds as they taste each other's mouths. She blinks several times, waiting for him to disappear like a mirage because she can't believe he's real. Any moment, she'll wake up from this fanciful dream, Bugs will be licking her face, and she'll settle back into her carefully crafted ways that have kept her safe.

Bryce is unwilling to share her with even her own thoughts. He reminds her that she's fully awake by angling his body forward. She leans her back into the sofa.

His heart and mind are aflame for her. His loins merely follow suit.

She extends her anxious hands and pulls his face to hers, feeling grabby and starved. Desire ignites inside of his eyes, gloriously oozing all over her. This is a moment that neither wants to end. Bryce gazes down at the delicate creature before him, wanting to protect her in this moment more than he desires to be inside of her.

At her tugging instance, he allows his body to rest atop hers. His generous erection throbs against her thigh, betraying his heart. Torturous cries of pleading escape her throat and she nibbles his bottom lip.

"Zia!" he sighs.

She gazes up at him. His eyes flicker with desire for her, but she's too blinded by her passions to see his conflict. Instead, she maneuvers her legs apart. His breathing changes. His chest rises and falls.

A stunned look adorns his impossibly perfect face. He attempts a daring escape from their building fire, but she denies him. Pulling him back down, she allows his manhood to press firmly against her damp folds. If her panties and his trousers weren't creating a barrier, he'd be inside of her, where she wants him. Where she needs him. He shudders, undulates his hips, and her clitoris tingles in response. She squeals with delight. He growls, and his movements cease.

"Zia, we should stop."

"I don't wanna stop. I want you. Don't you want me?"

"More than you could possibly wrap your mind around. But the last thing I ever want is regret. Yours."

"What makes you think…"

"You will, because it's too soon. Every disagreement we have, you'll wonder if you made the right decision. I don't want you to feel taken advantage of or used. Let's just take our time."

He kisses her lips and pushes himself off her with every ounce of strength he's ever known himself to possess.

She lies there with her legs slightly agape, humiliated. All she can think is how she just threw herself at him and he's rejecting her. Her eyes sting and her face grows hot. Her lips tremble like a child. His heart shatters like glass at the sight. She suddenly feels like a kid playing dress up and less like a woman being courted.

"Zia. Zia, no. It's not what you think."

He attempts to touch her face, but she snatches away from him.

"It's exactly what I think. You just don't want me and that's fine. I understand."

She grabs her purse, fixes her clothes, and dashes toward the door. He races ahead of her to block her exit. That act triggers her beastly anxiety.

"Bryce, move." She summons her calm, praying not to reveal her fault.

"Zia, just calm down. We had a perfect night. Let's just talk about this."

He has his palms in the air and his eyes plead for a do-over. Her nerves twist into angry knots. Her anxiety now has a knife to her throat, but she'd never pop a pill in front of him. Drawing her shoulders back, she holds her head high.

"There's nothing to talk about, so just move away from the damn door! Right now."

She clinches her teeth. Tears inadvertently stream down her cheeks. He drops his head and opens the door.

"Zia, please just—"

"Goodbye."

She runs down the stairs. Once she makes it to the street, she sprints as fast as she can. She smells the ocean water, but she can't see anything. She damns the Los Angeles area for not having plentiful taxicabs like New York City.

Allowing logical reasoning to return, she tells herself that she should have never allowed him to drive her to his home. She beats herself up for the entire experience. After she's jogged a few blocks in five-inch heels, she sits on a bench and cries into her hands.

"How could I be so stupid?"

Her phone rings, so she checks to see that it's Bryce. She rejects the call and blocks him. There are a flurry of texts from Jazz, but she decides that she'll reply when she makes it home. She launches the Uber app, books an UberX, and waits on the darkened road like the idiot she believes she's made herself out to be.

Headlights approach. Uber was swifter than she anticipated. She eagerly stands. The passenger window rolls down as she approaches.

"Zia, please. Please, just let me take you home. Please?" Bryce pleads from the driver's seat.

Her anger has dissipated somewhat, but she's still mortified.

"Bryce, stop. What are you doing? You don't have to do this," she replies with open arms for effect. "You don't have to pretend anymore. I won't tell anybody, if that's what you're worried about. Your little secret is safe with me." Her tears break free once again.

His facial expression changes and he exits the vehicle, leaving his door open.

"I have been very understanding and patient, but don't you ever, EVER say anything like that to me again!" He jabs his finger at her and his tone is scarier than she's ever heard.

What had she said besides the truth? He's clearly embarrassed to be associated with the freak that society has shown her she is.

"You are not a secret, Zia. I can't believe you said that. This—what I'm doing right now— is called respect. I am respecting you and treating you like the queen you are. You're so scarred you can't see that. You're living your life in the past while those people you spoke of have moved on. You can think what you want, but you'll think it *after* I've taken you home. Now get in the damn car." He yanks the passenger door open

She stares at him in disbelief. This is the first time a man besides her father has ever spoken to her so aggressively, without misguided rage, but authority and tenderness as the foundation of their words.

She inches slowly toward the car, unsure of what she should do. Should she walk away and leave him standing there? If she does, they'll never speak to each other again. The thought hurts her heart more than she cares to admit. She defiantly enters while maintaining her rebellious demeanor. He stands on the sidewalk with the passenger door ajar, ogling her.

"What?" she blurts in a tone that drips with annoyance and impatience.

He sighs and reaches inside to fasten her seatbelt. He inserts the buckle until it clicks and slams the passenger door shut.

They ride in silence. Heat radiates from him. He's upset, but so is she. She reasons that her anger is justified because she hadn't rejected *him*. She'd welcomed him into the most intimate parts of herself. She thought that's what he wanted when he sent all those expensive gifts. That's generally how men with means express their desire to *possess* a woman.

When they approach her condo, she begins frantically unbuckling her seatbelt, preparing for a swift exit.

"Zia, wait."

"Bryce, I…"

"No, just listen to what I have to say and then I won't stop you if you choose not to speak to me ever again." His voice is calm, low, and composed. His sadness overshadows his anger. He turns to face her, but she cannot return the favor.

"The first day I saw you, I felt—different. I can't explain it, but it's almost like your spirit called out to mine. It wasn't because you had a beautiful face or rare eyes. It was something else. Something intangible. Every single time I saw you, I knew I wanted you in my life." He places his palms to his chest. "My life, Zia. Not just my bed."

She glances at him from the corner of her left eye but remains too hurt to turn her head.

"There are a billion men who wouldn't hesitate to have sex with you, but there's only one who is going to love you and make love to you. That's me. So, if you're going to allow your bruised ego to keep you from a once in a lifetime spiritual journey, then I won't stop you. I just hope that you won't because—because I think I'm falling in love with you." He kisses her on the cheek.

A retort burns in the back of her throat. She has so much that she wants to say but decides not to bother. Instead, she swings the car door open.

"Goodnight," she mutters in the saddest voice.

She runs inside as fast as she can, back to the sanctuary where dating is outlawed. Where Bryce can't exist.

Chapter
FIVE

BURYING HER FACE into the pages of Chiseled Bone, she surrenders herself to Julius Kelp and his mysterious world. It's a nice reprieve because it isn't real, and she needs the escape. Couldn't have come at a better time. She doesn't want to think about Bryce. It's frustrating and hurtful. She doesn't know how to ever face him again, so she plans to avoid him altogether.

She takes a break to grab a bottle of wine. Bugs follows her. She gives him a few doggie treats to keep him quiet for a while. He curls himself up on his plush doggie bed in the corner of her room and she jumps back into hers, wrapping herself tightly inside of her blankets. She takes a few gulps of the sweet fizzy drug with plans to spend the entire weekend reading the manuscript while getting drunk.

As she swiftly turns the pages, questions develop in her mind. She grabs a notebook from the nightstand drawer and writes them down as she progresses in the addictive plot. She's also reading with an editor's eye.

She foresees Julius Kelp as a serial killer. As such, this book should be a series. The deeper she sinks into the layered story, the larger her smile spreads because she knows she has a winner on her hands.

Chiseled Bone will easily sell millions. If she can get Sasha on board, that is. Reaping's forte is crime, horror, mystery, and suspense, and they've had a very long dry spell. No one can push this through the way Sasha can. She's also been looking for the perfect project to shift the market and Zia's been searching for an author brave and talented enough to break through the monotony.

There's no better way to revamp an extinct genre than with an explosive, addictive main character, and a steamy thrilling plot. Somehow Baxter has developed something that's equally character and plot driven. That's true talent.

Zia arrives on the page where Kelp meets up with Sarah Smulders for the first time after they'd developed an intense cyber relationship. She's stunned by his appearance when she sees him in person for the first time because he doesn't look anything like his pictures. She slowly realizes that it's not the same person in the photographs at all. That's a serious red flag.

The only reason Sarah proceeds is because Julius Kelp is even more handsome than the person in the photographs. She completely overlooks the fact that she's just been catfished, and all because he's physically appealing to her eyes. As Zia passes her judgments on Sarah's character, she believes that other women will likely have a similar reaction. This book could be a lesson to make women smarter and more careful.

Kelp is tall, muscular, meticulously dressed, and speaks with a sexy Australian accent. When Sarah asks him why he lied about his appearance, he reasons that he wanted someone to love him for who he was and not what he looked like.

This is where he introduces his massive wealth. Sarah's so desperately taken by him that she accepts his answer and proceeds with their date—effectively dismissing his deceit. Sarah believes that she's hit the jackpot by having stumbled upon a rich handsome man with self-esteem issues. Or so she thinks. She completely lets her guard down and he easily gains her trust with a few lavish gifts, expensive vacations, and wild sex.

Salivating as the plot thickens, Zia jumps out of bed for popcorn, with Bugs right on her heels. She throws a bag of kernels into the microwave and walks around the house while it pops. From the hallway, she notices her cellphone illuminating on the nightstand. She has it on silent because she doesn't want to be disturbed at all this weekend. She sighs and decides to take a peek, fully expecting it to be a text from Bryce. When she realizes that it isn't, her heart sinks. It's an email from Baxter asking if she has any questions regarding the complex plot so far.

It's nice that he's making himself available. Though all the agents she knows, including herself, find this sort of thing annoying, she does have a few questions. Mostly about Kelp's childhood friend, Jason Donovan, who is now lead detective of New York's homicide division. The microwave dings so she drops her phone on the bed.

When she returns, crunching on the buttery popped kernels, she bounces onto the bed, retrieving the phone from underneath her bum.

She prepares to reply to Baxter with the questions she's scribbled down, but when she unlocks the phone, there's a text from Bryce. Oceans of relief cascade over her like California coastal waves.

"Zia, I can't stand this silence. Please, talk to me."

She sighs and decides that she'll respond later. She exits the text and returns to Baxter's email. She replies and continues reading the manuscript. Every couple of pages, Baxter sends an email and she replies. He has a wonderful sense of humor and she finds herself laughing throughout the evening. She truly needs it.

As the night progresses, they send each other dozens of emails, and sink into casual conversation. Baxter's personality is a breath of fresh air. Nothing like his main character. Kelp's mind is inescapably dark, while Baxter seems to be genuinely witty and easy-going. After several hours have passed, she decides to reply to Bryce's text. She keeps it short and sweet.

"There's no need to apologize. I'm not upset."

She dozes off mid-sentence of Kelp's dialogue with Sarah, as she slowly begins to realize that she's made a terrible mistake.

Bugs licks her face until she opens her eyes. She groans and turns over.

"Not now, Bugs. Five more minutes."

He barks his disapproval and pulls the covers from over her head.

"I should train you to fill your own bowl."

He barks again because he understands sarcasm and gripe in every language. She kicks the covers away from her feet and throws a tantrum before finally getting out of bed. She attempts to go into the bathroom, but Bugs isn't having it. He comes first.

"Fine! Let's go!"

He scurries ahead of her, into the kitchen.

She fills his bowl, then hurries into the bathroom while he drowns himself in his breakfast. She'll cook him a fresh meal tonight.

She quickly brushes her teeth, washes her face, and empties her bladder. She glances at herself in the mirror. The redness from crying makes her irises appear even lighter…and creepier, in her opinion.

Her curls haven't completely fallen either. She'll wash them out tonight because she wants them gone and any other remnants of that night to be scrubbed away.

She selects a random pair of blue jeans, a green shirt, and shoves her feet into white sneakers. Just because she's caging herself doesn't mean Bugs has to suffer. Even though that *is* what friends are for. He notices her dressing and barks his excitement. He grabs his leash and brings it to her.

"Traitor. Let's go."

She takes him for a slow walk around the community. There are a few other residents walking their dogs on this balmy Sunday morning. She just smiles and keeps walking. Minding her own business is more crucial than ever before.

She checks emails from her phone while Bugs wanders around. Baxter had replied after she'd fallen asleep. A smile spreads across her face. She responds that she's halfway through Chiseled Bone and should have more feedback for him tomorrow.

Bryce never replied to her text. She tells herself that she's fine with that. Deep down, nothing could be farther from the truth.

WHILE STILL SITTING in her car inside Fargo Tower's underground parking structure, Zia takes a few moments to gather her strength. She'll need it today. She needs it every day, but especially today.

She's disappointed that she's allowed her focus to be curved by a pair of beautiful eyes, a muscular chest, a few gifts, and a fancy date. She smacks her lips.

She'd finished Chiseled Bone last night and knows for an absolute fact that she'll be offering Baxter representation today. That's priority number one. The manuscript was clean and completely error free. He must've submitted it to a top-notch editor before subbing her. She appreciates that extra icing. Just made her plan go a whole lot smoother. She decides to put Bryce behind her and focus on Baxter, but she must pace herself, so as not to come off as desperate.

After finishing the manuscript last night, she'd had a nightmare about Julius Kelp. In Chiseled Bone, he sexually assaulted and then deboned Sarah Smulders. Gutted her like a fish before dumping chunks of her body along the Hudson River and Long Island Sound. He also murdered other women. His character viewed Sarah as special. So special that she got the worst of it.

She shakes the terrifying visions from her head, thankful that it's just a story. She takes a few more deep breaths before exiting her Prius. She calms her nerves by asking herself what the odds are of running into Bryce today. Fargo is a large building.

She walks in the direction of the elevators and gives the area a quick scan. He's nowhere in sight. She joins the crowd and enters the elevator with about a dozen others. She makes her way towards the back because she knows most will exit before her. She sighs deeply because Bryce isn't one of the dozen. The doors begin to close as everyone makes their floor selections, when someone shouts from the lobby.

"Hold that door!"

A couple of people in the front stop the doors from closing. Bryce squeezes inside and briefly glances at her. He thanks the other employees and presses the button for the 25th floor. She notices how the others immediately warm up to him after they realize where he works. Typical networking involves so much butt kissing that it makes Zia's arm pits itch.

Floor by floor, the elevator empties. After the seventh floor, it's just the two of them. He's standing in front of the doors and she's still in the back. She waits for him to attempt a conversation, but he doesn't turn around. He doesn't even speak to her. When they reach her floor, he steps aside. She exits while glancing back at him. He looks away as the elevator doors close.

She speeds past the front desk, into her office, grateful that Jazz hasn't arrived. As soon as she sits, her emotions sit with her, on top of her head and heart. He didn't speak to her. He wouldn't even look at her. She never imagined that it would hurt this much, but it does.

It's like a scorpion is stinging her, injecting her with poisonous venom. Her eyes water and she starts hyperventilating. She grabs her purse and frantically searches for the Xan.

She twists the cap off and swallows a capsule, dry. Only after she's swallowed it does she search for water. She grabs a half empty bottle of PH water from atop the file cabinet and chugs it down. She swallows too fast and starts choking. All of it isn't going down her throat. Some of it is spilling across her face as she wildly yanks her head back.

Her hands are shaking, and her sinuses are clogged. She sits, waiting for the drug to take effect. She's not sure how much time passes, but eventually the tremble in her hands cease and her sinuses clear. She dabs the wetness from her eyes and cheeks.

She sighs when the attack ends. Never again, she vows. She'll never let this happen again. She snatches her laptop open and presses the power button. It's time to finally rocket her career to the next level. After the OS loads, she launches her email. She skips over everything else and goes directly to Baxter's.

She wastes no time typing him a thorough message expressing her excitement, detailing the few concerns she has, and asking him questions about his professional life as well as his expectations for Chiseled Bone. Once that is done, she follows up with everyone else, and digs into her slush. She selects one hopeful from fifty and rejects the rest.

After printing out the sample pages of that selection, she composes an email to her golden egg, Sasha, who'd pushed three other authors of Zia's into publication already. Sasha's expressed how much she wants something similar to Chiseled Bone, so Zia is giving her first dibs.

However, Zia's made up her mind that if Sasha doesn't come correct, she'll open an auction. If that happens, Sasha will lose and that might hurt their professional relationship. Zia doesn't want that, and she hopes that Sasha doesn't either.

Every agent and editor just knows when they have something great. This time, Zia knows. She attaches the error-free manuscript and clicks send.

Next up, she contacts Lillia at TransMedia to follow up with her regarding StarFire. StarFire is one of her client's published book series. It's generated only moderate sales, but Yazz Network has expressed an interest in converting StarFire's characters into a televised drama series.

Lillia is trying to get the deal tabled soon, so Zia plans to have lunch in the cafeteria today. She decides that it's time to kick her own butt and force on the fake smile that others have mastered. She's ready to play the game.

Jazz arrives at 9:30 and she approaches Zia like she's just been released from a psych ward.

"Are you okay, bookie?"

"Jazz, I'm fine okay. Don't start."

Jazz stands motionless for a moment, squinting her eyes as if she's reading her friend's mind. Zia continues typing while occasionally glancing up.

"Jazmine, I'm fine." Zia actually forces a smile and a chuckle as proof.

"Mmm hmm, okay. If you need anything, let me know," Jazz grumbles while cocking her head sideways.

"I will."

"Lunch downstairs today?" Jazz warbles in a wary tone, challenging Zia's answer.

If Zia says that she's having lunch in her office, Jazz'll hound her for months.

"Yup, I wanna try their roast beef."

"Okay, okay. You win this round."

She closes the door and Zia shakes her head. Jazz is truly a great friend and she's right. Her compass is pointing in the right direction. Zia's just misleading her because she's not quite ready to discuss Friday's unpleasantness. Especially not since Bryce is ignoring her now. She's far too embarrassed to reveal that recent detail.

A new priority email arrives from Baxter. She vigorously grins as she clicks. He answered her many questions and addressed her few concerns. He's direct and thorough and has even included the link to his author website. She eagerly clicks it. There's only one photograph of him and a short bio.

She'd expected the site to be simple because he isn't published yet, but the bio is also scant, to say the least. It doesn't contain too much more information than he's already shared with her via casual conversation. She's satisfied that he has some type of internet presence.

She replies to his email, inviting him to give her a call to discuss further details. She then informs the switchboard to remove the block from her incoming calls which normally serves to direct everyone to leave a message, so she can return their calls when she has time to speak. A typical screening tactic.

Within the hour, her line rings. She answers without hesitation.

"Baxter Leopold is on line one," the nasally attendant announces.

"Thank you. Please, send him through."

"Hi, Mr. Leopold?"

"Miss Lennox?" his greets in an appealing British accent.

"Zia. You can call me Zia," she chuckles.

"Well, Zia, it's nice to finally chat with you."

She blushes at the sound her of name pronounced more eloquently than she's ever heard.

"Yes, same here."

"So now that I have you on the telephone, I can put you on the spot by asking you how you truly feel about my manuscript."

"Well, the truth is that I love it. It's an amazing story. That's what I wanted to speak with you about."

"Oh?"

"Yes, I'd like to offer you representation and discuss the details, if you're interested in establishing a partnership with me."

"Partnership? Hmm, that sounds appealing."

"Well, it'd be a professional one, of course."

"Yes. Yes, of course. Please, explain the details to me. What does it involve?"

She spends the next two hours chatting with him. The professional portion of the conversation lasts a meager forty-five minutes. The rest of the time, they converse about literature, authors, arts, and the market. They even discuss cuisine.

The conversation flows so effortlessly that she hadn't realized so much time had passed until Jazz sticks her head inside and taps her watch. Zia nods to acknowledge it's lunch time. She reluctantly informs Baxter that she must go.

"Oh no. Already?"

"Unfortunately, yes. But I'll send you a contract before the close of business today. Take your time with it. I recommend that you have an attorney look it over with you. If you decide to sign it, just email it back to me in PDF format. Once I receive it, I can go to bat for you."

"Oh wow. I like the sound of that. Very gladiator-like," he chortles.

Her face flames. This discussion was such a breath of fresh air for her. She now feels blessed to have made the connection.

"Well, I'll chat with you another time then, Mr. Leopold."

"Baxter."

"Okay, I'll talk to you soon, Baxter. Goodbye."

"'Til another time, Zia."

The sound of her name on his foreign tongue inexplicably warms her insides. She's quite enchanted, but she's done things out of order, and hopes that she doesn't regret it. She had no business sending Chiseled Bone to Sasha before Baxter signed a contract. If he decides to pass, Zia could be terminated.

"No negative thoughts, Zia," she murmurs to herself.

Sighing, she pushes away from her desk and grabs her purse. She takes Jazz by the arm and guides her towards the elevator.

"Come on, I'm hungry!"

Zia walks with bounce in her step and sample pages in her arms from a different author. They enter the elevator where Jazz eyes her suspiciously. Zia catches the glare.

"Why are you looking at me all crazy?"

"Just yesterday you were the darkness trapped inside of a spissatus cloud, as you so eloquently put it, and now you're suddenly on the moon? That's bipolar as hell Zee and you know it."

"Can't I be happy without there being a reason?"

"What the? Do you hear yourself? Hell no you can't be happy without telling *ME* the reason why you're happy, and after spending a weekend under a rock. Now spill it!"

Just as she finishes her rant, the elevator door opens. Zia loops her arm through Jazz'. She practically has to yank her friend from the elevator because she's in shock.

They pile food on their trays. Zia catches Jazz's squinty glares a few times but ignores them. Zia pays and leads them to a booth near the window that seats four. As soon as they sit down, Jazz continues her interrogation.

"Okay, Zee. What's going on? First, you're smiling and skipping around the office, and now we're sitting in a booth where others can join us?"

"Calm down, okay. I'll tell you everything. Just chill out. Don't make a scene."

Zia laughs and starts slicing into her roast beef with a plastic butter knife. Jazz patiently places her napkin in her lap while Zia pops a piece of tender beef into her mouth. She savors the flavors and licks her fingers. All the while, Jazz' scowl is heating up. Zia just smiles, teasing her, and relishing in the moment.

"Zee!"

"Okay, okay," she laughs—taking a sip of sweet tea. "Remember that manuscript I told you about?"

"The creepy one about bones? Duh, of course I remember. What about it?"

"Well, I read the whole thing and it's the *one*. The million dollar one."

"Okay, so give me a full rundown then."

Zia divulges all the juicy details about the book and spends several minutes discussing Kelp. She and Jazz agree that women fall for Kelp's shady glitzy type all the time and that women will definitely relate to the story.

"Dang, that's horrific. To remove pieces of someone's bones out of their body while they're still alive? Ugh," Jazz shudders.

She shakes off her chills, though Zia left out the part where Baxter made her blush. No need to go there.

"Well, I emailed it to Sasha at Reaping, as planned. Once she starts reading it, she won't put it down. After that, I'll give it a week for her to pitch. If she doesn't give me an offer worth my time, I'll open an auction."

"Whoa, Zee. Careful. You know how editors can be. She's looked out for you in the past, so don't step on her toes unnecessarily. We never discussed this part of the plan."

"No, of course not. I'm just saying that I know this is worth millions and any publishing house will see the potential. It wouldn't be right if she expected me to accept pennies just because we're colleagues."

"That's true, but other publishing houses may not give it the time of day simply because they've decided that the genre is extinct. Just try to negotiate with Sasha before jumping into an auction. You may make the money and lose a good ally in the process. You don't want that."

Knowing that she's right, Zia calms down and tries not get ahead of herself. Sasha has been great to her. She just sincerely hopes that this goes well because she desperately wants and needs this.

They sit quietly munching on their food when Lillia saunters over with her tray.

"May I join you ladies?"

"Of course," Zia squeals in a tone so crisp that it surprises even her.

Jazz heaves a look of noticeable surprise. Zia kicks her underneath the table before scooting over to allow Lillia to sit beside her. Jazz asks Lillia to join her on her side instead.

The three of them jabber when Zia catches a glimpse of Bryce paying for his lunch. They make eye contact, but he walks all the way to the opposite end of the cafeteria. The smile on her face evaporates into a pool of sorrow. She loses her appetite and quickly thinks of a lie that will allow her to make an exit.

"Hey, you guys, I need to get back upstairs and make a few follow up phone calls. We'll catch up later."

"Let's go out for drinks after work," Lillia suggests.

The offer is a bit of light seeping through the sudden darkness. Knowing how introverted her friend is, Jazz immediately begins shaking her head, preparing an excuse, but Zia cut hers off.

"Sure, let's do that. But tomorrow though. I have to type up a contract tonight."

The expression on Jazz's face is one of priceless astonishment. Zia dumps her entire tray into the trash, then makes a beeline for the elevators. As soon as she's back in her office, she decides that she's leaving early and will finish everything else from home.

Her mind leans into not coming in tomorrow. Possibly not for the rest of the week. She notifies the switchboard to direct all calls to voicemail, grabs her purse, and heads down to the parking garage.

She reaches the bottom floor, the elevator door opens, and Bryce is standing there.

"I figured you'd leave."

She walks right past him, towards her car, without saying a word. Her heels click loudly against the asphalt. He follows behind at a safe distance, with his aching heart in his hands.

"See, Zia. This is exactly why I haven't spoken to you. You want me to speak, only so you can ignore me. It's very hurtful."

She whips around to face him.

"That's not true. I did respond and then *you* did not. Besides, you're not the only one who's hurting."

Darn her big mouth. She didn't want to reveal that.

"Telling me that you weren't upset when I knew you were, isn't a response. Come on, let's have an adult conversation."

"About what, Bryce?"

He sighs. His head is telling him that no woman could be worth tap-dancing all over his pride this way. She unlocks her car doors, throws her stuff into the backseat, and swings around. Her smoldering eyes reinforces his heart's decision to fix this trivial thing.

She wraps her hands around her twenty-six-inch waist while impatiently awaiting his reply.

"About everything. We can move beyond this. That's what mature adults do. I want you to take the time to express your feelings to me and I will listen. I will understand."

He walks closer. Instead of flinching from the proximity, she averts her eyes. His choice of words rub her the wrong way and she decides to correct him instead of fearing him.

"Stop making references that I'm being childish because I'm not. This— right here— is me being humiliated. Humiliation will make any woman angry."

He's satisfied with the progress of the cruel irony she's dished. He reasons that if she didn't care for him, she wouldn't bother to argue with him or remember Friday night's conversation so vividly.

"I didn't intend to make you feel that way. I didn't expect things would heat up so quickly. That's my fault. I had no idea you even found me attractive until that moment."

Her facial expression reveals her shock.

"Talk to me, Zia. At my place, your place, the park, the zoo—I don't care. Just meet me."

She reluctantly looks into his soft and pleading eyes. They suck her right into him and she caves.

"Okay. Meet me for coffee at Genobia's on Santa Monica Boulevard at seven."

She turns to open her door, but he beats her to it. He holds it open as she slides into the seat.

"Thank you, Zia. Drive safely."

She starts the engine and speeds out of the parking structure, glancing at him in her rear-view mirror. He remains cemented with a grin on his face. She makes a right turn onto Wilshire Boulevard and heads home, dripping with relief.

Chapter
SIX

IS PHONE RINGS and he glances at the caller ID. Why, it's his dear old friend, Johnathan. Likely calling to feebly insinuate and hint about, hoping that their childhood friendship will eventually cause a conscience to appear from thin air.

"Ha, ha. Oh, Johnathan."

He allows the call to go to voicemail, only because Johnathan will call back. When the phone rings again, a grin stretches across his face. Everything must be on his terms. This time, he decides to answer the call.

"Hello, Johnathan."

"Hey. How are you?"

"I'm as blessed as any man can be in this world. How are the wife and kids?"

"They're great, thanks for asking. Look uh—there's been some really creepy stuff happening around town and I was wondering if you knew anything about it."

"This is New York, buddy. You must be more specific," he chuckles, as rehearsed.

"Well, female body parts have been discovered floating in Hudson and LIS. Have you heard about it?"

"Yes, I have. Terrible business there."

He takes a sip of his $30,000 aged Yamazaki single malt whiskey.

"Yeah, I'm sorry to put you in this position, but we have no leads. Literally, nothing. Do you think you can possibly use your connections to ask around a bit?"

"Oh, yes. Yes, of course. Anything for a dear friend."

"Thanks again and I'm really sorry for calling you with this. Let's have drinks later this week. If the billionaire is free, that is."

They laugh.

"Of course. That'll be just wonderful. I'll have my assistant clear my schedule. You just tell me the day."

"Great, I'll follow up with you in a few days."

"Alright. Well, give my love to Grace and the kids."

"Will do. Talk to you soon."

They disconnect the call. Each man, feeling ahead of the other. Truthfully, only one of them is. The most cunning and deviant of the two. The one who actually received the information he didn't even need to seek but was most assuredly supplied. He takes another sip of his whiskey and returns to the ripened chat room that's plump and spilling of juices for him to devour.

CHISELED BONE WILL officially be published. When Sasha came back offering a five-book deal with a seven-figure advance, Zia couldn't believe it. She didn't have to negotiate anything because she knew that was the best offer she could've ever hoped for. She was in a trance for weeks. Baxter tried giving her all the credit, but she refused it each time. He'd written the story. She simply placed it into the right hands.

She and Baxter sat on the phone for hours and hours saying wow every couple of sentences the day the offer came back and even longer when Reaping decided to push Chiseled Bone's release up by six months, which is now only a few weeks away. Reaping knows something that she doesn't, and she lacks concern for their internal politics. She cares about ensuring that Baxter's best interests are protected. That's her job. A publicity agent has been hired and marketing campaigns have been launched.

She's already received her official copies from Reaping and has forwarded Baxter his. Reaping believes that Chiseled Bone will help reestablish the darker side that they've always been known for in the past. Zia and her bank account definitely agree.

She likely would've gone on a little shopping spree if she didn't have Bryce to keep her sane. He's helping to grow her money and has been working with his billionaire B&F connections to maximize her returns since the firm specializes in investments.

She reimbursed Jazz for the $5000 hair cut at Selena's and paid off her Prius to eliminate that annoying monthly expense. Bryce wouldn't allow her to pay anything else off. Not even credit cards. He told her that would all come later.

A dazed Zia cooks breakfast for Bryce and Bugs. Her cellphone rings, breaking her from her reverie.

"Hello?"

"Come meet me so we can celebrate," Baxter pleads with her.

Her already chipper mood instantly skyrockets to the moon.

"I couldn't possibly just take off without making plans."

"Of course, of course. But why not?"

"Well, I do have a job, ya know."

"You're practically your own boss so cut it out. Come on," he whines playfully.

"Be that as it may, I still have to make plans for such a thing. I need to think about it and decide if I can even afford to travel."

"I'll pay for everything. Flight, accommodations, everything. You just made the deal of the decade and you should celebrate."

"I can't ask you to do that. I..."

"...you're not asking me for anything. I'm offering. Besides, I've completed the second book and I refuse to share it via email. So, you must come."

"That's not fair!" She laughs at his brilliantly cunning strategy.

He knows she's been waiting anxiously like a mad woman for the next installment. He chuckles a hearty one and continues pleading.

"Come on. Say you'll come."

She pauses for a moment and sighs, realizing that at some point she knew she would meet him, so why not now?

"Okay."

"YES!"

"Just let me talk this over with Spark and I'll have a definitive answer for you as soon as I can."

"Great! Fantastic! Till later then, love."

He disconnects the call and she removes the sizzling sausage from the pan—shaking her head at his uplifting enthusiasm.

"You're going to New York?" Bryce inquires, alerting her to his presence.

He's standing in the doorway behind her, shirtless, with his arms folded across his chest. She nervously wonders how long he'd been standing there.

"Well, yes, eventually. We both knew that I would have to go at some point."

"Yeah, I just figured that we'd discuss it when the time came." He kisses her and sits down at the breakfast table.

"And we will discuss it. Baxter just brought it up a second ago. I haven't given him a definitive answer yet. No dates have been set. No flights have been booked."

She smiles at him while grabbing a carton of eggs from the fridge. He playfully smacks her bottom.

"I don't like the idea of you traveling to New York to meet a stranger, alone. I can't take time off from B&F anytime soon either because I've already requested time for something else."

"I know, babe. I know. But he's not exactly a stranger. He's my client."

"Zee, he's a stranger. Period. Your safety is all I care about and I don't know him."

"Okay, okay. We'll talk about it some more. But right now, no business talk. This is our time." She tenderly kisses him on the lips.

He wraps his arm around her waist and pulls her onto his lap.

"Babe, I love you. If anything ever happened..."

"Stop it. Nothing is going to happen. Now how do you want your eggs?"

Bugs barks at them, jealous of Bryce. He's always come first and now he's sharing her with someone else.

"Sorry, Bugs. How would you like *your* eggs then?"

"Woof!"

They laugh at him as he goes to sit near Bryce's feet. He allows Bryce to pet him now and that's progress from just last month. Bugs whimpers at Bryce's churning gut. The thought of Zia traveling to meet her client just doesn't sit right with him.

The television is on. Bryce flips through the channels. There's nothing more soothing than watching the news on a Saturday morning over breakfast. He's waiting for the sports segment and she's waiting for entertainment to see if this agent Reaping has hired for Baxter is doing their job. As she whisks the eggs inside of the Pyrex bowl, the anchor's announcement captures her attention.

"More body parts of an unidentified woman have been discovered along the Hudson River this morning. NYPD have yet to release any further details regarding the discovery and whether this is in any way related to the remains discovered in Long Island Sound just last week."

She stops whisking. *Couldn't be anything more than coincidence,* she convinces herself. Horrible things are happening all over the world, all the time. Any likeness is clearly coincidental.

"Babe, you all right?" Bryce asks.

"Oh, yeah."

She pours the beaten eggs into the sizzling pan and clears her mind.

After breakfast, they take Bugs for a walk together. Bryce never just holds her hand. He locks their fingers together and massages the inside of her palm with his thumb. He truly is her dream come true. They sit on the bench and watch Bugs roll around in the grass.

"So, I was thinking—I want you to meet my parents," he springs on her.

"Oh."

She knew that would eventually become a topic of discussion because he's met her parents and they absolutely love him. She was so surprised at how quickly her parents became attached to him. Her mother squealed with delight when Zia told her that she'd flushed the Xan. She's not quite sure that his parents will feel the same delight.

She hates to state the obvious, so she doesn't, but it doesn't stop her from thinking about it. Now she understands why he can't request more time off from B&F to travel to New York. He's obviously been planning this trip instead. His family are southerners. Beaufort, South Carolina. The Deep South.

"Hey," he whispers while lifting her chin. "Don't overthink this. They'll love you."

"And if they don't?"

"Their loss. I love you and that's all that matters. Everything will be fine. Stop overthinking, Zee."

"Okay." She smiles and decides to believe in him. If he says everything will be fine, then everything will be fine. She removes tissue and bags from her pocket and shoves them at Bryce.

"Your turn."

Picking up after Bugs has never been fun. At least she has someone to share the exciting duties with now, and watching a thirty-year old man pick up dog poop is more satisfying than she'd ever imagined.

"How romantic," he replies while rolling his eyes sarcastically.

He kisses her. Fireworks erupt inside of his heart. He's never met any other human quite like her and he knows that she's the one.

She welcomes the blossoming feelings of joy and happiness that overtake the dreadful one of fear of abandonment.

SPARK ASSIGNED A temp intern to filter Zia's slush, but it's grown beyond a one-person job, so she happily digs into it as well. She's making the most of the assistance because, with Spark, you never know when they'll snatch the rug from underneath you. She doesn't fool herself into thinking that she has more time to spare. Instead, she thrusts herself even deeper into discovering more gems.

Baxter wants to chat all day, every day she's in the office and she does love conversing with him a little too much. She's in a relationship now, though she hasn't expressly verbalized it, she still keeps their conversations inside of the guidelines. Baxter laughs every time she virtually slaps his hand for venturing outside of the lines. His weird matches her weird and that makes for an easy professional duo.

"Hello?" Jazz screeches while snapping her fingers in front of Zia's face.

"Hey."

"I've been calling you."

"Oh, I'm sorry. I'm just lost in thought. What's up, bestie?"

She sits on the sofa and crosses her slender, toned legs.

"I think I'm gonna leave work early. I'm running on empty right now, I swear."

"Jazz, I don't recall the last time you've called off. Go home and rest before you crash."

"Yeah. Yeah, I will. What's going on with you? And don't say nothing because you know that I know better." She rests her head against the crest of the sofa.

"Jazz, you're not ready for this."

She snaps her head erect and leans forward. The thought of juicy gossip has resurrected her. There's a sparkle in her tired, red eyes. She slaps her palms together in anticipation.

"Spill it Zee, and don't play with me!"

"Mmmmmm…" Zia hesitates because she's not ready to admit it to herself, let alone her best friend.

"Is it Makayla? Has she tried to get with Superman again?"

"Bryce. His name is Bryce, Jazz, and no. She's still salty and sour, but I don't care. No."

"Well then what? Did corporate offer you a promotion? Come on, tell me already!"

"I've been talking to Baxter Leopold…a lot lately."

"Well, you're supposed to. He's your *it* client right now."

"No, Jazz. Read between the lines."

She moves her fingers around until the implication finally registers. She bulges her eyes and then scowls.

"Zee, why? Super—I mean Bryce is the perfect man. What could possibly have your mind wandering?"

"It's nothing like that. I just—I like him, and I can tell that he likes me too."

"But you've never met him. We can all be who we want to be over the telephone and internet. You know better."

"I know—I just—like him. That's all. I'm telling you because I need to say it out loud, so I can slap some sense into myself."

"Okay, well now you have. I don't care how handsome or talented he is, he's a stranger and you don't know him. He's a client. Keep it professional. There are Spark horror stories a-plenty and those agents never recovered from the scandals."

"Scandals?"

"Yes. Women tend to get swept off their feet by mysterious strangers, but those strangers always reveal some fundamental flaw that finally clarifies why they pursue women via the internet. It's never good."

"What scandals, Jazz? And don't play with *me*."

"Just two years before you were hired, there was a junior agent named Jillian. This was her office. She fell in love with her Dallas TransMedia client, got pregnant, and he turned out to be a serial polygamist. She never lived the humiliation down and eventually got canned."

"Damn."

"Exactly. Whatever he's offering, it's not worth it, but you can always talk to me about anything. No matter what it is, we'll figure it out."

"I'm glad you feel that way because I'm traveling to meet him for the official release."

"Have you talked to Bryce about it?"

"Sort of."

"Zee, come on. You're asking for it. If you deflect, he'll begin losing trust in you faster than you can earn it. You're smarter than this. Go home. Talk to your man." She stands and grabs her back like a senior citizen.

"We'll talk about this more after I've replenished my stores," she yawns.

Zia rushes over to hug her bestie.

"Thanks, Jazz. Text me when you get home."

After she leaves, Zia rethinks everything, resolving that no man, no matter how appealing, is worth losing Bryce. He's every woman's dream come true and he chose her. She decides to send her phone calls to voicemail to avoid hearing Baxter's voice. Text and email are perfectly sufficient, and both are far less intimate forms of communication.

She receives a priority email from Sasha informing her that Reaping has finalized the book tour for Chiseled Bone. Zia gulps and her stomach growls. She decides to go to lunch an hour early because she needs the time alone. She takes the partial she's printed to Sebastian's Pub eight blocks away where she can watch the news and catch up on the coverage for the release.

She's grateful the Pub isn't as packed as it'll likely be in an hour with the lunch rush. She requests a booth in the corner and anxiously places her order as soon as she's seated. Her server brings her a glass of wine and she wastes no time gulping it down. Her thoughts swirl around Baxter and how to prepare herself to end their flirtatious conversations.

There's no real way to ease into it. It just needs to happen, but she can't be rude about it. After officially thinking it through, she takes her mind away by reading through some sample pages of the partial she brought along.

She grins because it definitely has potential. She's already receiving better material and Chiseled Bone hasn't been released yet. Perhaps the announcement of the deal has turned polished writers her way. Feeling on fire, her optimism grows. The TV blares in the background, but it isn't saying what she wants to hear right now, so she ignores it.

Her food arrives and the aroma wafts into her nostrils. She wastes no time shoving her mouth. She reminisces on the cafeteria choking incident and slows down. She's in no mood to embarrass herself, but the bacon avocado cheeseburger is plump and delicious. It's hard to eat something so good slowly. Plus, the garlic steak fries are hot and fresh.

Tasty foods should include choking hazard warnings. She decides she'll risk death and recommences scarfing while occasionally glancing up at the TV.

> *"The human remains discovered in the Hudson River and Long Island Sound several weeks ago have been identified as Rebecca Horton of Brooklyn, New York."*

A picture flashes across the screen and her jaw droops.

> *"Rebecca Horton was a 26-year-old secretary of Paradigm—the largest conglomerate in the nation. No one noticed that she was missing until nearly a week had passed and she hadn't shown up for work. We contacted her family for comment, but they have declined at this time. According to the autopsy, Rebecca was tortured and sodomized before and after her grizzly murder. Her body was mutilated, with portions of flesh having been cut away from the torso and legs. No further information has been released by the NYPD at this time. More on this developing story—"*

So many questions bombard her mind. How could no one notice that a human being was missing for an entire week? That's absolutely horrible. Portions of flesh were removed from her body? Zia's appetite jumps out of a moving car somewhere. She pays the bill and rushes out of the restaurant.

Chapter
SEVEN

THE BOOK SIGNINGS are proving to be successes. The current line is out the door. Baxter extended his three-hour signing, at the owner's request, to ensure that everyone's purchased copy gets signed.

Zia patiently waits off to the side and watches both of their dreams come true. She texts Sasha to request the sales numbers. Her reply contains only digits and emojis.

"*80,000* 😊"

For a debut by an unknown author, Zia can hardly believe it. In fact, she doesn't believe it at all. Sasha must've accidentally added a zero in there, so Zia texts again. Sasha replies with the same calculation. Zia closes her eyes to allow reality to sink in. Baxter looks over at her and smiles.

Zia picks up a newspaper and flips through it to pass time. At the bottom of the front page, there's a headline about a serial killer on the loose. The police believe the same monster that murdered Rebecca Horton has struck again just last week. This time, the killer completely removed the victim's ovaries. She slams the paper down, unable to read anymore.

After everyone's had their book signed, Baxter expresses his gratitude to the owner and joins Zia, who also thanks the shopkeeper for their hospitality.

"I saw a look on your face a moment ago. What was that?"

"Reaping reports that Chiseled Bone has sold all 80,000 copies. They're printing more as we speak."

"Is that even possible?"

"It's a reality. You did it!"

She throws her hands up into the air and he embraces her. The contact shocks her, but she manages to slowly wrap her arms around him and squeezes very gently.

"Let's celebrate, yeah? Over dinner?" he suggests.

His eyes do something weird to her, so she blinks rapidly, hoping to break the budding spell.

"Sure."

There's nowhere else in the world she'd rather be right now. He grabs her by the hand and hails a taxi. Her adrenaline is pumping and her smile spreads its wings. She recalls Makayla and other agents bragging about their success stories and she could only imagine the feeling. She no longer has to imagine. It's actually happening.

Eighty-thousand copies in one week has exceeded any crime/thriller debut author in Spark's history. She's now convinced certain genres are intentionally oversaturated until they dry out, so things like this appear phenomenal. She just happens to be the first one to stick her toes into the wet sand on a deserted beach and it feels mighty good.

They sit and order their meals. Baxter orders a bottle of champagne and Zia finds herself anxious for a glass of it. She's over the moon with happiness and his smile matches hers.

"You know, when you write something, you never imagine that anyone else will like it. You just hope. I was so afraid to present my work to anyone. You're the only agent that I queried."

"The only one ever?" she asks in disbelief.

That's quite a rarity. Most writer's compile a list of agents to query and systematically check their names off the list as the rejections come back.

"Yes, the only one. I had actually decided not to publish until I attended the Fire Pages conference. After hearing you speak, I had decided you would be my one and only attempt. If someone with your knowledge, vision, and passion would reject me, then there was no need for me to proceed."

"But one agent's rejection is subjective."

"Be that as it may, I was unwilling to alter my character in ways I suspected most would've wanted. It was imperative Julius Kelp remained exactly as I had penned him. Otherwise, all was lost."

Zia most certainly understands where Baxter is coming from. Kelp is the kind of eerie character that frightens the timid masses and intrigues the daring.

The waitress arrives with their food. Zia lifts her fork while the waitress fills their glasses with foaming golden bubbly.

"A toast?" he offers, raising his flute into the air.

She abandons her food to match his elevated glass.

"To the very best and soon to be, richest, literary agent in the world."

She blushes and clinks her glass against his. She seriously doubts she'll be the richest, but it's a nice thought just the same.

As they eat, his eyes burn a hole through her. She swallows nervously. The flavors in her mouth evaporate as different parts of her body tingle in delight.

"You know, I'm actually not very hungry. Would you like to leave now?" he entices.

"Yes."

Her response was swift and anxious. He smiles and requests the check. After paying, they take a taxi to his place. When they enter, the lights in different rooms turn on by themselves, obviously by motion detectors.

"Make yourself at home. I'll grab us a bottle of wine."

He removes his tie and jacket before disappearing. She ventures off to absorb the scenery. Expensive paintings adorn the walls. There are spiral staircases leading upstairs and downstairs.

Light glows from another room, so she follows it. The fireplace has been lit inside of the bedroom and music is playing very faintly in the background. A gentle breeze floats underneath her frilly pastel dress.

She turns around.

Baxter is extending his hand with a glass of wine.

"Thank you."

She gulps it down while keeping her eyes trained on him. He devours his in two large gulps, then removes the glass from her grasp. He lifts his shirt over his head and tosses it onto the floor. Her mouth waters as she stares at his physique. There doesn't seem to be an ounce of fat on him. His pale skin glistens under the moonlight seeping into the room. The flickering reflection of the flames dance on his chest.

He slowly saunters toward her with his eyes scorching, and his sculpted muscles, rippling. For every step he advances, she retreats, until he has her cornered. He leans into her until his erection jabs her rapidly swelling clitoris. She can't help but sigh.

He swallows her breath and fills his hands with her eager breasts. She gathers a bit of strength to lean forward, pushing him away and slapping his face as hard as she can.

"Mmmm," he growls.

She assumes that he's upset and will return the favor, but when he turns his face back to hers, he's even more overwrought with passion. He gazes intensely into her eyes and she decides right then that he will be inside of her. He traces his fingertips across her lips, creeping down to her crevice.

He effortlessly lifts her by the waist and slams her back into the wall so hard that she cries out. A painting crashes to the floor. He smothers her mouth with his. She fiercely bites into his lips. He groans like an animal when she wraps her legs around his waist.

He carries her towards the bed and tosses her. As he frees his erection, revealing that he's much more endowed than she had imagined, she slams her thighs together. The look on his face terrifies her, so she scoots backwards—rethinking her decision.

No way will her body accommodate all that he has to offer with the meager experience she's had. She fears that he'll tear her insides apart. Her reservations do nothing but fuel his fire.

He grabs her thighs, pulls her back to the edge, and glowers in a way that compels her to submit. She reluctantly spreads her legs apart for him. He grins and rips away her delicate panties with no effort.

She's simultaneously petrified and concupiscent. She can't help but retreat as he pursues her, until the crown of her head smashes into the headboard. There's nowhere left to run. His eyes hunger for her. They reveal his intent to gain entry. He thirstily tastes her lips as she sinks into the pillow.

"Don't be afraid, love. I won't hurt you." A mischievous grin spreads across his face momentarily, but disappears as he turns serious. "Not too much, anyway."

As he traces his tongue across her throat, she becomes more and more anxious. Her wetness spreads and her heat ascends. He makes his way lower, until his steamy breath tickles her entrance.

She squirms as he places his hands beneath her bottom and squeezes. The warmth of his tongue against her cleft sends her to a place she's never been. She moans and grabs the pillows. He licks and flicks his tongue as she digs her nails into his shoulders. He glances up to gauge her reaction.

"Is this what you want?"

She doesn't have the breath to answer him, so he shoves his tongue completely inside of her until her knees crash into the mattress. He moans while she runs her fingers through his hair and she smashes his face into her vagina.

"I must have you now," he groans.

His tone is both demanding and beseeching. He mounts her, but hovers for a brief moment, gazing deeply into her eyes, allowing the tip of his thick pulsating member to graze her dampness before entering. She squeals as he buries himself inside. He loses his composure and cries out in a way that she never imagined a man like him ever could.

Her body miraculously expands to allow more of him and he daringly attempts to fit every inch. Her cries of pleading reveal the pain and pleasure of having his shaft caress her walls so aggressively.

Hungrily, he undulates his hips as she clamps her knees against his waist—trying desperately to control his depth. She can barely stand the pain, but she doesn't want it to end. She commands her body to obey and adapt. But with every thrust, she buries her bottom deeper into the mattress until he pins her in a way she cannot escape him.

Tears form in her eyes. He kisses them as they drip from the corners.

"I'm so sorry to hurt you. Do you want me to stop?"

"No," she breathlessly replies.

His kisses become more intense, as do his thrusts. While dominating her gaze, he lifts himself and spreads her legs completely apart, pinning her knees against the mattress. Her fear resurfaces. He's effectively limited her movement in this position, and from the looks of things, he's only had half of himself inside of her this entire time. She fears that if the rest won't fit, he won't enjoy her, and she'll be humiliated.

"Bax, I—I'm scared. You're too big and I can't..."

"...shhhhh, yes you can."

He thirstily drinks the fear in her eyes and the tone of his voice changes. It becomes tender and supplicating.

"You worry for nothing. You feel so amazing, I never want to be out of you. Can I stay inside of you? Please, tell me I can stay inside of you forever, love?"

She can only whimper and moan her responses as he massages her insides. His strokes are gentle. Her pleasure escalates. His rhythm increases and tears well up in his eyes. Her insides become itchy, tingly, and warm. The mounting sensation is foreign, and she can't stop it. She can't control the feeling. Her vaginal muscles spasm as she climaxes.

Her body jerks and her head swirls. He leans forward and shoves the rest of himself inside of her and they both cry out to each other. His flesh gets caught under her nails as she fiercely digs into him. He growls like a beast when he peaks. He collapses on top of her and lays his head against her soft breasts.

ZIA STIRS AS the sun on her face alerts her to the dawn. As soon as she moves her limbs, pain spreads. She winces and reaches down to inspect herself. She pats her hands against her swollen labia. Visions of last night flood her thoughts. She smiles and glances over at an empty spot on the bed. She sits up to rest her back against the headboard and groans.

"Bax?"

Delicious aromas waft into the bedroom, but she's too sore to snoop.

Just as she's making her way out of bed, Baxter enters carrying a breakfast tray. She can't help but to beam at him.

"Good morning, sleepy head." His smile is warm and inviting. He's shirtless, wearing only pajama bottoms.

"Good morning. What's all this?"

"It's called breakfast. Sit back and have some."

"Wow, thank you."

It's such a sweet gesture and she thoroughly appreciates it. He kisses her while placing the tray over her lap. He's cooked everything. Sausage, eggs cooked inside of buttered toast, orange juice, coffee, and oatmeal. Her eyes linger on the delicious eggs.

"Egg in a basket," he offers.

"Huh?"

"I saw you eying the eggs suspiciously. We call them eggs in a basket over in England. Try one."

He feeds it to her. She bites into the buttery crisp bread.

"Oh God, it's delicious!" She instantly falls in love with the flavors.

"I figured you would."

He beams proudly as they share the breakfast he's prepared, conversing about their plans for the day. She'd honestly prefer to remain locked inside of his condo with him, making love, eating, and sleeping, but he reveals his intentions to venture out.

He makes a telephone call and asks the person on the other end to send a car for them within the hour. Must be nice to have such a service at your disposal, she thinks.

Zia showers and allows the hot water to massage her aching folds. Baxter has requested that she be dressed and ready in an hour. She decides to use a full forty-five minutes relaxing underneath the hot water. As she lathers her body, he yanks the shower curtain open and joins her. His lust for her has overpowered his other functions.

Initially, she presumes they're going to take a romantic shower together until he devours her mouth. She drops her loofah and wraps her arms around his neck. His fingers massage her swollen vulva. She flinches. He grabs a fistful of her hair and forces her body back to his.

He licks her lips and face like an animal in heat. Her body tingles against her will. Placing his hands on her shoulders, he turns her body around and bends her completely over. The water splashes her face and drenches her hair. She cries out as he shoves himself into her once again. Having only the slippery shower wall to grab on to, she holds on for dear life.

"Your bum is amazing!"

He squeezes and smacks it multiple times. She reaches back to place her hands against his hips in an attempt to slow his thrusts, but he slaps them away—digging even deeper. Piercing screams fill the steamy shower stall as he grabs her wrists and binds them together with his hands.

Her breasts jiggle with every thrust. He repeatedly yells out her name, madly and passionately. He whimpers, revealing his weakness. A weakness that ignites her lust. Her aching genitals expand and retract around his shaft as he yells expletives, demanding that she confirm the pleasure he gives.

She pleads with him as he demands an answer.

"TELL ME!"

He dives completely inside of her. She shrieks at the top of her lungs, unable to bear the pain much longer. She submits to his every command. The pain begins to subside as she arches her back to allow him more access.

He gasps, releases her wrists, and grabs her bouncing bottom with the palm of his hands. He's whining and sobbing like a child. With her climax imminent, she wickedly plunders his last ounce of control by slamming herself backwards, as forcefully as she can.

"Zia, I—I'm not gonna be able to make it. I—I can't..."

He howls while emptying himself inside of her—spurting and squirting all over her insides. Refusing to exit, he pulsates inside of his new home. His body jerks with each tiny explosion.

Just when she thinks his orgasm has ended, he pulls halfway out and slams himself back into her—expelling even more. His hands wrap tightly around her waist as her orgasm finally peaks.

Tears stream down her flushed face. She shakes her head in disbelief.

He finally attempts to exit, and she slams herself backwards into him, denying his request. He shrieks, and his softening penis grows hard again. A growling rumble escapes his throat as he lifts her upright. He gently yanks her hair as he massages her insides for a second time.

"I need to see your eyes," he murmurs in a soft voice.

She turns to face him. He steps out of the shower and pulls her with him, guiding her down to the floor where they take each other again on the warm hardwood, effectively burning every calorie they'd recently consumed. With each thrust, Zia surrenders herself to the addiction she's formed, vowing never to relinquish her access to such pleasure.

They're still lying breathless on the bathroom floor when the doorbell rings. They scurry to their feet and hastily dress. Baxter answers the door as Zia continues dressing. She glances into the mirror and barely recognizes the person looking back. She once gazed into the eyes of an innocent girl and now, she sees a blossoming woman, full of passion. She ignores the guilt bubbling in her stomach and joins Baxter in the bedroom.

"I hope you're in the mood to fly," he says while shoving his feet into his sneakers.

"Fly?"

"That's right. New York only has so much to offer, so we're taking our curiosity elsewhere."

She's never felt such excitement. Instead of asking him a ton of questions, she allows herself to be surprised. They meet his driver downstairs and are chauffeured to a massive tower next the Chrysler building. She gazes up at the sky while he guides her through the revolving glass doors. They enter an elevator and exit rooftop where a chopper awaits them on a helipad. She freezes. He squeezes her hand for reassurance.

"Don't be afraid, love. I've been flying since I was twelve."

She's terrified, but eager. They fasten their seatbelts and secure their headsets. After he checks the controls, the blades slice through the air, and they take off. Zia looks down at the shrinking Apple below and smiles in amazement. She has no clue where they're going, and she doesn't much care, as long as he gets her there in one piece. She wonders how far they could possibly travel in a chopper anyway.

About fifteen minutes later, they land. He all but yanks her towards a private jet. Baxter prides himself in being spontaneous. Sincere human reaction is his aphrodisiac.

Considering all that's taken place, she now finds it appropriate to question him about his professional life. They board and take their seats. He summons the attendant to order lunch and drinks. He also informs them that he's ready to take off.

Zia gazes out of the window, fascinated.

"Are you feeling alright?" he asks.

"Oh, I'm great. Hungry," she gushes, recalling this morning's escapade. He chuckles and then sighs.

"I'm a bit famished myself. Brunch should be along shortly."

The engines roar to life.

"Bax, where are we going?"

"You'll see."

After they ascend into the air, the sun comes closer.

"What exactly do you do for a living, besides writing awesome books?"

"I'm majority shareholder of a major corporation," he flatly replies.

"What corporation would that be?" she asks, smiling, and excited to learn more about this mysterious man that she's formed an attachment to.

"Vex Enterprises," he spits the name as if it's nothing.

Her smile evaporates as she allows his revelation to sink in. Vex is the third largest conglomerate in the Eastern United States, not to mention seventh most profitable in the world. She immediately feels out of her league. Far more out of it than she ever could have imagined. He's a zillionaire.

"Zia, are you all right?" Concerned that he's upset his most precious cargo, he places his hands atop hers.

She doesn't know how to respond because any response could result in a shift. She likes their chemistry just the way it is. If she allows something like this to affect how she deals with him, all is lost.

"Yes, I'm fine."

"Are you sure? Most are intimidated by Vex, failing to recognize that

I am not Vex. I am Baxter, a completely separate entity," he smiles, with hope materializing in his dazzling eyes.

"Yes, I'm absolutely sure."

He sighs, then settles back in his seat. The male attendant arrives with their food. It's lavish and complete. She normally doesn't have such a large appetite this time of day, but she's expended far more energy in the last twenty-four hours than she ever has in her life. Her cheeks grow pleasantly hot with guilt. He snickers.

"You have another message from John," the attendant announces.

Baxter glares intently at him.

"I'll hold all of your calls until further notice."

"Thank you."

The attendant swiftly retreats. The spacious airbus coasts, tilting just enough to allow sunshiney sparkles into the cabin. Zia squints as the yellow light dilates her delicate pupils. As she devours the delicious pastries and fruits, her mind drifts.

She tries to imagine how many women have come before her. How many he has courted, flown around the world, had passionate sex in the shower, and intimidated with his wealth and power?

The thoughts most certainly rob her of her special feelings, so she rebels against them, though she's suddenly grateful for the IUD she had inserted after her last breakup. It must be difficult for a man like him to spend time with someone who isn't focused on his professional responsibilities.

"Zia."

"Huh?" she replies, sounding like quite the doofus, with a mouth full of squishy melon.

"I haven't been this happy in a very long time. Thank you."

She just smiles and swallows the sweet quaggy fruit, confused by his gratitude. She's sure that he means well, but her woman's intuition kicks in. She's never had a man thank her for sex. Not outright or verbally, for that matter. She won't reveal her true thoughts about his statement. That's just more conversation than she's willing to have.

Her thoughts immediately shift to Bryce. Though she shouldn't, she compares the two men. They don't correlate in any form, from any angle. Bryce stands at complete contrast in every way. Superior, except for one glaring detail; passion. He doesn't seem to have it for her nor professionally. He seems quite complacent. His only ambition seemed to extend as far as bringing her into his life. Beyond that, none.

She's extremely ambitious and rarely settles professionally. She's always thinking of different avenues to explore, beyond becoming a mere partner at Spark. She dreams of starting her own agency and even more.

Bryce is an investment attorney. Quite a boring job from her point of view. She can't imagine too much excitement transpiring in a work day for him. Lit agents live inside of vivid worlds, sparking their interests in ways that won't allow them to become complacent. Perhaps she and Bryce are incompatible in that way.

Then there's Baxter. She gazes over at him fumbling through documents as they're presented to him by the attendant. He's already plateaued professionally. That would explain why he decided to venture into writing. It might provide him a different world to explore. He expresses his passion for life in various ways. He draws outside of the lines and seems quite adventurous.

He's wealthy beyond the imagination. He's powerful, witty, and cultured. He's awakened parts of her she never knew existed. His desire for her is her aphrodisiac. He's extremely well endowed and unafraid to express himself sexually. He couldn't be too much older than Bryce but seems to possess more confidence.

On the other hand, she wonders how he could pursue her knowing that she's in a relationship with another man. She's in no position to judge, for sure, but wonders if he views her as a garden flower to be plucked for his pleasure or does he hope she'll leave Bryce for him? What has she gotten herself into? Though clueless on both fronts, her swollen vagina throbs inside of her panties, reminding herself she cannot turn back.

Chapter
EIGHT

BITTERSWEET EMOTIONS SATURATE Zia's atmosphere as she revels being back in Los Angeles. The last time, it was simply sweet. This time, guilt has followed her home. She's missed Bryce, but she no longer feels worthy of him. He deserves someone who wouldn't do the things she has.

Her conscience is overwhelmingly guilty, but her love for Bryce is so strong that she acknowledges her inability to let him go. She musters as much courage as possible before sticking her key inside of her condo lock.

Walking through the front door, she expects Bugs to knock her down with a greeting. Instead, her eyes are filled with hundreds of sparkling white lights streaming from the ceiling and stretching across the walls. The dining room table has been elegantly decorated with a white linen cloth, vanilla-scented votive candles, red and white roses scattered about, and a bottle of wine chilling. But it's eerily silent.

"Bryce?"

He walks out of the bedroom, dressed in a lavender collared shirt and dark blue jeans.

"Bryce, what's going on?"

"Welcome home, babe." He rushes over and wraps his arms around her.

She squeezes him, buries her face into his neck, and inhales his fresh clean scent. He peels her bags away from her shoulders.

"Babe, what's all this?" she asks again.

He takes her by the hand and leads her into the bathroom where the tub is outlined with tea-light candles. There's another bottle of wine nearby in a bucket of ice. White rose petals are floating atop sudsy water.

She gazes in delight at her warm homecoming as Bryce undresses her. First her shoes, then pants, and the rest. He buries his face into each part of her body. She trembles when the warmth of his breath caresses the face of her pubic area.

After all her toiling and torture, she wonders if he's finally going to make love to her. Then it dawns on her that she's dirty in a way that no bath can cleanse. She won't allow that, so she flinches away.

"Bryce."

"Shhhhhh, come." He guides her over to the tub, then helps her to slowly submerge her body into the soft warm water.

It's so heavenly she leans her head against the tub and sighs. Her fatigue finally catches up with her. She wraps herself inside of the liquid blanket and closes her eyes.

"I'll be right back."

He disappears and returns with a pillow that he gently places it behind her head. He kisses her and traces his fingertips along her jawline, adoring her. He's missed her so much that every day she was gone, he surprised himself with an aching and longing for her return.

"I missed you so much," he whispers.

His eyes overflow with such love that she knows she can never let him go. She just made a mistake. Bryce deserves the very best and she intends to be that. Not break his heart and then hand him off to someone else who won't appreciate him or have patience with the hurt she caused. All those things ruin a person's ability to love and be loved. She decides that she will be better and do better.

He pours her a glass of red wine. She eagerly reaches for it, wiggling her fingers in the air so aggressively that he laughs.

"Rough trip?"

"I'm glad to be home. Now give me my drug."

He hands her the glass and she hungrily devours the luscious sanguine liquid in four large gulps. She smacks her lips, savoring the tart sweetness on her tongue before dangling the empty glass in the air. He refills it and she chugs it down.

"I'll go chill another bottle. If you need anything, just call me. I'll be in the bedroom."

He kisses her lips several more times before disappearing. She revels in this moment of his untainted happiness. Though he's done all of this for her pleasure, the feeling is all his. She doesn't know how she lucked up on Bryce, but she thanks God he chose her. Of all the beautiful women in this wide world, he chose *her*.

She attempts to quiet her thoughts, specifically the guilty ones, but they won't relent. Visions of Baxter's eyes on hers summon her lower parts and they respond in kind. Her clitoris tingles and throbs. The way he invaded her body brings tears to her eyes.

She wants Bryce to desire her the way Baxter does, but he just doesn't seem to. Sometimes she feels like a teenager making out, wondering when they'll get to third base. She wonders how a thirty-year-old man cannot desire the woman he lays next to every night. She rarely ever feels his erection anymore. It's almost as if he's found a switch and flipped it.

That familiar frustration opens the door to her anger and she allows her hand to wander lower. She gulps down what's left in her glass and discards it. Using all ten of her fingers, she explores her folds in an attempt to quench a desire that she knows Bryce will not. She doesn't want to be frustrated. She yearns to be satisfied.

Just as she plunges her fingers into her folds, Bryce calls out from the bedroom.

"Are you okay?"

His voice startles her. She snatches her hands away. He appears in the doorway just as she reaches for the wine.

"Are you alright? You didn't answer me."

"I think I dozed off for a little bit. I'm fine."

She pours the last few drops into her glass and he takes the empty bottle away. Her head swirls as the heat rushes to the back of her neck. It spreads to her breasts. She sighs deeply. He runs his fingers through her hair.

She throws her head back, wanting him so much. Needing him inside of her, but tired of expressing it only to be rejected. Seems that if they ever make love, it'll be when *he's* ready. She'd always thought it was supposed to be the other way around. That's another dynamic that makes their relationship unconventional. Whatever *it* is, it's theirs.

He kneels beside her and gently washes her skin with the loofah. She maneuvers her perfectly curved body to allow him to scrub every inch. Standing up, she places her right foot on the basin, and carefully gauges his reaction to her boldness.

She watches his eyes twinkle with delight at her wet, naked skin. She stands completely still with her legs apart, waiting for him to clean the most delicate part of all.

His erection swells torturously against his left thigh, desiring her so much that he could cry.

She's empowered and ready, not just for sex, but for comfort and acceptance. His chest rises and falls as he delicately sponges her labia. She sighs but maintains eye contact with him. He fidgets, alerting her that he's reached his limit. She requests a towel and disguises her annoyance with fatigue. He assists her out of the bathtub. She pats herself dry as he releases the water, allowing it to drain.

"I'll be in the bedroom," he mumbles.

He makes a swift exit and she shakes her head. It seems that he can't stand to be near her when she's nude. Even if he wanted to wait until marriage, she'd like to think he would want to be comfortable going into it. Not that she's considering marriage. It's not something she ever thought about until Bryce brought it up a while back.

Now, she just wants to crawl into bed and fall asleep. Sleep is the safest escape from reality a human being can get. She moisturizes her entire body and dumps the damp towel into the hamper.

When she exits, a red nightgown awaits her on the bed. She touches the silk fabric. She quickly scans for a price tag, but alas, there isn't one. She slowly slips it over her head, allowing the soft texture to caress her skin. Just as she prepares to dive underneath the covers, she remembers that the living room is lit up like a Christmas tree, so she goes in search of Bryce.

There's a gentle banging coming from the dining area, like the clinking of metal pots. She assumes that it's Bugs, but as she rounds the corner, Bryce is placing a metal cover over a plate.

"Ahhh! Please, sit."

He pulls her chair out and she sits, suspiciously scanning the table. It's more elegantly decorated than most restaurants she's been to. The meat covers look to be antiques, silver with Georgian designs.

"More wine?"

"Yes, please. Bryce where—"

"Please, no questions. Bugs is with your parents for the night."

He removes the covering to reveal the feast he's lovingly prepared. Grilled white fish covered in pesto, cheddar stuffed mushrooms, and creamy polenta. She's stunned because she had no clue he could cook meals of this caliber.

"Wow, babe!" she squeals.

He beams while placing the red linen napkin on her lap before taking his seat across the small table.

"I truly hope you enjoy it. It took me several hours to prepare."

"I'm sure I will love it, thank you. Wow!"

He chuckles and offers the blessing. Taking her tiny hands into his, they bow their heads.

"Thank you, Lord, for bringing us together. For uniting us and allowing us this precious time. Lord, you have been most gracious to bless me with this beautiful woman in my life and I thank you again and again. Together, we thank you for this meal you have placed before us. We ask that you remove all that is not of You, that this food will be a blessing to our temples, and not harm us in any way. In His name we pray. Amen."

"Amen."

He has effectively wowed her yet again. She's left astounded, speechless, and most of all, grateful. Even his prayers are tender. She silently prays for God to please fix her so that she can be the best woman to him. She prays to be his blessing and not his curse.

On the other side of the table, Bryce's nerves threaten to rock his core. He's determined to maintain his cool throughout the evening that he's thoughtfully planned.

"Would you like to discuss your trip?"

His attentive and considerate request catches her off guard, so she stutters her reply.

"No. I—nothing much really happened. I mean it was just, well ya know…New York. I'm not sure if you've ever been before, but umm, it was okay, I guess."

"Okay," he giggles, "I have been several times and I've always enjoyed myself."

If she continues to downplay her trip, he'll know that she's hiding something. Her pulse increases. If she were connected to a polygraph machine right now, it'd be buzzing like hell. Liar, liar, liar. She wishes he could see through her, so she could escape the harshness of confessing.

She takes slow bites of delicious food that turn into ash in her mouth. She again wonders how he's surviving their relationship without sex. Testosterone isn't exactly a mild hormone. Her pessimism wonders if it's possible that he has someone on the side. She drops her fork. It clinks loudly against the plate. Her loins have led her into sin and now her mind is seeking a way out of the guilt.

"You don't like your food?"

"Oh, yes. I love it! It's delicious."

She resumes shoveling forkfuls into her mouth and he breathes a sigh of relief.

"I'm actually a bit jealous," she confesses to break the silence.

"Really? Why is that?" He sets his fork down and awaits her reply.

"I don't think I've ever cooked a meal this great for you. Don't think I ever could."

His laugh is one so hearty that it sends waves of relief through her. He shares the adventures of his week and she asks him several questions to keep the focus on him. They finish their meal and he clears the table. He won't allow her to lift a finger and she's clueless as to why. She grows nervous in wonderment, hoping that she hasn't forgotten some milestone moment.

He returns to escort her to the sofa. They sit facing each other and he takes both of her hands into his. This is the "confession" and "bad news" pose. Her thoughts splinter and sprint in every direction.

He fidgets so much she fears that he's going to confess some awful affair, or worse, call her out on hers.

"Bryce, you're scaring me. Is everything okay?"

"Zia, when you left for New York and I went home, I realized a few things."

Her heart thumps ferociously enough to shatter her ribcage. Her breathing catches in her throat. She prepares her apologies just as he speaks.

"My life, my heart, and my home are with you. You are all those things and more. It was torture crawling into bed without you. I missed you in such a way that I just knew. My soul just knew it was missing its other half. You, Zia. You're my other half."

He kneels before her in the exact same way he did that night in the cafeteria and removes a burgundy velvet box from his pocket. He pries it open and the biggest diamond she's ever seen sparkles.

"Zia, I'm in love with you and I want to spend the rest of my life making you happy. Will you do me the honor of becoming my wife?"

Her breathing spasms and she bursts into hysterical tears. She hyperventilates because she believes she doesn't deserve this proposal. This is supposed to be the happiest moment in her life, but she's spent the last four days allowing another man to have her. Her spasms scare him, so he gathers her up into his arms.

"Breathe, baby. It's okay. Just breathe."

He holds her face in a position that allows her to focus on his.

"That's right, just focus on me. In and out. It's okay."

They sit down together, and he caresses her arms.

When her breathing normalizes, and her sinuses begin to clear she notices the uncertainty and sadness in his eyes. He bows his head. She hasn't given him an answer yet.

"Yes."

He snaps his head back up.

"Yes?"

"Yes, I will marry you."

His eyes lighten several shades and he swoops her back up into his arms. He pummels her with kisses. A smile stretches across her face. His happiness is her happiness.

"Oh my goodness. Oh…I…" he stutters while removing the ring from the box.

He places it on her left finger. She silently gazes at it in amazement.

She pleads with herself to please be worthy of his proposal.

"I love you, Zia."

"I love you too."

He carries her into the bedroom and lays her on the bed. She's truly anxious now because she hopes that they're finally going to make love, but as he pulls the covers over her thighs, her hopes are dashed.

"I'm sure you've had a long and exhausting trip. Get some rest. I'll clean up."

He kisses her on the forehead once, and several times on the lips before leaving the room. She sighs and finally unwinds. She glances out the corner of her eye at the sequel to Chiseled Bone peeking out from her bag on the floor.

As the sandman makes his way, her thoughts scatter. She's returning to New York in a few weeks to attend a meeting at Reaping. She wonders how she'll face Baxter knowing they can never be intimate again.

She turns onto her right side and stares at the huge diamond adorning her finger. She can't believe this just happened. Life seems to be rewarding her for her sins. It doesn't feel good.

RUNNING HIS SLENDER manicured fingers through his meticulously groomed dusty-blond crop, he contemplates his next move. There is someone he's come to desire more than any other. One fairly reminiscent of his most beloved. Now, the others satisfy an immediate aching need, but nothing more. She prolongs the inevitable by preventing the flames from devouring him just long enough to complete his purpose.

The world hastens their destruction by continuing to breed disease like cattle. Women. They should not have been created. They should *not* exist. They're the single greatest threat to the existence of human peace. To *man*kind itself.

His mind twists and twirls around the possibility of their extinction. He can manage no grin, but the one plastered inside of his befouled thoughts. *Men require complete freedom from the slithering influential beast of the female presence.* He presses the send button on his modified phone and orders his assistant about—dispensing with such trivialities as greetings and polite vocal tonality.

"Have the car here promptly within the hour."

"Yes, sir."

"Have the chopper ready and the jet fueled as well."

"Yes, sir. Anything else?"

"Yes. $100,000 U.S. currency in small denominations on the jet please."

"Yes, sir. Very well."

He disconnects the call and swivels his chair around to face the computer screen. Every twenty-four hours, he wipes the hard drive. Every seven days he flies to a remote location of random selection, but from a carefully crafted directory, to completely dispose of the hardware, and purchase a replacement.

His favorites are the Muslim nations because they share similar beliefs. Today, he has chosen the country of Qatar. Quite a lovely people. Yes. Their female citizens are nothing more than slaves to barter and he has plenty of cabbage to shred. There, he can dispose of many without a lash to bat.

"So many fish. So little time to cast."

He gracefully lifts his 6'4 frame from the imported leather chair, grabs his designer jacket, and tosses it over his muscular shoulder. Very much in similarity to supermodel, David Gandy, but with more definition and yes, more money.

Chapter
NINE

BRYCE GRABS THEIR luggage from Charleston International airport's baggage claim while smiling his fiancée's way. She smirks, though her fingers tremble.

"Zee, don't worry. Everything is going to be fine."

"I'm not," she fibs.

She doesn't think that she's convinced him because he releases the luggage handle to caress her cheek. He doesn't say anything, he just kisses her, and lingers until she smiles.

She's not ready to meet his family. She was never ready to meet the family of any man she's been involved with. There's something unsettling about being introduced to critics for the purposes of judgment and acceptance.

She'd always felt judged. Never welcomed to be a part of their familial unit. In the past, it annoyed her to the point where she avoided being thrust back into their midst. They all thought she had something to hide, when she honestly just didn't care for the environment.

She bravely places one foot in front of the other and before she knows it, she follows Bryce out of the airport. She's unsure how far the drive is from Charleston to Beaufort, but she hopes it's a long one.

There's a black Lincoln Town Car waiting curbside. Bryce approaches the gentleman holding the rear passenger door open and shakes his hand. Zia wonders how well Bryce knows this person.

"Nick, I'd like you to meet my fiancée, Zia. Zia, this is my good friend, Nicholas."

She slowly shakes the stranger's hand, allowing her confusion to seep through.

"It's an honor and pleasure to meet ya, ma'am. Welcome to South Carolina."

His southern twang is even more prominent than Bryce's.

Nicholas escorts her into the backseat. The two men chatter as they load the luggage. Zia texts Jazz to let her know that she's touched down. At the same time, there are multiple texts from Baxter. Just as she taps the reply button, Bryce swings the door open. She turns her phone off. Not on silent—OFF.

There's a twinge of bitterness in her regarding the order things are happening. Bryce should've introduced her to his parents before he proposed. Now, she fears his mother will resent her. The ring screams of how she *has* to love and accept Zia now that she's going to be her son's wife.

Bryce scoots into his seat and reaches over to secure Zia's seatbelt. He kisses her and smiles. His excitement is so obvious a blind man could see it.

The car accelerates from the airport and onto the highway, toward a future that she can never turn back from.

They approach a winding road with a large cobblestone carving.

Weingart Manor is sprawled across the front.

Her nerves disperse. Bryce squeezes her hand.

"Welcome home, suh," Nicholas twangs over his shoulder.

Her eyes bulge as she catalogs the massive grounds. The cascading mansion is erected on lush grounds that stretch farther than the eye can see. Various people are out tending the gardens, dressed in white and cream uniforms.

"Bryce?" she mumbles in fear.

"Uh, Nick just drive around towards the back. I don't want to make an entrance."

"Yes, suh."

"Bryce."

"Zia, calm down. It's just Momma and Daddy's estate. It's been in the family for generations."

She's not as stupid as she may appear. This is clearly a *family* estate. Of which, he is also a part. *Weingart*. Where has she heard that name before? Just as her curiosity catches steam, the car stops, and Bryce exits.

"Stay here while I help Nick unload the luggage. I'll be right back."

He kisses her.

"Don't move."

Her nerves have scooched far too close to the edge to move. There's a couple playing tennis on the court. The swimming pool is to their left.

Her heartbeat fills her ears and she wishes she had the Xan to turn to. Maybe there's a loose one floating in the bottom of her purse somewhere. She yanks her bag open and frantically searches. Finding only coins, she sighs. Bryce opens her door and extends his hand.

"Shall we?"

She takes his hand and slowly exits the car. The warmth of the sun caresses her neck. She gazes up at a sky that seems to have banished clouds for the day. Only the beaming yellow sun and coasting birds are present.

Bryce tenderly wraps his arm around her waist and guides her towards a house that's much more than she ever expected. She fears she won't fit in, being a simple girl from Los Angeles. South Los Angeles, for goodness sakes.

As they enter the house, a black man dressed in a suit greets them.

"Mister Bryce, welcome home."

"Thank you, Gregory. This is my fiancée, Zia."

"Nice to meet you," she shyly greets the stranger.

"It's a pleasure ta meet such uh beautiful young leddy."

"Gregory, have you seen my parents?"

"Uh, yes suh. They out playin' a few rounds of tennis. I'll fetch some lemonade."

"Thank you, Gregory."

"Thank you," Zia nods Gregory's way.

He scurries off.

"Welcome to Weingart Manor," Bryce whispers.

"Wow."

He takes her on a very brief tour. She gazes at the lavish furnishings in astonishment. Antique and modern alike. Everyone in the world knows there's no money like Southern money. The kind that goes on forever.

Now she has to worry his parents will mistake her for a gold-digger. She despises the pressure. Had she known Bryce descended from wealth, she would've never dated him.

They sit on the white leather sofa that's trimmed in gold leaf. She tries not to sink into the luxurious fabric for fear of leaving a crease. Her clothing looks even cheaper against the Italian backdrop. Within moments, a middle-aged woman with shiny golden hair appears.

"Bryce!" she squeals.

"Momma!"

They tenderly embrace each other as she examines her son's face, just as Zia's mother does when she visits. His mother removes her white visor and beams over at a nervous Zia through her light brown Bette Davis eyes.

Zia's smile is effortless because his mother's eyes are sincere.

"Momma, I'd like you to meet Zia."

Zia extends her hand.

"It's an honor to meet you, ma'am."

She eyes Zia's hand awkwardly.

"Ma'am? Now we'll have none of that. My name is Lucille, but you can just call me Lucy."

She hugs Zia so tightly, it initially shocks her, but she quickly returns the warm embrace.

"Aren't you just as lovely as the day is sunny? My, my, my. You're gorgeous! Bryce, honey, you never mentioned she was this strikingly beautiful."

"Thank you," Zia gushes.

"Momma," Bryce playfully warns.

"Well," Lucy shrugs.

Her perfect smile spreads across her gorgeously tanned face. She's fit and slender, but not skinny. Her smooth golden thighs wink from underneath her dusty rose tennis skirt, complete with a white spaghetti-strap shirt. A gargantuan diamond ring adorns her left finger. How her demure hands carry that beast around, Zia will never know.

"Hi, Daddy."

Everyone turns toward the tall and ruggedly handsome man entering the parlor. Enthusiasm is absent in his overall demeanor. He's quiet and his face reveals no happiness.

"Nice to see you, son. Welcome home."

Bryce approaches his father with apparent reluctance. They shake hands. Not quite the warm welcome he received from his mother.

"Daddy, I'd like you to meet Zia."

He motions for Zia and she walks over. Unsure how to greet him, she extends her hand.

"Hello. It's an honor to meet you."

His eyes are icy and judgmental, tracing every visible inch of her. Gregory enters with drinks for all. Zia drops her hand, realizing his father made no attempt to grab it anyway.

These are the types of situations she detests and accordingly, avoids. It's usually the mother who forms all types of negative judgments in her head or decides that Zia's trying to steal her son away from her. Not this time.

Lucy approaches with a different temperament.

"Turner, the young lady has greeted you. Don't be rude."

He glares at his wife before reluctantly extending his hand.

"It's a pleasure to finally meet you, Zia. My son has told me many wonderful things about you."

He forces a smile that doesn't reach his eyes and Zia glares at his hand. Now she's the one who doesn't want to oblige. She doesn't care who it is, if they start off on the wrong foot with her, she doesn't feel the need to cater to a bad attitude.

Bryce clears his throat. For him, she softens, reluctantly shaking Turner's hand before quickly releasing it. Everyone grabs a glass of lemonade from the silver platter Gregory passes around. Everyone but Turner, that is.

"Gregory, I'll have a bourbon on the rocks," Turner orders.

"Yes, suh," Gregory nervously bows before sauntering off.

The sweat still adorns Turner's brow from the tennis match he just played against his wife. Zia secretly hopes he lost.

"Momma, Daddy...Zia and I—"

"Son, I'm dripping with perspiration, as you can see. Allow your mother and me to refresh ourselves before we continue any further. Quite rude to address such a beautiful young lady in this state. I'm sure you've had a long journey yourself and would like to freshen up. Wouldn't you say?"

"Uh, yes. Of course."

"Very well. Let's all take a leave and meet in the family area in an hour," Turner concludes. He extends his arm and Lucy grabs it. Turner tells Gregory he'll be taking his bourbon upstairs and they disappear.

Zia turns to Bryce with discontentment pouring from her eyes.

"Come on. I'll take you upstairs."

They ascend the marble staircase and enter a bedroom that's larger than her entire condo. A few silver-framed photos of Bryce are scattered about. He's smiling and seems rather happy in some photos, but not so much in others. The ones with his father.

"I'll start the shower for you."

When he kisses her, she relaxes, bounces onto the bed, and contemplates what she'll wear to the family interrogation. With the way she's feeling, it'll be more like a séance. They may need a medium to break through her stubborn mood to awaken the spiritual light buried inside.

"I don't feel like unpacking right now," she tells him when he reenters the room.

"All of our clothes have been unpacked and put away."

He opens the drawers and closets to show her. He's battling his own crankiness as well.

Though she doesn't fault him, she can't bear to see him sad.

"Babe," she coos while grabbing his face.

She gazes into his beautiful eyes. He doesn't turn away.

"Talk to me."

"After you shower. Go ahead. The water is warm."

He needs a moment alone to fix his mood. She kisses him, and they embrace before simultaneously undressing. She steps into the steamy shower. The humidity and warmth instantly work to relieve her tensed muscles.

She again wonders why Bryce never told her about this place before or why he never mentioned he was rich. She's not upset with him; she merely wonders why he felt the need to keep it a secret. She reaches for the soap. Her hand hovers over an embossed gray bar of extreme luxury. She sighs at the $40 bar of soap, knowing this will be a long week.

Bryce escorts her into the parlor, where fresh beverages await them, and the house servants are readying the dining area. She loathes the existence of servants, but she's more disturbed by the fact that they're all black. They scurry about, lighting the fireplace and setting the dining room table. Zia sighs as she takes her seat on the plush sofa.

Bryce leans over and whispers in her ear.

"I know this might be a bit much but try to give it a chance. Please."

"$40 soap, Bryce?"

"I know. That's the way of life my parents have chosen to live. Try not to judge them for it."

She accepts he's right on that front. It's their money and they can do whatever they want with it. Zia imagines what she'd do if she had unlimited wealth. She immediately decides she wouldn't waste it on expensive soaps when a $1 bar works just as well.

She can imagine until the cows come home. A person can never say with certainty what they'd do until a situation becomes a reality, so she tries to cease her judgments. As long as his parents aren't too uppity, she can manage.

He squeezes her hand. She squeezes back.

"I know you're full of questions. We'll talk all about it tonight."

He kisses her cheek and she thinks they probably should've spoken before, but they're here now. She crosses her legs and scoots farther back on the sofa. He leans to remain in sync with her.

Zia suddenly has an epiphany. She remembers where she's seen the name Weingart. She suppresses her gasp just as his parents enter the room.

Lucy gracefully adorns a pink starburst sundress and appears to be floating on air. Effervescent and radiating positive energy, she smiles as she approaches them. Turner is dressed more formally, but still very handsome.

His powder-blue collared shirt stands out against his tanned, weathered skin. His icy cold eyes drill a hole into Zia's forehead. She doesn't know what she's done to make him so angry with her, but there's not an apologetic bone in her body for whatever Turner's issue may be. She glowers right back.

"Dinner is ready," Gregory announces.

After they're seated at the vintage table, Turner wastes no time.

"So, Zia, where are you from?"

"Turner! Excuse my husband, dear. He has a tendency to be more direct than he should. How was your trip?"

Bryce squeezes Zia's hand underneath the table. She unclenches her teeth.

"Our trip was nice, thank you," Zia manages. "I've never been this far south before. You have a very lovely home."

"Why thank you, dear!" Lucy exclaims. "Though these drapes *have* run their course."

Bryce beams, utterly disregarding his father's rudeness. Not that Zia minds answering his question, she just despises interrogations of this sort. She's not interviewing for a job. Nor are they. Families that behave the way Turner is behaving are usually the sole cause of the entire family's misery.

The servants flurry around, offering appetizers, and crisp beverages with fresh fruit slices. Lucy expresses her gratitude as she is served, but Turner does not. He doesn't even acknowledge the servant's presence.

Zia's gut warns her that Bryce and Turner's relationship is strained, so she decides against adding gasoline to that fire. For Bryce's sake, she'll remain positive.

"Zia is from Los Angeles," Bryce brags. "Born and raised."

Zia smiles at him while slicing into the shrimp scampi.

"I've visited Los Angeles quite a few times," Lucy admits. "The weather there is absolutely magnificent."

She's so positively radiant Zia wonders how Turner lucked up on that pot of gold.

"The weather is indeed the best part of L.A. It's usually fair," Zia agrees, taking a sip of her lemon infused water.

"How did you and my son come to meet, if you don't mind me asking?" Turner inquires.

"We met at work. On his first day, in fact," Zia smiles while reminiscing.

"Are you an attorney dear?" Lucy asks in a curious tone.

"Oh, no. I'm a literary agent for Spark Worldwide. Banks & Filmore is located in the same tower."

Turner is satisfied with the information he's receiving, and Lucy's entertained by it.

"Zia just happened to be on the elevator," Bryce adds, rejoining the conversation. "As soon as I saw her, I just knew."

"Knew what exactly, son?" Turner demands, creasing his brow.

"That I would love her."

"Oh, how wonderful!" Lucy cries, clasping her palms together in delight.

Women do love these types of stories.

Turner huffs and dangles his empty glass in the air. Gregory quickly refills it with bourbon. Perhaps the liquor is reason he's so unhappy. Although, Zia always assumed liquor was intended to have the opposite effect.

"Well Zia, I am so glad you met my son. I haven't seen him this happy in forever."

"Thank you, Mrs.—"

"Ah, ah, ah…"

"Lucy," Zia politely revises.

"Yes, we're delighted," Turner acidly adds.

She doesn't even attempt a smirk because he's rapidly pushing her to her limit. The servants bring in the main course. Roast duck, artichoke hearts, and baked potato. Zia's never tasted duck, though she's heard that it's gamey. She abhors the chewiness of gamey meat, but because this is

Bryce's family and the duck is likely a million dollar selection from a golden pond, she gives it a whirl.

Lucy blesses the food as they bow their heads. Turner wastes no time resuming his original line of questioning afterwards.

"So, Zia, please tell us more about yourself. Your family history perhaps?"

"Um, well my ancestors originated from Louisiana as far as I know. Concordia Parish, if I remember the childhood stories correctly."

"Ah, Concordia. So, you're of French Creole descent?"

Zia's fork clinks against the expensive blue leaf-lined china. Turner hasn't known her for more than a few hours and he's already asked her 'The Question'. She sighs, so Bryce steps in.

"Daddy, Zia is African-American. More importantly, she's human. The most beautiful human being to ever exist. Let's move on."

"Sorry, son. I didn't mean to offend anyone. Just trying to get to know her a little better."

"You haven't offended me. I just don't understand society's fascination with certain physical traits when it comes to people of color. That's all."

"Well, we can certainly understand that, dear. Can't we Turner?" Lucy asks her husband with squinty eyes.

He nods.

"Very well. Moving on. Would it be too intrusive to ask what started you in the literary business?" Turner continues.

"I love books. I love the various worlds created inside the minds of people all over the world. I can travel without ever leaving my office."

"I can't imagine it pays very well."

"Turner!" Lucy yelps, clearly exasperated by her husband's rudeness.

"Alright, Daddy. That's enough! Let's just get this out of the way now, since you're incapable of being civilized. Momma, Zia and I are engaged."

Zia gulps. This was not the way she'd imagined it happening. It should be good news and introduced into pleasant conversation. Turner has made that impossible. Zia bows her head for a moment while awaiting their reaction.

Turner's disappointment is evident. He sighs and dangles his empty glass in the air for a refill. Lucy's eyes water and she dashes around the table to embrace her son. She hugs Zia as well.

"Congratulations to both of you! This is wonderful news. Just glorious!"

"Thank you, Momma."

"Thank you, Lucy."

Turner remains in his seat with a knotted expression, guzzling bourbon. Zia no longer cares for his misery. The assumption may be that Zia loves Bryce for his money, but the Finks will probably never know that she had no clue about their financial status until she arrived. She decides to mentally block all of Turner's negativity.

Bryce, on the other hand, is more vocal.

"You know, I didn't really expect you to express any sincere happiness for me. But I'd be lying if I said that I didn't hope."

"Momma, Zia and I will retire early. We'll see you in the morning for breakfast."

He kisses her on the cheek, they say their goodnights, and disperse. The sound of Lucy telling her husband how disappointed she is in his behavior echoes upward as they wind the staircase in silence, hand in hand.

Bryce, right on cue, undresses her first and then himself. They climb into bed. He holds her tightly against his chest until they fall asleep.

Chapter

TEN

ZIA WAKES BEFORE the sun and immediately checks on Bryce, who's thankfully sound asleep. She ever so gently pries herself from his grasp, scoots off the bed, and tip-toes into the restroom to empty her bladder. She grabs her cell phone along the way and locks the door.

After last night's uncomfortable dinner, they'd gone right to bed without discussing anything. She'd fallen asleep with several unwelcome thoughts swirling. Turner's disrespectful behavior and Weingart were in the backdrop of her thoughts, with Baxter at the forefront. She's certain that he's feeling some type of way because she's been M.I.A. for 24 hours.

Just the thought of him makes her clitoris tingle. Last night in bed, the heat kept rising to her nipples. She continuously pressed her bottom against Bryce's manhood—tempting him to take her. All he did was groan tortuously, sinking the tips of his fingers into her flesh, but he didn't bite. Now she's awake and hornier than ever.

She powers up her phone while relieving herself. She sits nervously on the warm toilet, complete with bidet, while repeatedly whipping her head towards the door, praying Bryce doesn't wake up.

As soon as it loads, a flurry of text messages populates. A dozen from Baxter and a few from Jazz. She texts Jazz first. Next, she reads Baxter's many texts. First of concern, then they slowly become presumptive, and eventually, angry.

She swiftly moves her fingers to reply, concocting a believable lie about meetings and fatigue. Baxter knows she has a boyfriend and she doesn't understand why it seems like he wants her to keep repeating that fact.

What he doesn't know, is that Zia's boyfriend is now her fiancée. She's wondered if knowing this will change anything for him. For some reason, she doubts it. Baxter doesn't seem like the type of man who is accustomed to losing. Being spoiled by money can make people feel entitled to things and people that aren't theirs.

Though she cannot deny she still desires him, their affair must end, and she needs to hurry up and end it. Just as she lifts her bottom, there's an incoming text from Baxter. Apparently, he's been waiting.

> *"Although I am upset with you, I'm relieved that you're okay. My world had disappeared when I thought something happened to you."*

She gulps as his words reveal the feelings he's caught. The kind she hadn't expected. This will be tougher than she thought. She dismisses him by explaining that she requires more rest, so he won't worry or inquire too aggressively while she's in Beaufort.

She powers off her phone and washes her hands. Now that she's pacified him, thoughts of Weingart come rushing back. Questions upon questions.

Weingart isn't a common name, so she knows she has the right one, though she doesn't know much intimate detail. All she remembers is that it's a multi-billion-dollar tobacco and oil company dating back to the 1800's.

She has no right to be upset with Bryce for not telling her about his family's wealth. Especially not when she's had a torrid affair she's yet to completely end. She simply hopes he'll be open with her. This does explain how he was able to afford all those expensive gifts for their first date.

She dries her hands and opens the door. Bryce is sitting on the edge of the bed.

"I'm sorry. Did I wake you?"

"No, no. I guess my body just knows when you're not near."

She wraps her arms around his neck and holds him, while nonchalantly dropping her phone onto the bed. Every single time she's in his arms, she knows he is her forever home. She's never known a human being more beautiful.

"Zee, we should talk."

"Okay."

"I owe you an explanation and…"

"Babe, you don't…"

"…shhh, yes I do. We're a team. I should've talked to you about this a while ago, but I was afraid."

"Afraid of what?"

"Either scaring you away or worse…seducing you with money."

"Bryce…"

"I just need to use the restroom and then we'll talk…about everything."

He slowly walks into the restroom and she bounces backwards, against the headboard. Every honest and gracious act on his behalf, adds more weight to her already heavy conscience. Before she can blink, it'll be too much to bear. He washes his hands and climbs back into bed. He cuddles her against his chest.

"Okay, where should I start?"

"Anywhere," she whispers.

He sighs deeply and tightens his embrace.

"Well my great-grandfather, Weingart, started out as a sharecropper—like many others during his time, when food was scarce. Farming didn't quite suit him. He wanted different. Not necessarily more. He didn't want the world, he just wanted enough to take care of his family for generations to come."

"He decided to invest in tobacco when he and his friend, William Filmore, received a tip. Long story short, they made a fortune that they weren't expecting. The money caused Bill to change into someone great-granddaddy couldn't trust anymore. So, he bought Bill out. After that, he invested in oil. It changed his life forever."

"In 1923, he became the first ever reported U.S. billionaire. Of course, the effects of the tobacco took their toll and he died. My grandma, Tess, was his only child so he left everything to her. Of course, Momma, as Grandma's eldest, was rightfully the next heir to the Weingart fortune.

This attracted a lot of ravenous, slithering men. One being Daddy, Turner Whittle. He won her heart and they married, much to Grandma's disapproval."

"Whittle?"

"Yes, Daddy's a Whittle. Not a Fink."

"Well then, how did you?"

"I'll get to that in a minute. I want you to understand everything."

"Okay."

"Grandma Tess absolutely despised Daddy. There was just something about him she didn't like. They never got along. Momma said after I was born, she lightened up on Daddy a lot. Momma said it was because of me, Grandma *tolerated* Daddy."

He chuckles and smiles to himself.

"Well, Grandma Tess and I were close, like two peas in a pod. She taught me from a very young age about true love and business. Mostly how to recognize one from the other and keep them both separate. She taught me the value of true human companionship, as opposed to money. She taught me the value of time spent."

"Well, eventually Grandma got sick and she couldn't physically run the company. She appointed Momma. Momma stepped in and quickly decided to put Daddy in charge. This upset Grandma because she didn't trust Daddy and was fearful Momma would blindly sign over the family business to Daddy out of love."

"So, Grandma changed her will, naming me the heir…with conditions. She gave Momma 30% and Daddy had already purchased 4%. Of course, Grandma knew what Daddy was doing in secret, seeking to quietly hold the majority because he had Momma under his thumb, so Grandma left me 62%."

"After she passed away, Daddy expressed nothing but rage as the rest of us mourned. I was 17 and had just lost my best friend. Watching Daddy act the way he did was my first time seeing him without rose-colored glasses. You see, Grandma never spoke negatively about Daddy to me. She was better than that. She just always told me no human being is above sin and all those who love us will hurt us because it's in our nature. We just have to find those worthy of forgiveness and our continued presence."

"What were the conditions of her will?"

"In a nutshell? Marriage. She worded it to be true love. That's what she ultimately wanted for me. She saw true love as being the rarest experience in the world. Especially for the rich. Momma would control the company until I married, and my funds would remain in a trust."

This explains why Turner hates her so much. She's a direct threat to his hold on Weingart.

"I had courted a few young ladies the year after Grandma passed. They were all nice, Southern belles from elite families and so on. Daddy, of course, hated them all. Eventually ran them all away with his evilness and sabotages. Not many women want to endure that for long."

Zia can only imagine.

"Then, there was Salairya. Sally for short. She was just a normal, nice girl. Born and raised in Charleston. Her family was average working class. We became fast friends and eventually, we fell in love. I asked her to marry me. Thought it'd be forever."

"Right on cue, Daddy mistreated her. He was rude, and I had even heard he threatened her family at one point. Flexing Weingart's muscles and such. She wouldn't budge. None of his tricks worked. At least, that's what I thought until the day I went to take the Bar. I passed and I was so excited. Couldn't wait to share the news with Sally."

"I ran up the driveway with my papers in hand. No one was in the main house, so I went out back to the pool house. Sally loved it there because she despised being anywhere near Daddy. I put my hand on the knob and I—I froze. I saw them through the glass door."

"Saw who?"

"Daddy and Sally. On the couch. I—I didn't even alert them to my presence right away. I just stood there and watched for a few moments because Grandma's teachings were right in front of me. I hardened my heart as I watched in horror and disgust. It wasn't just sex. Not for Sally. I could see that she was in love with Daddy. The way she was touching him and looking at him. But I could also see that Daddy wasn't in love with her."

Zia squeezes him as his memories pour and his flesh grows warmer from the intensity.

"I gathered my strength and entered. Sally lept from the sofa and began stuttering her apologies. I was disinterested because I couldn't take my eyes off the wry smirk on Daddy's face. He had succeeded in the most awful way. He didn't just end the engagement and relationship. He ended my ability to love another woman."

"He had donated five-hundred thousand dollars of my family's money to Sally's family in order to sway her into the affair. I never exposed them because I didn't want to hurt Momma. She didn't deserve to hear it from anyone but Daddy. I've been tempted many times to tell her, but something tells me she already knows who she's married to. No Southern woman is that oblivious."

"Anyway, I continued working for the family business until I couldn't take it anymore. I set my sights on Los Angeles and passed the California Bar when Filmore offered me a job. I took it. Before I left for California, I legally dropped Whittle from my hyphenated name, and just went by Fink. For better or worse, that's what it should've been from day one anyhow."

Zia absorbs all he's told her and she appreciates him even more. She now understands in more depth why he guarded his family history. It's riddled with scandal. But aren't there deceitful leaves on every family tree? Everyone's human, capable of the worst and best.

Bryce went out on a limb and laid out the truth, allowing her to take it or leave it. He's given her the choice, rather than stealing it away by lying or omitting. When will she have enough courage to do the same for him?

"Thank you for trusting me with the truth. I'm so sorry that you had to experience something as horrible as that. I can't even begin to imagine what that must've been like for you."

She kisses his lips several times.

"I've made my peace with it over the years. I don't hate him. I love him. He's my father. My spirit has long since forgiven him, but my mind cannot trust him because he hasn't changed. When someone wrongs us, and we love them, we have faith they'll reform. After so many years, I doubt he ever will."

Sadness oozes from his voice and eyes. The love of money is poison. Those who worship it, render themselves incapable of anything good. Zia immediately thinks of her career and what she'd once sought. Not only that, but *why* she had sought it.

She desired financial freedom and accolades, but not one dollar of her recent income has brought her happiness. Only Bryce has done that. She no longer wants the money she'd been chasing in her career. She wants him. Only him.

"So now that you know how crazy my family is and that my father will undoubtedly never accept you, will you still marry me?"

She lays her body on top of his, straddles him, and cups his face. Staring into his eyes, she speaks slowly and clearly.

"I love you, Bryce Cunningham Fink. I will always love you. You are my eternal and I *will* be your wife. Your family is your family and you are who you are. I'm marrying you. Not them, not the money, not the past. Just you."

His bottom lip trembles and his eyes glisten with tears. He rolls over on top of her and they kiss until they fall back to sleep.

CLICK, CLICK, CLACK. Tap, tap.

The sound of his fingers dancing swiftly across the laptop keys is the classical overture of his life. More divine than Bach, Mozart, and Bala-kirev combined. Comforting to his ears and soothing to his purpose… to the tune of utter extinction.

Hastening his plan by committing to several hopefuls within the week keeps his mind from drifting off into a chaotic murderous rage. Murder-ous rage is perfectly acceptable and always serves a purpose, but never wild and senseless. He'd had his fun with that as a young man when his hormones controlled him. Good riddance to those reckless days. He's in control now.

He sips his coffee, resisting the temptation to smash the ceramic mug into the mahogany desk. How dare a subhuman keep him waiting?

"Stupid low life whore!" he yells.

He dares not admit to himself that this woman has gotten under his skin. Her perceived morality robs him of patience and he has very little to spare these days. But he's not quite ready to do away with this one yet. There's something more to be had from this human stain. However, she'd better get in line or he'll abandon all and scatter her organs along Red Hook Grain Terminal.

Chapter
ELEVEN

FLOATING INTO SPARK this morning, Zia's light on her toes. She's already told Jazz about the engagement, but Jenn notices the ring when she collects her messages.

"Oh my God!" she exclaims, pointing at Zia's finger with bulging eyes.

"Shhhhhh! Not in the office. Please," Zia pleads with her.

She still values her privacy, so she promises to tell Jenn about it over lunch. Jenn bounces excitedly in her chair. Zia just smiles and sashays into her office.

By the time the ladies sit down for lunch in the cafeteria, a flurry of TransMedia and B&F secretaries stop by to congratulate Zia on the engagement. She politely thanks them and rolls her eyes at Jenn, presuming she's the one who spilled the tea. It's not even her business to tell, and Zia had specifically asked her not to run her mouth. As she mentally crosses Jenn's name off her 'maybe friend' list, Jenn raises her hands defensively.

"I haven't said a word, Zia. I swear."

"Well, who else would?"

"Uh, perhaps your fiancée? Duh," Jazz interjects.

Leave it to her to make Zia feel like a moron. Of course. B&F and TransMedia do work closely together.

"I'm sorry, Jenn. I'm so sorry I accused you. I shouldn't have assumed."

"Don't worry about it," she smiles.

Zia apologetically rubs her arm.

"So, how long before this gets back to Makayla?" Zia sighs.

Jazz bursts out laughing. Zia giggles too. Jenn is oblivious to their inside joke and they decide not to clue her in because she's Makayla's friend. That would be sloppy of them.

"Makayla's dating Lonnie Filmore now so I don't think she'll care much about your engagement," Jenn adds, dropping a G-bomb on them.

Their forks and jaws drop.

"What? I thought you knew," Jenn shrugs.

She's either excellent at modesty or she truly thought they knew.

"Oh my God! Filmore has to be sixty years old by now," Jazz informs them with disgust and excitement.

She's still pumped from the juicy piece of gossip she just received. Zia, on the other hand, is already over it.

"Oh well, good for her. Now I don't need to worry about her having a sour attitude with me anymore. She bagged the boss. Case closed."

Zia's relieved, but still surprised by the news. She wouldn't dare think the couple was truly in love, because she isn't sure Makayla is capable. Besides, she's heard that Filmore is the asshole of the legal powerhouse duo. Two assholes like Makayla and Lonnie together might be explosive for everyone involved. She decides to ask Bryce about it later. It's nice to have an inside track upstairs.

She bites into her crispy, but gooey, grilled cheese sandwich while listening to Jenn and Jazz recommend wedding plans. Zia doesn't know how to break it to Jazz that she plans to have an extended engagement. When people rush into marriage, it always fails. She'd rather Bryce have the time to truly decide while remaining content that they're solid.

Based on what Zia's seen from the edge of many planks, men have a tendency to change their minds when a woman's skin wrinkles or they've simply had their fill of fun. One thing a human can never get back is their time.

It may sound pessimistic, but it is realistic. Zia doesn't believe that Bryce is one of the common, but trust isn't automatic, though it is required for leadership. She will not blindly follow. She's yet to completely earn his trust and he has yet to earn hers. Exchanging vows is serious and she doesn't plan to take hers lightly. She needs time to get better, to rise above her mistakes, to end this affair, and the reverberating feelings attached to it.

As Jazz and Jen chatter on incessantly among themselves like Zia's isn't there, she turns her eyes towards the latest installment in the Kelp series; *Skeletal Flesh.* The most disturbing thus far. Kelp is no longer just killing because he's dark and twisted. He's developed a specific plan to kill every woman he can get his hands on. If he wants every woman dead, that will only leave men. Kelp is clearly a misogynistic homosexual who is resentful of his desires instead of just embracing them.

"Zee, you okay? You're all frowned up over there."

"Oh yeah, I'm fine. Kelp keeps surprising me with how far into darkness his mind sinks. I'm just so grateful he isn't real. If he were, the world would be in serious trouble."

"Lay off it for a while, babe. It'll give you nightmares, like the daily news. I couldn't get past the first book."

Jazz shakes off her memory of Chiseled Bone. Yeah, it has that effect on people. It's still selling like hotcakes too. Skeletal Flesh is the third installment and Zia's anxious for the final two for a few reasons. One, she'll be able to gracefully step away from Baxter, and two, she wants Kelp to get his comeuppance. If she's denied that ending, she'll lose her mind. It's like bingeing on a television series, only for it to be cancelled before you get closure. His evil needs to die inside of her thoughts.

Jenn bites into her sandwich as she tells them about the latest news.

"If you think that Kelp character is bad, you should see what's been going on in New York lately."

"Oh, right. The murders," Jazz reminds Zia, tapping her arm.

"Some maniac is on the loose up there. Hacking women up, removing their organs, putting their heads on spikes. Just terrible, horrific things," Jenn adds.

Heads on spikes.

"Jenn, the heads on spikes—did the news specify anything about that part?" Zia asks.

"Yeah, so the lunatic is removing the flesh from their heads. You know, like in the Predator movies? It's very scary."

Skeleton heads on spikes, just like in Skeletal Flesh. Another coincidence or does Baxter have an inside track to these murders as he writes? When you have money, you have connections. Maybe he has a friend with the NYPD or something who's feeding him information. Zia's definitely disturbed by the similarities.

"Hey guys, I have some work to finish in my office. I'll catch up with you later."

Zia rushes off before they can ask her anything. She wants to talk to Bryce about this, so she can get his opinion, but as soon as she dials his number, she hangs up. She can't do that. He will never, ever, in a million years, trust her to go to New York alone again. That will make him investigate and she doesn't want that. She wants to confess this affair because a discovery is even more of a betrayal. She decides to look into it herself. She remains paused in the hallway.

She has close to a million dollars now and Bryce is still watering it. She can just take some of that money and hire an investigator to run a background check on Baxter. Something she should've done a long time ago.

"Zee, what's wrong?" Jazz asks, sneaking up behind her.

"Nothing."

"Don't shut me out. We're in this together remember? Talk to me."

Zia looks every which way before grabbing her arm and leading her down into the parking structure.

"Okay Zee, you're scaring me a little bit now. Where are we going?"

"Just get in the car. We're going to take an extended lunch and grab some coffee."

"I need to let Jenn know."

"Okay, so call her."

Jazz makes her phone call and Zia makes hers to Bryce. They drive to a barista a few miles away and sit in a corner booth, away from eavesdroppers.

"Okay, Zee. Spill it. I've never seen you like this before."

She sighs, knowing that she can never go back from what she's about to tell her.

"I—I'm having an affair."

Jazz sighs and goes in.

"Zia, I told you! Didn't I tell you?"

"Come on, Jazz. I'm coming to you for help and I'm trusting you with my secrets, knowing that I've made a mistake. If you're my friend, then be my friend. I know I've sinned. Don't spend more time judging me than helping me. Please."

Tears spill over because this is her first time speaking the words.

"Okay, okay. I'm sorry. I've messed up a whole lot of times. Who hasn't? We're all chameleons adapting to survive in the jungle of life." Jazz slides over to hug her dearest friend.

"We're going to figure this out, together. Look at me. Together, okay?"

"Okay." Zia sniffles and wipes her tears.

"Okay, give me the bullet points so I'll know where we are."

"Well, I started crushing on Bax before Bryce and I started dating. It was innocent. Then Bryce and I got serious and I couldn't pull away from my connection with Bax. Long story short, I fell for Bax because of the passionate sex. But I think it's because Bryce wouldn't touch me and now I feel so addicted that I can't stop," she rambles in a frazzled tone.

"It's okay. Take your time."

"Well, I'm going to New York this weekend for a meeting with Sasha and I plan to break it off once and for all."

"Okay, so you made a mistake. A terrible one. A horrible one. A scandalous one…"

"I get it, Jazz."

"I'm just saying, but you can fix it. You still have time to break it off and confess to Bryce."

"Do you really think I should?"

"Actually, no I don't. Men aren't as forgiving as we are when it comes to sexual affairs. It's a double standard. Quadruple for rich men. But I'd be a bad friend if I recommended that you pile a lie on top of lies. As long as you end it, you can move on in your life, learn from it, and never do it again."

Zia sniffles again.

"Zee, you're about to marry the heir to a multi-billion-dollar fortune and you don't even care about the money. That's what makes it perfect. He's been betrayed before. If you tell him, it'll ruin him. Only you know what's best for your relationship, but that's just my two cents."

"There's more."

"More than an affair? Nothing can top that but go ahead."

"Something is suspicious about Bax's writing."

"You mean like plagiarism?"

"No, I mean that his stories are very similar to the New York City serial murders."

"Similar or identical?"

"Similar, but eerily similar."

"Okay, that's normal Zee. A lot of authors are inspired by things taking place in the world and they write stories about it. I've seen it a hundred times. That's nothing to freak out over. Focus on ending this affair."

"Okay, right. You're right."

"Lil ole Zee has two billionaires fighting for her heart and here the rest of us are—single as hell. Get it together, girl," Jazz murmurs under her breath as she orders her coffee.

Having spoken the words of her suspicions aloud has allowed Zia to realize how ridiculous it is. Of the trillion men in the world, what are the odds that she'd end up in the arms of a serial killer?

◠◡

HE SITS PATIENTLY inside of the abandoned, darkened hole in the wall. Mary twists her wrists against her reinforced bindings as if on the thousandth try, they'll magically loosen in a way that will grant her freedom. *These beasts never know when to quit.*

"If you do not stop whimpering and moving, I'll torture you until you're still. Trust me, this is not what you want."

Tears stream down her splotchy apple cheeks. Normally, this would sexually excite him, but his thoughts are on another. Mary is here because it is her time and no other reason.

He turns to face her and nonchalantly twirls the knife in the air as he speaks.

"Mary, do you understand the disease that you are?"

She shakes her head and whimpers. He snaps the black latex glove against his wrist like a doctor readying to inspect a patient.

"No, of course you don't. Nor does the swine. It is not your fault. It is the fault of *your* god. He created you in error. But what your god should have done is flip the pencil and erase his mistake. As forgiving and hopeful as I've been told he is, he apparently awaits your change. But you're incapable of the required change. That's where I come in. My purpose is to cleanse this world of those of you whose purpose is unclear and yes, misguided."

Mary can scream as loud as she pleases. No one will hear her. Her cries will echo into the cold, dead, vacant night. He takes pity on her and decides to kill her mercifully before using her insides to decorate his canvas. He walks behind her, grabs a hand full of her hair, and yanks her head backwards—exposing her neck.

She chokes for a few seconds before eternal sleep envelops her. Time to return her bones to the dust from whence they came. The act triggers his memory and his mother's face appears. Her eyes, wide with more disbelief than fear. Her final moments were the most sparingly gracious ones he's ever granted a female, and he gave them unwittingly. The incidental mercy is contributed solely to his mother's own doubt that her baby boy would be the one to remove her human stain from existence.

Thirty cleansing years later, he remains above suspicion. White privilege paired with worldly riches are an exquisite combination.

He prepares Mary's body for deboning and dismemberment, starting with her head.

Chapter
TWELVE

As Zia retrieves her luggage from JFK's baggage carousel, only one thought ripples through her mind.

End this affair. End it. End it.

She'll be meeting up with Sasha at Reaping tomorrow and closing with Baxter on Sunday. The man hasn't stopped calling and texting since she told him she was coming for the weekend.

His childlike excitement tugged at her heart's strings. In his defense, he didn't know what he was getting himself into with her. She's the monster here. She yanks on the handle of the suitcase, angry with herself.

She plans to avoid Baxter as much as humanly possible until she meets up with him to tell him that it's over. Intimately, anyway. No way to avoid this affecting their professional relationship. Thankfully he has more corporate experience in these matters and should be able to take this in stride.

Just as she prepares to hail a cab, she notices him standing by the curb to her right, leaning against a black limousine, with his hands in his pockets, dressed to the nines. His face brightens as soon as their eyes connect.

She asks God why, when she's trying so hard to do right, and to be right. As long as she doesn't look into his eyes for long, she'll be okay.

"Zia!" He embraces her and lifts her from the ground.

She can only manage a smile while hiding her disappointment with his unforeseen presence. She expected him to be pissed because she's been avoiding him so much. Any grown man would notice the boomerang curve she's been throwing, but here he is, acting utterly oblivious. He's ruining her carefully laid plans with all this good cheer.

"I missed you so much! Put those bags down."

He whistles. His driver appears and tucks her luggage into the trunk. He takes her by the hand and they slide into the limo. What she'd sought to avoid has become a reality in .01 seconds after her feet touched the New York asphalt. The devil sure is working overtime. Oh well, she needs to rise above the situation.

"Bax, honey I told you I had a meeting with Reaping, and I'm pretty jetlagged. I wanted to be nice and fresh before we met up. I look a frightful mess."

"Nonsense. You look more radiant than I remembered. I just couldn't wait another second."

He leans over and kisses her passionately. Her insides are quickly oozing into a pitiful mess. He's demanding and forcing eye contact. Every attempt she makes to look away, he denies. His gaze burns a hole straight through her.

"I need a shower and I…I've had a long flight. You should drop me off at—"

"You're coming with me. Any needs that you have will be provided for, including showers." He traces his fingertips along her jawline as he speaks, continuing his gaze, devouring her with his eyes, tucking her runaway curls behind her ear. He hasn't taken his eyes off her since she arrived.

She gulps.

After a bit of a drive, they arrive at a quaint house.

"Where are we?"

"Greenwich. Come."

They enter the building. It's absolutely gorgeous inside. Modest, but he undoubtedly spared no expense in hiring a designer to furnish the place. She cares only to be pointed in the direction of the restroom, so she can shower and regroup.

"Bax, I…"

"…your shower has been prepared for you. This way."

He leads her upstairs and into a bedroom where there's water running.

"Everything you could possibly need is already inside. But if you'd prefer your own things, they'll be up shortly."

"Thank you."

No sense in fighting him, seeing as how he'd planned her abduction quite carefully.

"I'll be downstairs."

He leans in for another kiss and she turns her face, directing him to her cheek. He backs out of the room and closes the door. She wastes no time discarding her clothing and hopping into the stall.

She takes the longest shower she ever has before in her life. She even washes her already clean hair. She keeps expecting the hot water to run out, but it's never-ending. These rich folks are really starting to grate on her nerves. Then she remembers that if she doesn't check into her hotel room, Bryce will become suspicious.

She steps out, pats herself dry, and tosses the towel into the hamper. She moisturizes her entire body with the expensive creams aligning the counter before entering the bedroom for clothing to find an odd selection of cotton pajama gown with fleece socks lying neatly on the bed. Men generally like frilly foo-foo, silk gowns.

She's too grateful for the comfortable medley to pick apart his reasons. She slips it on, then rifles through her suitcase and yanks out a pair of pink sheer panties. She slides them on and leans back against the bed.

She calls the hotel and checks in. Next, she calls Bryce and assures him that she's arrived safely. He expects she'll shower and hop into bed. After her confession, hopefully that won't be a lie.

She'd planned to tell Baxter when there was no time left on her trip and now, plan B is to just get it over with. She straightens her posture and heads downstairs.

He's dicing food on the island counter in the kitchen. His hair is damp and he's wearing only a pair of black briefs. His rippling muscles glisten under the recess lighting. He looks up and smiles. He's impossibly gorgeous. She decides to hurry up and tell him before losing her nerve.

"How was your shower?"

"It was wonderful, thank you. Bax, we should talk."

"I'm making lamb chops. Do you like lamb?"

"Yes, I like it fine. But we need…"

"...and we will. But for now, come over and keep me company."

She walks over to stand next to him as he slices and dices. He handles the cutlery like a professional chef. At least from what she's seen on TV cooking shows. She hadn't known he was skilled in the kitchen.

She senses that he requires control, so instead of trying to force the conversation on him, she opts to make him beg for it. Her last-minute plan only requires two things—total silence and to be in close proximity to him.

She initiates her plan by standing even closer to him, allowing her 36D breasts to graze his arm. He chatters on about lamb and various ethnic seasonings. She just occasionally glances into his eyes without responding. After only a few minutes, he caves.

"Okay, Zia. What is it?"

He drops the knife and wipes his hands with a cloth.

"Just spit it out and get it over with."

"Bax, you already know that I have a boyfriend."

He folds his arms across his chest, unmoved.

"Yes?"

"Well, he proposed."

She pauses, but he doesn't say a word.

"And I accepted. We're—engaged."

His face and eyes simultaneously change color.

"We can't do this anymore. It's not right."

"You cannot tell me that it isn't right to love you or to desire you. That, you cannot do."

"I know this comes as a shock to you but—"

"You're mine."

"What?"

"You are *mine*. You belong to me. You belong *with* me."

"Bax."

"Say that you're mine."

She retreats, with her lips parting, but no words escaping.

"Say it or I will make love to you and force you to say it."

"I...I..."

"Submit."

She's breathing heavily. Her pulse races as her body disobeys her commands.

He pushes her against the refrigerator. The stainless steel is like a block of ice against her flaming skin. In trademark fashion, he licks her lips and face like an animal in heat. His massive erection bulges through his briefs, stabbing her like a sword.

With both hands, he grabs fists full of her collar, yanks her away from the refrigerator, and then flings her onto the island counter. Bowls of food crash to the floor. She's truly frightened by the look in his eyes. She's never seen him this way before. He's both angry and full of passion. She can't tell what else is going on inside of him, but she knows for a fact that he's going to be inside of her…right now.

He kisses her and aggressively bites down on her lips, nearly breaking the skin. She can't help but to cry out. He stares directly into her eyes as he issues commands.

"Open your legs."

She hesitates.

"I won't ask again."

She slowly spreads her knees apart. Dissatisfied, he pushes them, grabs her bottom, and scoots her to the edge. Slipping his forefinger into her panties, he keeps his eyes fixed on hers. Just when she thinks there's going to be foreplay, he rips the fabric, and shoves himself inside of her with one forceful thrust.

She gasps for air and squirms backwards. He clutches her bottom with both of his hands, so she can't escape, and shoves himself deeper into her neglected, aching, throbbing wetness that has longed for him despite her resistance.

He cries out with every thrust. Torturous struggle wells up in his eyes. He can see hers pleading with him to stop and continue. His thrusts are like whippings for her naughty behavior. He's punishing her, and she deserves it. She yearns for it. It inspires her desire for control. She leans forward and bites both of his lips, licks them like a wild beast, and twists her arms around his neck, locking him in her embrace.

She wraps her legs around his waist and climbs on top of him, taking it all. His groans grow loud and fierce. She smiles fiendishly at the reversal of power and wants more. She bounces up and slams down on his manhood until he starts to lose his balance and his sanity. He stumbles backwards until they end up on the floor, with her on top—riding him all the way into another dimension of pleasure.

He's incapable of controlling his limbs, his breathing, or his facial expressions. Just the way she's learned to love it. She repeatedly lifts and slams down hard until he jerks violently. Spurting, thick and hot, all over her insides. She knows she should stop, but she doesn't. She can't. She growls and lean backwards.

"Zia, I can't take anymore! I can't."

"Yes, you can, and you will."

Her words and voice surprise her. She can't believe how far she's tumbled. She takes his hands and positions them around her neck. His eyes widen.

He doesn't squeeze, so she slaps his face. His eyes bulge with excitement and surprise. She compresses her vaginal muscles around his shaft. He tosses her onto her back.

She spreads her legs open as far as they can go. He mounts her and eyes her carefully. She lifts her chin, exposing her neck to him.

"Do it!"

He sinks himself into her folds. She bites down on her bottom lip as his grip around her neck closes like a vice. The tighter his grip, the tighter she retracts her muscles around him. He moans her name so many times that it quickly becomes hypnotic.

Just like that, her orgasm is at hand, but she can't get any oxygen. His grip is far too tight. He's still thrusting, but she can't breathe. She attempts to loosen his hold, but he won't let go. She slaps his arms and claws at his hands.

He looks at her as she squirms and fights for air. The harder she struggles, the wider he smiles. The room spins, and she nearly slips into unconsciousness.

A high-pitched yelp fills the room before the oxygen gloriously returns to her lungs. She chokes and turn over onto her stomach.

"Are you okay?" he asks.

"You almost killed me! What the hell is wrong with you?"

"I'm sorry. I thought—I didn't know. Let me get you a glass of water."

He rushes off and returns with a glass. She angrily slaps it out of his hand, still rightfully furious.

"Zia, love. You have to know I would never hurt you."

He places the palm of his hand on her back and she jerks away.

She's not so sure of anything he says anymore. She saw the look in his eyes and it was pure sadistic joy. He lifts her into his arms and carries her into the bedroom. He examines her neck before grabbing his cell phone.

"Who are you calling?"

"A doctor."

"No!"

She can't end up in the hospital. Bryce may find out.

"I need to make sure you're okay. I'm not taking any chances."

"I'm not going to any hospital!"

"I have a private doctor."

She tries to snatch the phone from him, but he's too fast.

"Violet, get the doctor to Greenwich immediately. No questions."

He disconnects the call and returns to his examination of her neck.

"It looks to be a little swollen, but I don't feel any broken bones."

"I'm fine."

He lowers his head in shame.

"I should have never done that. I thought that's what you wanted. I thought it would bring you pleasure. I didn't mean to hurt you."

He appears to be crying, but he's hiding his face. She softens, and her anger subsides. She is the one who initiated the act, so she's equally culpable.

"Hey, it's alright. We just got carried away. I know you didn't mean it."

"I'll never forgive myself for hurting you." He turns away, walks out of the restroom, and closes the door.

It's just as well. This is nothing less than what she deserves for falling victim to her lust, again. She came here to end things and have only made them worse. The first step to letting go is admitting she has feelings for him.

Maybe this incident might help. Maybe Baxter will be so ashamed of himself that he'll let go and this tryst will just end all on its own. The Kelp series only has a two more installments left in the contract, and then she'll be free.

Zia wonders if Baxter will allow her to taxi herself over to Reaping. His protective nature is beginning to make her feel like a captive. She brushes her teeth with one hand, while rubbing her neck with the other. Evaluating the damage in the mirror, she decides that she's definitely wearing a turtleneck or scarf today. She gargles and clears her lumpy throat.

"Are you alright?" Baxter asks from the doorway.

"Yeah, uh hem. My throat is just a little sore," she replies in a cracked voice.

He sighs while approaching. He delicately touches her throat with his fingertips and kisses her all over her bruised neck. He apologizes profusely between each kiss. Sobbing, he drops to his knees.

"I'm so sorry. I'm sorrier than I've ever been. I don't expect you'll ever forgive me, but I'll never stop apologizing until you do. I would never hurt you. You must believe that."

She looks down into his eyes, unwilling to believe that anyone is this great of a pretender. His tears are real. Perhaps he was simply lost in the moment of rough sex. She'd played a part in it too, losing herself as well, to the point where she didn't recognize her own thoughts and feelings. She opts not to make this situation any more complicated by holding a grudge.

"It's okay, Bax. I know you didn't mean it."

He leaps to his feet and hugs her tightly.

"I'll make you some tea."

He kisses her tenderly on her forehead before leaving her to dress. She's so lost, unsure of what to do anymore. She'd told him. She told him that she was getting married. She convinces herself that when she leaves New York, he'll fill his bed with some other woman. He's rich, handsome, and women flock to him.

She's prepared for what she must do when she returns home. It's all about actually doing it. She picks up her cell phone and dials.

"Mom, I need to talk to you. I'm in New York right now, but when I get home, I'm coming to see you."

Chapter
THIRTEEN

"OH, MY GOODNESS. Zia baby, you're trembling. Are you okay? Did somebody do something to you?" Zia's mother asks her only child.

"No, Mom. No. Where's Dad?"

"He's golfing. Why?"

"Good, I don't want him to know about this, so can you promise me that you won't tell him?"

"Tell him what? What's going on?"

"Mom, look at me. Promise me you won't tell Dad."

"Okay, I promise I won't tell your father if it isn't life threatening."

"It isn't."

"Well, then. What is it?"

"Mom, I need your advice because I've done something bad."

Vivien holds her daughter's hand tightly and braces herself for the worst.

"I'm having an affair with one of my clients. I tried to break it off, but I think I love him."

"You *think* you love him?"

"I think I do, but I'm not sure. He lights a fire inside of me that I've never felt before."

Vivien pats Zia's hand and sighs.

"Oh Zia, baby. That's not love. That's lust. Now I won't sit here and tell you that makes it okay. You're still in the wrong."

"I know, Mom. I know."

"You're a young woman, and you're engaged to a decent gentleman who's properly courting you. That abstinence can make a young woman feel starved."

"That's exactly how I feel, but I sometimes feel like Bryce isn't sexually attracted to me."

"I raised you to be smarter than that. Anybody with one good eye can see that man loves you more than anything on this planet."

"But Mom, I mean..."

"...I know what you mean, baby. Too many people have been faced with the same decision, including me. But let me ask you this; between the two men, who have you doubted?"

Vivien sees the answer in Zia's eyes.

"Exactly. So, while this client may light a temporary fire inside of you, eventually you'll grow bored, and so will he. If you were truly torn by love, you wouldn't have tried to break it off. Consistent acts of true love have already separated the two men. You just need to listen to your heart and not your vagina."

"Mom!"

"What? I have a vagina too, ya know. So, I know how they work."

"Arrggghhh, Mom! Can you please stop saying vagina?"

"You *do* know that you came out of mine, right?"

"Mooooom!"

"Fine."

"Okay, okay so I know that Bryce is the one. What should I do?"

Vivien playfully smacks the back of her daughter's head.

"Ouch, Mom."

"Stop telling yourself that you're *going* to break it off with this person and actually cease all contact. Go cold turkey. That's the only way."

"He's my client."

"Uh huh. And?"

"I can't just cut him off."

"Yes, you can. You just don't want to."

"No, Mom. I do. But he—he scares me."

"Now I know for a fact he's not the one. Women don't fall in love with men they fear. Why does he scare you?"

"I don't know. There's just something off about him. I can't put my finger on it."

"He sounds like all kinds of trouble. Stay away from him."

"His books are making my career."

"You can make your career with a client who doesn't frighten or tempt you. It's not like you'll struggle without him. You're marrying a billionaire. If you're smart, anyway."

"Mom. I don't care about the Weingart fortune."

"I know you don't."

"Okay, so I go cold turkey...then what?"

"You and Bryce need premarital counseling. Ask him about it. If he's the man that I'm sure he is, he won't object."

"It's not really fair to drag him into counseling when I'm the one who did wrong."

"Zia, that man has been through some things and so have you. Premarital counseling isn't about whodunit. It's about learning to understand each other, communicate more effectively, and think as a team instead of one against the other. You'll be helping each other to heal so that open wounds don't rip your marriage apart before it begins."

This is the best advice Zia could've ever hoped for. That's precisely why she came to her.

"Thanks, Mom. I love you." She squeezes her mother tightly.

"Now, let me treat you to dinner. Come on. Get dressed," Zia offers.

Vivien squeals in delight and runs off to fix herself up.

WHEN ZIA RETURNS to work, there's a stack of mail on her desk that she doesn't bother touching. Not yet, anyway. She has other work to do, so she plops down just as Jazz bursts through the door.

"Hey, Jazz. Sorry I'm late getting back. I went to see my mom."

"Zee, have you heard?"

"Heard what?"

She pauses with a poker face.

Zia's pulse races.

"Jazz, what is it?"

Jazz breaks out into a smile.

"Lillia came by with this," she confesses, slamming a document onto Zia's desk. Zia immediately inspects it but is unable to believe what she's reading.

Elysium Motion Pictures has won the film rights to the Kelp series for $140 million dollars. What that means for her, after Baxter insisted that she take 50% instead of 20%, is a $70 million-dollar profit.

"Jazz, is this a joke? I—"

"No, it's for real baby girl. You're a millionaire in your own right."

"We did it. We did it!"

They scream and hop around in circles.

"I'm going up to see Bryce! I gotta tell him, if he doesn't already know. B&F seems to know everything that goes on in this building."

"Zee, do you know what this means?"

"Yes, it means that everyone can stop assuming I'm marrying Bryce for his money."

"No, it means that after the payment is finalized, you can pass Baxter off to another agent or recommend he seek representation elsewhere."

"Yeah, you're right," Zia concurs in a low tone.

She'll be free. Her sin will finally be behind her and she can move on.

Zia hugs Jazz once more before yanking her office door open.

"Oh, and some guy named Kevin called a couple of times. He said it's urgent," Jazz adds while handing Zia the messages.

She dashes towards the lobby and into an open elevator. She waits until the elevator door closes before looking at the message slips. Kevin Phillips is the private investigator that she'd hired to run a background check on Baxter. She didn't want him calling the house, her cell phone, or sending any mail to where Bryce could see it. The first few slips all ask for a return call. The last one only contains three words.

Check your mailbox.

She's anxious but decides she'll check it in a bit. She doesn't want Baxter anywhere near her thoughts while she's in Bryce's presence. She exits on the top floor. The snobby receptionist instructs her to have a seat. Bryce comes out in a matter of seconds.

He greets her with much enthusiasm.

"It's always a treat. Come on back."

He guides her into his office. As soon he closes the door, she's in his arms. He kisses her like he never has. His level of spontaneous passion is foreign to her. Her whole body tingles.

"Wow, babe. What was that for?" she breathlessly asks.

"Do I need a reason?"

"Hell no!"

They laugh and devour each other's mouths again. If they don't stop now, she's unsure what side of her will come out, and she's afraid he won't like it, so she douses the flames with conversation.

"I have some great news."

"What is it?"

"Elysium won the film rights to the Kelp series for $140 million."

"Are you serious?"

"Yeah. I can't believe it!"

"Oh, my goodness. Congratulations, babe! Wow!'

He hugs her tightly, beaming with pride.

"Thank you! When Elysium initially expressed interest, I figured that's as far as it would go. But after recent book sales, I guess they decided to move forward."

"Wow! That's like $28 million for you, before taxes."

"Babe, no."

"No? Isn't that standard?"

"It is. But when I sent my client the contract in the beginning, he had his attorneys modify the percentage."

"Modify it to what? What did you sign, Zee?"

"Bax insisted that I take 50% of everything instead of 20 or 15."

"Bax? Since when do you start calling him Bax? He's a client, Zee."

Unable to believe that she'd let that slip, she swiftly follows up with rationalizations.

"I know, babe. I know. We work together, and I shorten quite a few of my client's names. You know that. I call Cindy, Cin and you don't flip. Come on, babe. It's just a name."

His brow is still creased, and his fingers are clasped together. He analyzes her intently before eventually relaxing his posture.

"You're right, you're right. $70 million dollars. I am so damn proud of you."

"Thank you, but my cut will be $60 million, not 70."

"How do you figure?"

"Jazz gets a cut. I couldn't have done it without her."

"Right, of course."

He hugs her tighter than usual and sighs into her hair.

"I love you so much. You know that, don't you?"

"I love you too."

Concern saturates his tone. His spidey senses are boinging all over the place.

They rub noses like two little kids and kiss again.

"Do you think your Dad will cut me some slack now?"

"Nope. It doesn't matter how much money you have. What he wants is Weingart. His days are numbered, and he knows it. As soon as we marry, I'm firing him."

"Then what?"

"Replace him."

Zia hopes that Bryce doesn't suggest they move to Beaufort because she has zero interest in leaving L.A.

"Are you saying?"

"No, I don't ever want to move back to Beaufort. I like it here. Our life is here. But I may have to temporarily fill the spot until a suitable replacement is found."

"Bryce, honey, I've been thinking...we should start premarital counseling."

Recalling her mother's words, she patiently awaits his rebuttal.

"Sure, I agree. Set it up."

She doesn't hold back her smile.

"Why are you surprised? Did you really think I'd object to something that can only help us?"

"I wasn't sure how you'd react."

"Sign us up," he cheerfully bellows.

This man is absolutely, positively, perfect for her and she's certain they're going to have a great life together.

After leaving Bryce's office, she heads back down to Spark to grab her mail before heading home. Not only does she not want to be at Spark, she officially doesn't have to be. She mentally hi-fives herself.

She enters Spark's lobby where everyone applauds. One by one, her colleagues come up to congratulate her. Most of them, she doesn't even know because they never speak. $70 million dollars later, suddenly she's worthy of a greeting. From everyone except Makayla, who remains plastered against the far wall with her arms folded across her chest. Zia smiles politely, expresses her thanks, snatches the mail, and swiftly exits. Her life is finally coming full circle and she couldn't be more excited.

She decides to go shopping.

After purchasing a few things, she heads home. Bryce won't be in until 7 or 8. That gives her at least 3 or 4 hours to read Kevin's packet of information and properly dispose of the evidence without rushing. As soon as she opens the door, Bugs attacks her.

"Hi, baby! I missed you so much. Yes, I did!"

He jumps around and barks his excitement. He always knows her every emotion. Happy, sad, or in between.

"Guess what I have for you little guy?"

"Woof!"

"A nice, juicy steak dinner."

Bugs doesn't like anything more than food. That's his thing. She waives the doggie bag from the restaurant in front of his face and he goes crazy. She laughs and fills his bowl. While he digs in, she gets comfortable by kicking off her shoes and pulling her dress up over her head. There's no place like home.

She bounces onto the bed while opening Kevin's envelope. She carefully reads through his summary. He couldn't locate any public files on Baxter Leopold, which doesn't seem right because the man is president of a major corporation. There should be a heaping pile of information on him.

No social security number. No birth records. No addresses. Nothing. She grabs her laptop and decides to conduct a search via Garble. She's livid about having paid an investigator thousands of dollars to give her nothing. She's annoyed, but tenacious and determined.

Garble leads her to the author site that she's previously seen. Next, she ventures to Vex's website. She clicks on every link. About Us, FAQ's, etc. She locates a list of the board of directors and officers. Baxter's name is nowhere on it.

The top men in charge are Frank Sarkisyan and Dwight Fairfield. There's no photograph for Fairfield. Above Sarkisyan's name is a photo of a middle-aged white man. She hops back on Garble to search Fairfield's name, when her phone rings. It's her father. Hoping not to lose her train of thought, she continues typing as she talks. The search generates oodles of links. She cheats by clicking on the images tab, but not one promising image appears. Only those of people who couldn't possibly be Fairfield.

"Hi, Dad."

"Zee Bee, your mom's been in an accident."

HE STRETCHES HIS limbs underneath the starry winter sky, pleased with himself because he exercised more restraint than he'd thought possible. The patience he has for this subhuman is surreal.

No female has ever survived more than a few days and his mother doesn't count. Fancying himself in love, he smiles. This love, as they call it, has assisted him in discovering a more effective way to fulfill his purpose.

He could just as easily eliminate anyone he identifies as a threat. Instead, he showed mercy to a stranger for the sake of his joy. After all, he desires to continue playing with his favorite doll. He doesn't want a broken one. He likes her shiny and content.

He checks his watch. Johnathan is late. He considers tardiness a major and unacceptable sin. Just as he decides to leave, an unmarked squad car pulls up to the curb. Out steps one of New York City's finest.

"Hey, Dwight! I'm sorry that I'm late, but there was an emergency I couldn't avoid."

No fucks are given, but Dwight manages a smile—wondering why he hasn't ceased John's existence yet. Oh yes, because missing U.S. police officers bring too much heat.

"Don't worry about it, Johnny Boy. You're keeping us safe out here and that's no easy job."

The two old friends shake hands and enter the pub together. John's mind is sprinting, and Dwight's? Too far ahead to break a sweat.

They sit at a table beside the bar and order drinks. John has his usual—a Heineken with a whiskey back. Dwight orders a martini.

Since middle school, John always had an uneasy feeling about his friend. He's always sensed darkness in him, but denial was strong. Now, as a seasoned cop, 20 years on the job, he knows with absolute certainty that his friend is evil. Whether his friend has acted on that evil is what John's determined to find out.

Dwight's not interested in catching up. He only agreed to meet with John so as not to arouse his suspicions any further than necessary. Cops have a ridiculous disease called hunches. They take those hunches into court, spin webs of theories around them, and imprison people on that basis, rather than facts.

Dwight loathes the man that Johnny Boy has become. The world was once his oyster and he chose corrupt law enforcement instead of the pearl. What a disgrace. Before his disgust bubbles over, Dwight decides to open the dialogue to move this along.

"So, how's Grace? The kids?"

"They're great. Well, great might be an exaggeration. They're all healthy."

"Healthy is great."

"You're preaching to the choir man. Every day I clock in at work, I could clock out in this world, so I know."

Dwight enjoys the sound of that. Death is the only form of mercy God has bestowed upon the human race, though most don't view it that way. They fear it. Dwight does not.

"We always talk about me. What about you, Mister Millionaire? When are you gonna jump the broom again?"

"Aahhhh, I don't know. I guess when I meet the right person."

Dwight can't imagine marrying a subhuman without divine purpose. He's been there, done that.

John has always found it odd that Dwight didn't rebound after his wife's death, as if he was grateful to be free of her. Men who look like Dwight have no problem where women are concerned, but he rarely even opens a dialogue about women. John thinks his friend might be gay.

"Well, she's out there somewhere. You're one of the few men who could have any one of them. What does that feel like?"

"It all gets old and boring after a while. Now, just true companionship is all I hope for."

"It's funny how that works. It's what we should hope for in the beginning. But the hormones—well, that's a different story."

The two friends simultaneously chuckle. Neither of them genuinely finding any humor in the statement. They're both ready to interview the other. Dwight just has a different and skilled way of going about it.

A devious grin spreads within his thoughts. He allows John to drive the conversation because they always end up at the same destination regardless.

Chapter
FOURTEEN

ZIA FRANTICALLY RUNS down a sterile hallway aligned with beds and patients. Worried faces are everywhere.

"Dad!" she tearfully screams as she flies into her father's arms.

"Dad, please tell me that she's okay."

"She's going to be fine, Zee Bee. A few broken bones, but no serious internal damage."

Carson wipes his baby girl's tears with his thumbs. She sighs and hunches her shoulders. She can't imagine life without her parents. They're her foundation. Her father has always been a rock, but his eyes are swollen and red from crying. The sadness in his eyes overwhelms her heart.

"Can I see her?"

"She's knocked out from the meds, but you can go in."

She kisses him on his cheek before rushing into the room. Beeping noises from the machines give her the creeps. Vivien's lying on her back, swaddled in white hospital blankets. Her hair is spread across the pillow. Both of her eyes are blackened. Her lips and face are bruised.

Zia caresses her hand.

"Mom, I hope you can hear me. Everything is going to be alright. I love you."

She kisses her mother's forehead and returns to her father. They walk hand in hand into the main waiting area.

"Dad, what happened?"

"I don't know yet. We know she wasn't drinking. They said it's possible she fell asleep behind the wheel because there were no tire marks indicating that she deployed the brakes," he sighs. "We just don't know yet."

As long as she's going to be okay, they can figure out everything else.

"You look exhausted, Dad. I'll go get you some coffee."

As soon as she turns around to locate the sign for a cafeteria, she notices Bryce at the nurse's station.

"Bryce!"

He jogs over and grabs her. He hugs her so tight that the bones in her back crack.

"What happened?" he demands.

"Mom was in a car accident."

"Oh my God! I'm sorry. Is she okay?"

"She's going to be fine. She has some serious injuries, but she's alive."

He hugs her again.

"I'm so sorry, babe. How are you holding up?"

"I'm fine. It's Dad that's not so good. That's his soulmate in there."

Bryce looks past her and walks right over to Carson.

"Mr. Lennox, I'm so sorry."

"It's alright, son. Been a long night, but God is good."

"Yes, sir. He is."

They hug and pat each other's backs.

"Dad, we're going to grab you some coffee. Are you hungry?"

"I can't eat anything right now, even if I should."

"Okay, stay with Mom. We'll be right back."

He nods and rushes back into his wife's room. Zia and Bryce locate the vending machines. Her stomach is in Merovingian knots.

"Sit down, babe."

"I'm fine."

"No, you're not."

The tone of his voice is enough to make her take a seat. She leans her head back. He purchases the coffee while she prays her thanks to God in Heaven.

"How does your father take his coffee?"

"Black, two sugars, piping hot."

"Okay, I'll stick it in the microwave."

Bryce is a winged angel. He dropped everything and came running. After he prepares Carson's coffee, he reaches his hand out for Zia. They take the coffee inside, but Carson is slumped over Vivien's lap, snoring. Zia places the coffee on the table, kisses her father, and they leave.

Zia's still jittery and her nerves are terrible. Bryce insisted that she shower as soon as they walked through the door. As the hot water splashes across her face, she quietly bursts into tears. She'd almost lost her mother. Her fears may cause her to become overprotective, though she can't treat her mother like a child just because she's afraid of losing her. She knows she wouldn't like it if someone wanted to suspend her driving privileges because she had an accident.

She washes the hospital scent from her skin and hair, turns off the shower, and steps out. After wrapping the towel around her damp body, she notices how quiet the house is.

"Bryce?"

He doesn't respond. She blots the excess water from her dripping hair before entering the bedroom where he's sitting on the bed, facing the window, with his back to her, reading something.

"Babe, are you alright?"

"What's this?" he asks while lifting the documents into the air.

Sensing the tension, Bugs lifts his head.

"I don't know."

He walks around the bed and shoves Kevin Phillip's investigation summary on Baxter into her hands. Bugs stands protectively near her.

"Babe..."

"Is this where the $5,000 from your account went?"

"Well, yes but—"

"Why are you hiring a private investigator for your client?"

"Because it's something I should've done in the first place."

"Okay. But why are *you* paying for it and why *now*?"

Bugs looks at her and tilts his head, just as curious to see what she comes up with.

"Because—because Sasha at Reaping was telling me some horror stories when I saw her. She scared me into thinking I might've signed a contract with a fraud. I just wanted to make sure."

Bryce lifts his chin, still suspicious of her.

"Why wouldn't you tell me? I'm an attorney. Why did you keep it a secret from *me*?"

"It wasn't a secret. I just didn't think it was important enough to bother you with. I mean, unless something bad came up and it didn't. Just because you're an attorney doesn't mean I want to bombard you with every little issue I have at work. I want to be able to take care of small things by myself."

"Zee..."

"If it were a secret, I wouldn't have the documents sitting on our bed."

She's getting too good at this lying business. She needs to get out of it before she completely loses herself.

"Next time, tell me. I don't care if you think it's trivial or not. You let me be the judge."

"Okay. I'm sorry, babe. I will."

"I want to see the contract tomorrow. I'll go over it myself."

"Okay."

He kisses her, touches her hair, and gazes distrustfully into her eyes.

"I'll make you some dinner."

"Bryce, I'm not really that hungry."

"But you need to put something in your stomach."

While he cooks, she gathers the documents, and shoves them into her satchel. That was a close call. She'd gotten sidetracked by the accident. Otherwise, she would've burned the documents in the fireplace before Bryce came home.

Now he won't be 100% satisfied until he figures things out for himself. She needs to beat him to the punch, so she can confess her sins in the right way. She has information that isn't on any documents yet. A name.

She grabs her laptop from where she'd left it on the bed. Her touch wakes the screen from hibernation. The Garble search results are still there. Thank goodness Bryce didn't see this. She can't imagine what lie she could've concocted to explain away going the extra mile. She closes the open tabs and clears the browser history. She also makes a mental note to contact Kevin when she gets to work tomorrow. She has a new name for him to investigate.

Dwight Fairfield.

VIVIEN'S AT HOME being nursed back to health by her husband, allowing Zia to concentrate on other things. She's at work with a different focus. She'd signed a new client by the name of Larson Francis and her work is spectacular. She's penned a crime/thriller series that Reaping has fallen in love with.

Zia's all but ceased regular communication with Baxter after emailing him a recommendation to seek other representation. She'd cited her mother's recent accident because that's all she could really think of at the time. She just knew she needed to start somewhere.

She can't break away from him if she's talking to him all the time. Her body continues to yearn for him, but her heart has changed. She's 100% in love with Bryce and that'll never change.

Bryce probed Zia's contract with a fine-tooth comb. He'd found that it explicitly specified that all fees would be paid from Baxter's percentage, leaving hers intact, and upon closer inspection, leaving Baxter with very little. Bryce frowned upon that glaring abnormality.

He'd concluded that the percentage differential itself was outrageous enough to justify his suspicions. He just couldn't wrap his mind around why an author would increase their agent's cut so dramatically. Zia had told him not to worry about something that was done and over with. She'd also explained that Baxter was already rich and he didn't need the money. That's the only thing that calmed Bryce down.

Elysium processed the payment and forwarded it to Spark. Spark has B&F on retainer to divide the monies, etc. With Bryce on top of things, she'd barely given the process much thought.

Spark has made all her flight arrangements to New York for this weekend to meet with Reaping to finalize everything for Larson, who'll also be there. She's looking forward to meeting the author and the PR agent they've hired for her.

Zia informed Kevin not to send any documents to the office nor to her home. She specified that email was the only acceptable form of communication, unless otherwise instructed. She reasons that it doesn't really matter what Kevin reports next because she's done with Baxter.

Jazz interrupts Zia's thoughts when she opens the door.

"Zee, the payment's been processed. Bryce has already instructed them on the tax percentage, yada-yada. Corporate wants to meet with you in B&F offices before lunch to sign the paperwork."

"You're coming with me."

"They'll wonder why I'm there."

"I don't care what they wonder. I couldn't have done this without you. You're going."

"Alright, alright boss lady. Let me square some things away and we can head up."

"Sounds good."

She pauses in the doorway.

"How is Baxter taking the separation?"

"I don't know. Haven't spoken to him."

"Not even an email? Text?"

"No, neither. I changed my phone number."

"I'm proud of you."

They exchange smiles.

She's not proud of herself because her inner fire still burns for Baxter. That part alone fuels her ongoing guilty conscience. She still desires him and wonders when that feeling will go away. She phones Bryce to let him know that she's on her way up.

Zia and Jazz enter B&F's large conference room. Jazz sits down on her left. Bryce, on her right. Spark and B&F executives sit parallel from them. The meeting is swift. Numbers are discussed. Documents are signed. After forty-five minutes, Spark executive, Steven Moss, hands Zia a cashier's check for $50.4 million dollars while offering his two cents along with it.

"No client in Spark's history has ever done this for an agent."

"I find that hard to believe," Zia nervously responds.

She glances down at the pink and blue gradient check. Jazz is perfectly calm. One would think that Jazz received $50 million-dollar payments on a daily basis as calm as she is. Zia hands the check to Bryce before shaking Steven's hand.

Many congratulations are spoken. Although Zia resents him for speaking on Baxter's modifications of the contract in her favor, she's certain that Bryce's mind will eventually let go of it. The three of them exit the conference room together.

They walk toward the elevators. Once they're out of sight, Zia hugs the abnormally calm Jazz.

Zia's just about ready to scream. Bryce, as her legal representation, speaks in his lawyerly voice.

"Jazmine, I'll have the bank wire your portion within seven days. If it takes any longer, I'll let you know."

"Thanks. No worries. Let's go out to lunch and celebrate."

"Yeah, babe let's go."

"I'm sorry ladies, but I have a few more meetings, so I'll be working right through lunch."

"Awww," Zia whines. She's disappointed because she wanted Jazz and Bryce to spend more time with each other.

"I'll see you at home later," he says with a kiss. "Congratulations, big timers."

The ladies giggle as he scurries off.

"Jazz, I've wanted to say this for a long time. Let's go home early because—wait for it— we don't *have* to be here!"

They high-five each other and head back to down to Spark to gather their things. When Zia goes into her office to shut the computer down, she notices a new email from Kevin. She smirks and hits the power button, not caring to see it right now. She wants to float on cloud nine for as long as possible.

SEETHING WITH ANGER, Dwight sits in front of the large bay window of his condo, opening and closing the drapes by pressing the corresponding blue button on the remote control, over and over.

Click. Skweeee. Click. Skwoooo. Click. Skweeee. Click. Skwoooo.

His left leg is draped over his right and a glass of whiskey is clutched in his left hand. His thoughts are angry, but eerily focused.

This.

This is why the subhuman must be eliminated. They use their sexual influence to enslave men's hearts before destroying them. A man with a vacant heart is incapable of functioning as needed. Men make better partners for each other. They simply need to be rid of the wicked female option to see that.

Not only did Zia toy with his heart, she cut him off. No woman has ever been given the opportunity to do such a thing. His grip tightens around the glass of whiskey.

Even after he'd showed her mercy by sparing her father's life when he could've orphaned her. Her mother's survival was purely a stroke of luck. He had intended for her to die.

He assumed that Zia would come rushing into his arms after her mother was pronounced dead. His disappointment grew exponentially when he discovered that the job had been botched. His hired hand paid for that mistake with his life.

Then she goes and signs a new client. A subhuman, no less—adding insult to injury. The glass shatters inside of his hand.

He picks up the phone and calls his assistant a second time.

"I placed an order for him an hour ago. I don't like to be kept waiting."

"Yes, sir. He's on his way up as we speak."

This acquired young male flesh will take the beating that Zia deserves. The difference is, this young man will like it. Dwight stands and prepares himself. The doorbell rings. On the other side is a youthful brown face.

"Hi. My name is Levi."

Dwight doesn't return the greeting. He merely opens the door to allow the young man inside.

"Take off your clothes."

Levi does as instructed.

"Turn around."

Dwight inspects the merchandise, ensuring there are no marks of any kind on Levi's body. The final measure involves the eyes. He'd requested gray.

Dwight steps closer and grabs Levi by the jaw. He tilts the boy's head from side to side. No other human being on the planet will have the same eyes as Zia, so Levi's will have to do.

She should be here, with him, in his bed, with those strange translucent eyes gazing up at him as he tears into her flesh with his own.

He will have her. Dead or alive. If she continues to ignore him—dead.

Chapter
FIFTEEN

APPREHENSION QUICKLY EVAPORATES as Zia stands curbside outside of LaGuardia airport. Though there's no way Baxter would know she's gone out of her way to avoid him by flying into LaGuardia instead of JFK this time, she still looks to her left and right before rushing into a taxi and heading to the hotel.

Once inside of her room, she bounces on the bed. Guilt instantly ravages her insides. Certain off-putting behavior that results in radio silence can sometimes be explained away, but when someone you're intimate with changes their telephone number and doesn't give you the new one, that's undeniable.

She didn't set out to hurt Baxter, but she's convinced that she has. She never thought she was capable of hurting a man who had everything. She hunches her shoulders and starts unpacking her suitcase.

The hotel phone rings. She just stares at it, wondering who would be contacting her on that line so swiftly. Holding her breath, she gently lifts the receiver.

"Hello?"

"Oh my God, Zee. I thought something happened to you!"

She exhales in relief.

"Bryce."

"Why aren't you answering your phone? I called you 100 times."

She glances over at her purse on the bed, feeling like an idiot.

"I completely forgot to take it off airplane mode. I'm sorry, babe."

She'd lost her focus while trying to avoid someone who's clearly already gotten the message.

"It's okay. Just don't make me worry. Turn your phone on. Are you okay? You're breathing heavy."

"Oh, I was unpacking, trying to lift my suitcase. Packed a little heavier than I thought."

She chuckles nervously.

"Oh," he yawns.

"Babe, go to sleep. I'm fine. I'm going to finish unpacking, shower, and hit the sheets. Big day tomorrow."

"Okay, I love you."

"Love you too."

She laughs at her Drew Barrymore 'Scream' moment and turns back towards the bed.

The phone rings again. She smiles this time before answering.

"Babe, I said that I'd—"

"I always thought I was worth more to you."

Her heart all but explodes inside of her chest. She slowly sits.

"Bax, I…"

"…Zia, I don't know what I ever did to deserve such treatment but let me just apologize to you. Since I wasn't afforded a respectable opportunity to do so, I decided to take it for myself."

"I'm really sorry that…"

"…although I deserve an apology as much as you do, I no longer want it. Not under these circumstances. Not as a consolation."

"That's not what this is. I—"

"Yes, it is. We both deserved closure. You've had time to make peace with this. Maybe one day, I'll be able to as well."

The pieces of her exploded heart shatter into a billion tinier portions. She's destroyed someone who didn't deserve it. A fat tear splats against her collar bone.

"Don't cry, beautiful Zia."

"I didn't mean for things to go this way, Bax. I truly loved you."

"Loved? Has it dissipated so swiftly?"

"No. You know what I mean."

"So, you do still love me," he concludes.

"I think I always will."

"How cliché," he chuckles.

"Not when it's true."

"If I meant anything to you, please act like it. Cutting me out of your life in the various rude ways that you've selected is not befitting of love. Don't turn our time into a stain. If it's going to end, let the remembrance be great."

He's right, though she's too distraught to speak.

"I will always love you. I will always protect you and I will always look after you, but you must meet me half way if this is truly your choice. If you mean any of what you say, let your actions mirror your words."

She just can't see him. If she sees him, she knows that she'll fall right back into him.

After she doesn't reply, he sighs.

"I didn't mean to bother you much. I truly phoned to hear your voice one last time. I love you with my entire spirit, Zia. Enjoy your stay and good luck."

The call disconnects just as her brain catches up. She breaks down and sobs uncontrollably. Just last year, her life was blissfully uncomplicated, and now her desires have complicated it. She's angry and disappointed with herself. She doesn't regret the feelings she'd had for Baxter, only the web of deception that she spun around it.

She drags her feet back over to the bed and dumps the contents of the suitcase onto the floor. She abandons her plans of unpacking and showering for some fresh air. She's in the Big Apple and it's about time she actually takes a bite.

She grabs her purse, changes the setting on her phone, and then heads out. She aimlessly walks until she comes across a cozy restaurant. She ducks inside for a meal.

After a delicious Italian course, including 3 bottles of wine, and a trip to the restroom, she resumes sightseeing. Everything is so large and vibrant. The tourists' heads are pointed towards the sky and the natives scuttle hurriedly towards their destination with frowned faces, glaring forward. Her stride is a cross between tourist and native.

All the different sights do a fantastic job of emptying her head, which is spinning a bit. She relishes in the feeling of lightheadedness. She makes a few purchases and stops at a bar for a couple of shots. She gets on and off the train a few times without caring which direction she travels.

She strolls along, allowing the crisp air to cradle her face. Feeling ready for bed, she pulls her head out of the clouds to finally gauge her surroundings. It's dark and there aren't many people anymore. Only a few cars pass and most of the businesses are closed for the evening.

She hastens her stride a bit, but not too much. She walks close to the curb, so she can hail a taxi, should one pass. So far, no such luck. Her lone footsteps echo into the night, making her feel that someone is behind her. She nervously looks back. No one's there.

Accepting that it's all in her plastered mind, she continues walking. A shadow appears alongside hers. She turns her head to the left. A man speeds up, walks past, then makes a left around a corner. She breathes a sigh of relief.

A car approaches in the distance, so she prepares to step off the curb—in case it's a taxi. Before her foot touches the street, there's a hand over her mouth, and an arm around her waist, pulling her backwards. She drops her bags and flails her loose limbs every which way. The cool, sharp tip of a blade is jabbed into her neck.

"Stop moving and don't make a sound or I'll slit your fucking throat. Do you understand me?"

He yanks her head sideways and the tip of the blade breaks her skin. Stormy tears cascade down her flushed cheeks.

"Do you fucking understand me?"

She nods yes.

He drags her backwards, deeper into the darkness, away from the street. Her anxiety spills over as the light slowly disappears.

"If you scream, no one will get to you fast enough to save you from me. You got me?"

She nods again. He removes his hand from her mouth and shoves her against a wall, near a dumpster. He's wearing a mask that's blackened his face, but the blade is now underneath her chin.

"Ooohhh, looks like I caught a pretty one. Nice."

She squirms and does the only thing she can think of.

"Please, don't kill me," she pleads.

"Shut up!"

"Okay, okay."

She shoves her hands into the air and completely freezes.

"What the hell is wrong with your eyes? I ain't never seen that before."

"I—don't know."

"Shut up!"

He jabs the knife at her. She tries to back up, but she's already plastered against a wall. He snatches her purse, breaking the strap. He rifles through it, takes the cash, and tosses the rest.

"Empty your pockets. Now!"

She turns the pockets of her blue jeans inside out. A few dollars fall to the ground. He scrapes them up.

"Is this it?"

"Yes."

"Bull! You look like you got money. Where is it?"

"I...I..."

"Oh, I know where it is. Where all women keep their money."

He chuckles fiendishly as he steps forward.

She turns her head, avoiding the repulsive lust in his eyes and the sickening scent of his rotten breath. Her lips tremble. He yanks her blouse, ripping it vertically, and again, horizontally. He slowly slides the tip of the knife underneath the center front frame of her red lace bra. All she feels next is the stale night air against her exposed nipples.

She can't help but cry as his gloved hand cups her left breast. She squeezes her eyelids completely shut, refusing to watch. Then she decides better of it. Before she can think too much, she brings her right knee up into his crotch. The cartilage makes direct contact and he doubles over.

She balls her left hand into a fist, reaches all the way down to Mississippi, brings it back up, and Ali's his face with every ounce of strength in her. He stumbles backward. She quickly tucks her engagement ring into the palm of her hand and aims for his eye. As he yells out, she runs as fast as her legs will carry her. The darkness blurs past, but he's right on her tail.

"I'm gonna kill you, you stupid whore!"

Before she reaches the sidewalk, a familiar voice calls out her name. Her eyes haven't yet come back into focus.

"Zia?"

She runs full steam into the arms of the willowy figure.

"Help me!"

"What's going on?"

She looks up, into Baxter's face. A beautiful sight, to be sure. She feebly points in her attacker's direction while her head spins. Baxter shoves Zia behind his body and follows her finger.

The stranger reaches the sidewalk and pauses for an instant before darting south. Baxter is on his trail. As they run off into the night, she falls backwards onto the pavement, out of breath. She just sits with her knees against her chest and her head down, rocking back and forth.

She's unsure of how much time passes, but her body registers being inside of Baxter's arms. She refuses to remove her hands from her face and she can't stop crying.

"Zia? Zia, please look at me."

Reluctantly, she uncovers her face. They're in the backseat of a car or limo. She can't tell, and she doesn't care, as long as she's safe. She gazes at him with overwhelming relief. A tear falls from his eye.

"I should've never given up so easily. I should've...I...this is my fault. Did he hurt you?"

"I'm—okay."

He wraps his arms around her.

"I'll never let anyone hurt you ever. Never ever again."

"Why are we still here?"

"We're waiting for the police. I've retrieved your things."

"I don't want to talk to the police. Please, let's just go. Now!"

She can't let this get back to Bryce. He'll never let her out of his sight and she has no interest in being treated like a child when she returns home.

"But...if you don't give a statement right now, the police might..."

"I don't care. Just get me out of here."

"Okay. Driver, let's go!"

The car jerks and they speed away. He cradles her in his arms while they ride in silence.

The car comes to an abrupt stop. She lifts her head before sitting up. They're in front of her hotel. She swallows repeatedly. Her throat is dry and lumpy like she's swallowed sand. Some small part of her had hoped he would take her back to his condo where she wouldn't be alone, but then that would make him appear pathetic. No, she'd asked for this. Now she must face it.

He gazes at her with an abundance of love and tenderness in his eyes. She doesn't feel she deserves to be in his presence. He wants to say so much, but refrains. He just caresses her cheeks with his fingertips. He gawks for so long that she becomes convinced he's trying to memorize her face.

She hesitantly gathers her things with one hand, while clutching her mangled bra with the other. She prepares to exit when she loses control of her breathing. She doesn't know how, but she goes from zero to 100 as soon as she pulls on the door handle. She falls backwards and her surroundings fade. He calls out to her, but she can't respond. She slips into a void.

WARMTH AND BRIGHTNESS slice though Zia's closed lids. She throws her hand up, squinting and attempting to open her eyes. It takes a few tries before she succeeds. She sits up and looks around the room. It takes a full minute for her to realize she's in Baxter's condo. As soon as she registers that fact, last night's events come flooding back.

She clutches the incredibly soft lavender bedsheets against her bare chest, worried that they might've made love. She peeks underneath the sheets to see that she's still wearing panties.

No vaginal tenderness is present, so she's satisfied that they hadn't had sex last night. She hears him in the next room on the telephone. She creeps over to the doorway to eavesdrop.

"Yes, yes. I understand. I've already come down and allowed you to question me for several hours. You have my official statement. Uh, yes.

Well, she can't make a statement if she's unconscious, now can she?"

She elongates her neck even further.

"Besides, she was the victim here. I've already confessed to the—"

He pauses and sighs.

"I'm the one who—yes, but you're aware that she has legal representation. Hold on."

She runs back to the bed and tries to appear as relaxed as possible when he enters. She glances back at him as he ends his phone call.

"I'll call you back in a bit."

He walks around the bed and kneels in front of her.

"How are you feeling?"

"I'm fine."

He smiles and kisses her on the forehead. His blue eyes drip with sincerity.

"Whenever you're ready to talk about it, I'll be here."

"I just want to forget it ever happened."

"Hmm."

"I heard you on the phone. What was that about?"

"That was law enforcement, Zia."

"I'm not pressing any charges. I refuse to have anything to do with anything. It's over and I want to move on from it."

"Zia, listen—"

"No, Bax. I've made up my mind."

"Zia, stop and listen."

The timbre in his voice frightens her a bit. He sighs and sits beside her.

"I'm not sure how much you actually remember from last night. There's no need to press charges, but you will need to make a statement to the police."

She sighs in an exaggerated fashion to express her disagreement.

"It's important that you listen to me if you truly want this nightmare to end."

He places his finger underneath her chin before continuing.

"I will never put you in harm's way. I won't let anything happen to you. Ever. Do you understand?"

She nods.

"But you must listen and allow me to protect you. Now, I'm not sure if you recall what happened after I found you."

She attempts recollection, but a black spot appears after Baxter intervened, frustrating her.

"Well, when I arrived, you were running away from your attacker, right into my arms. When you pointed him out, I gave chase. I caught up with him a few blocks away."

She gulps.

"Needless to say, he will never harm anyone else."

"Bax, is he?"

"Yes, love. He's dead."

Her breathing spasms at the thought of someone having died last night. Though, it could've been hers, a human life was extinguished just the same. He rubs her back.

"Did you? Did he?"

"He gave me little choice. He attacked me with a knife."

Yes, that knife. She doesn't think she'll ever forget it. She touches her neck and flinches.

"Let me take another look. The doctor said you didn't need stiches. It's just a tiny puncture wound that should heal swiftly. He recommended Mederma to prevent scarring. I've already purchased it for you and applied it as you slept."

"What do the police want with me?"

"Like I said, just a statement. I've secured legal representation for you already. You won't say anything that may expose you to criminal charges. I'd never allow that."

"Criminal charges? I didn't do anything. I was attacked!"

"Shhh, I know. They know that. The legal system has a disgusting way of re-victimizing the victim. That's why we're meeting with the attorney. He will make a statement to the police on your behalf. You don't even need to speak with the detective directly."

She lowers her head.

"Hey, look at me. I've got you now. Don't worry about anything.

Anyone who wants to get to you, has to come through me, and no has ever been successful at that. Including law enforcement."

Well, the man *is* worth billions so she's certain there's much truth to his statements. He's so rich that if he woke up with her piddly millions, he might kill himself. Zia's newly rich, but he's generation wealthy. She suddenly feels safe with him. There's something about him that tells her he isn't the one to mess with. He's killed for her. She shrugs the horrifying thought away.

As her senses return full circle, she recalls the meeting at Reaping.

"What time is it? Where's my phone?"

"It's only an hour past sunrise. Plenty of time before your meeting. Your phone is on my desk, next to the rest of your things. I'll grab it for you."

"Thanks."

He retrieves her phone and hands it to her. Before he walks away, she grabs his hand.

"Thank you. For everything. I don't deserve any—"

"I'll make you some breakfast," he interrupts.

"My clothes…I don't have anything."

"Yes, you do. In the closet." He points to the proper door before disappearing into the kitchen.

She's anxious to call Bryce. Before she hits the send button, she steadies her nerves and reminds herself that he knows nothing about what happened last night. She aims to keep it that way.

"Good morning, sunshine!"

"Good morning, babe."

"Did you sleep well?"

"I did," she lies for the umpteenth time.

"Good. I'm glad you called. Didn't think you'd be up this early."

She remembers the time difference.

"I'm still a bit tired, so I may sleep for a few more hours before heading over to Reaping."

"You need the rest. Just be careful out there. Only go where there are lots of people. Don't wander around alone."

"I won't," she promises.

"I've got a few meetings this morning. I'll be working through another lunch. I've worked through so many, I've forgotten what lunch is like."

His laughter waters her parched soul.

"Well, we'll talk later, and I'll fill you in on everything. I love you."

"I love you too, Zee. So much."

Just as she hovers her thumb over the red button, he yells out.

"Oh! When you get back home, we need to start planning the wedding."

"Yeah, starting with setting a date."

They both laugh.

"Talk to you soon, babe."

"Okay, bye."

She lingers this time, hoping he'll have more to say, but the call drops.

She walks across the room and swings the closet door open. She enters an entire bedroom of a closet. She spots her luggage to the left and recalls dumping the contents onto her hotel room floor last night. She unzips it to find her belongings neatly folded.

She wonders how he could've gained access to her hotel room. Then it dawns on her that the key must've been inside her purse or pocket.

She then notices that her purse is missing. She ventures into the living area, then into his study. Atop his desk, lies her purse and bra. Gazing at the mangled items, she decides that she never wants to see either of them again.

"I'll incinerate them for you, if you like."

He leans against the doorway.

"Yes. Please, destroy them."

"Of course."

She empties the contents of the purse before handing it to him. He quietly disappears. She's impressed and grateful by his respectful demeanor. The average man who had their heart broken the way she broke his, would want revenge. Or at the very least, they'd take advantage of the situation. He's being a perfect gentleman.

Perhaps she'd judged him too harshly. Perhaps she'd mislabeled her feelings for him based on the advice she was given. She hasn't seen an ounce of lust in his eyes. Only love.

Chapter
SIXTEEN

THE MEETING AT Reaping was a resounding success, although Zia had postponed it to 4pm. Larson was as wonderful as she'd expected, but that wasn't the surprising part. What shocked her back into reality was discovering that Makayla is now Baxter's agent. What's more, she's already negotiated a new book deal with Reaping on his behalf.

On her way out of Reaping, she rebukes her inner jealousy, but it remains as constant as the rising sun. Her pettiness rears its thorny head as she takes comfort in the fact that her deal was worth more money than Makayla's.

Baxter's driver picks her up. She rides silently in the back seat, denying her jealousy, and desiring to pummel Makayla's face. She must be careful not to reveal her feelings to Baxter. After all, she's the one who'd pushed him away. She rolls her eyes and decides to call Bryce for a mood booster. They discuss wedding plans and Weingart. She hangs up feeling much better.

The driver stops in front of the condo.

Before she can exit, Baxter joins her. He plants a kiss on her cheek, smiles, and scoots her over.

"Uh, am I missing something?"

"We're going to meet with the attorney and get it out of the way."

She'd forgotten about those plans and she's anxious to be done with it.

They arrive and exit curbside. She gazes up at the skyscraper, draws her shoulders back, and allows Baxter to lead her inside—31 floors into the sky. As soon as they exit the elevator, the receptionist greets them.

Within seconds, a tall graceful redheaded woman approaches.

"Mr. Silverstein will see you now."

They follow her into a corner office where a stout gentleman, dressed in Prada, greets them.

"Tom, this is Zia. Zia, this is Tom Silverstein."

She shakes his hand and exchanges greetings before sitting. Tom gets right down to business.

"Let's start by stating the obvious and go from there."

"Okay," she agrees.

She glances at Baxter as he rests his back against the chair, completely relaxed.

"Based on the information I have, you were attacked in an alley last night in the Bronx," Tom states as he flips through his documents. "Castle Hill, from the looks of it."

"Yes."

"Mmm hmm. Before I interview you, I'll summarize the information the NYPD has already received."

"Okay."

"On the evening of September 13, 2019, at approximately 11:12 pm, you were traveling north on Norton Avenue by foot. Male perpetrator, identified as Guzman Lopez, grabbed you and dragged you into an alley, where he robbed you at knife point and attempted to sexually assault you. You struck the assailant with your fist and ran for help. While running away, you collided with my client."

She doesn't recall telling Baxter the details of what had transpired in that alley, but she does have many black spots in her memory from last night, so she may have.

"You pointed to assailant Lopez and my client gave chase. The events that followed were out of your range of sight and hearing. Is this information correct?"

"Yes, sir."

"Okay, if you wish to make any amendments, don't hesitate to stop me. Now, after my client caught up with Lopez, he himself, was attacked. Lopez attempted to stab my client and was met with brute force. My client and Lopez struggled over the knife, until the blade was forced into the assailant's neck. The assailant later died from massive blood loss."

This is her first time hearing the details and she's sure this version has been cleaned up for her benefit. She swallows and allows Silverstein to continue.

"Now, because there was an assault that resulted in a death, statements must be made by all involved parties and witnesses. Although you did not witness the altercation between my client and Lopez, you were at the scene. All you need to do is confirm the timeline of events that I've provided, and I'll handle the rest."

"That's pretty much what happened," Zia confirms.

"Did you witness the altercation between my client and Lopez?"

"No."

"Did you hear anything? Possibly that you did not see?"

"No. Once Bax ran after him, I fell to the ground and covered my head."

"Bax? Oh, oh, of course."

She's yet to learn to be more considerate when using his nickname. Baxter squirms, then leans slightly forward, ready to go.

"Okay, so basically, you were attacked. My client chased down the assailant, hoping to apprehend him. The assailant then attacked my client with a knife. After a struggle over the weapon, Lopez was struck and later died from his injuries. Do you both agree?"

"Yes."

Baxter simply nods.

"Okay, that's all I needed. I'll prepare your statement and forward it over for your signature. Once you sign it, I'll deliver it to law enforcement. You will make no statements to any law enforcement agency, media, or other individual regarding this incident without first consulting with me. Are we clear on that?"

"Yes."

"If for any reason you're contacted by law enforcement, direct them to me."

He hands her a business card.

"Do you have any questions?" Silverstein queries.

"Has my name been released to the media regarding this incident?" Zia probes.

"The police have bigger problems on their hands. Lopez was a career criminal with a conviction record spanning longer than you've been living. No family or friends have come forward, so law enforcement doesn't have anyone to answer to. So, no. It's not media worthy, my dear."

She sighs. The last thing she needs is to end up on the news when she hasn't told Bryce about it. She's exhausted with keeping all these secrets. They say their goodbyes and head back to the condo.

Zia doesn't want to go anywhere or do anything. She's already shopped and taken in the sights. Look where that got her. She easily decides she's safest indoors.

Baxter unlocks the door. She enters the foyer and freezes. There are luxurious black candles and white roses everywhere. The candles are decorated with rhinestone bows. The atmosphere is saturated with vanilla and floral scents. On the dining room table are two ice buckets, wine glasses, and miniature white trees made of pure light. The door closes so gently behind her that she doesn't bother to turn. She can't pry her eyes from the decorations.

The walkway is aligned with white rose petals, leading into the bedroom. She slowly follows the trail. The bedroom furniture has been rearranged, leaving a larger space in the center. The fireplace is lit.

There's an array of black boxes lying on the bed, along with a large linen card with her name on it. Before she reaches for it, she's drawn to the tiniest black velvet box atop the others. She pries it open. A humongous diamond ring twinkles in her eyes. She slams it closed. She flips the linen card over. There's only one word written on it.

Upstairs.

She drops her new purse on the floor and makes her way up the winding staircase. She's never ventured into the upper and lower levels of his home until now. When she reaches the top of the staircase, flickering light captures her right eye. She looks back and around.

"Bax?"

She enters the lit room where a large ovular Jacuzzi bathtub, filled with sudsy bubbles, and white rose petals, steal the show. Black candles enclose the tub and are also scattered throughout the room. The tub faces wall to wall glass, overlooking the Manhattan skyline. The scene is breathtakingly gorgeous.

A pair of soft, warm hands are on her shoulders. She glances over her left shoulder, into his face. She's never seen his eyes this way. The blue pools are calm and patient. He slowly, and very delicately, undresses her, one item of clothing at a time. She doesn't resist.

He's wearing nothing but briefs. He sweeps her into his arms and carries her into the tub. They submerge together. He has her cradled in his lap, underneath the fizzing water.

The bubbling heat is so heavenly that she closes her eyes and inhales the steam. Stroking her cheeks, he adores her face with his eyes. His doll is a picture of pure perfection.

"Our entire lives, we're taught what love is," he begins. "What it should look like and how it should feel. We take those teachings as truths without ever questioning why. Passion is mistaken for lust and we're told that the feeling is wrong. Everything that feels right to us, we resist because— well, love doesn't look or feel that way. Partner after partner, we end up feeling failed and the world faults us for it."

She listens intently. His tone is so tender that he's momentarily a stranger to her.

"We sometimes even marry someone because they present them- selves in the way that they've also been taught love is to appear. But love is indescribable. If you can put it into words, it isn't love. Love is more colorful than the existent spectrum. It is many things. Why just choose one or a few? Why not have it all?"

She notices his erection isn't as solid as it usually is when they're this close. Plus, he's still wearing briefs, so she doesn't feel he's trying to romanticize her with his words in order to get into her pants. His per- ceptive words are heartfelt.

"When I first saw your face at the Fire Pages event, I wondered what you were. Not just who—but what. The way you moved about and spoke just gave me so much pause. You were not what I had been conditioned to believe that love would appear as, because my body reacted to your presence in a way that society categorizes as lust. But as you continued to speak and smile, I knew it was something else."

"The way you spoke of arts and literature moved everyone in the room. But it was the glimmer in your eyes, the confidence in your tone, and the movement of your fingers that spoke to me. When you looked right through me, my heart sank. That had never happened to me before. Not that I had never been ignored by a woman, but how it affected me was a new experience. Having believed myself to be superhuman before, you humbled me as a human being that day."

Wow, she thinks.

"God sent you to me. He sent me to you. To love, care for, protect, and change. I believe our experience of being together is a blessing and I'm grateful for every second it has lasted. I don't know when our time will be over, so please understand that as long as I have you, I will love you."

He kisses her in a way that he never has before. He doesn't lick her lips or face. He maintains her gaze and strokes the back of her neck with the tips of his fingers.

"Let me bathe you."

He turns her body to where they're both facing the quixotic, starry skyline. He lathers the loofah and gently washes away all negativity and stress. She lays back in his arms, closes her eyes, and allows him the control she's spent every second of her life trying to maintain.

When he stands, she opens her eyes. He extends his hand to help her up. He continues to wash every inch of her. He doesn't pause. He is completely comfortable with every portion. She tingles all over as he rinses the suds from her skin.

He steps out of the tub and grabs a plush towel. He wraps it around her before scooping her up and carrying her out of the tub, and all the way back downstairs to the bedroom. He pats her dry in front of the fireplace. She can't take her eyes off him. She's never seen him this subservient. She wonders if it is because she's marrying Bryce and if that's why he'd strategically placed an engagement ring on the bed.

As doubt materializes into multiple questions, he applies oil to her skin.

When he kneels and caresses the face of her vagina, she flinches away.

"I'm sorry. I didn't mean to hurt you."

"You didn't."

Confusion and uncertainty pool inside of his eyes. A first that she's ever witnessed. He's always been in control and never truly vulnerable, until now. As he kneels before her by the crackling fire, she stands erect like a Queen. The dynamic of their union seems to have changed, allowing her control where she once felt she had none. She'd always felt victim to their passion. Even enslaved by it. Gazing down at him, she no longer feels that way.

He wraps his arms around her waist and buries his face into her stomach, kissing it. He gently kisses her everywhere. Slowly and tenderly while occasionally glancing up at her. She grabs his face and lifts it. She doesn't say a word. She simply gazes into his eyes for the longest time.

Instantly, she's in his arms. He sweeps her off her feet and carries her to the bed. He pushes the gift boxes onto the floor before gently laying her atop the rose petals. The velvet brushes against her softer skin.

He takes a petal and massages her with it, starting with her thighs, before adventuring to her hips and toes. His eyes are absent lust and spill over with loving desire.

"You are beautiful in every way any human being can be," he whispers.

His words soften her heart. A tear escapes the corner of her right eye. He lies on top of her and wipes the tear away, kissing her again and again. His girth is now as hard as a rock, but he doesn't move between her legs, so she spreads them apart, and pulls his briefs down.

"Zia, are you sure?"

"I want you."

He sighs when their wet heat connects. They cry out to each other. He moves slowly inside of her, allowing her the pleasure of enjoying the very feeling of him. She desires to experience more. Her body registers his crest, shaft, and testicles as they delicately massage her perineum. Moist juices from her insides flow down, into her anus.

He shivers and whimpers with each thrust. She buries her fingers into his back, pulling him deeper. He calls out her name like an infant child.

She strokes his face and hair. They maintain eye contact throughout. His mouth opens and closes. His rhythm steadies and his speed increases. She moans his name. A tear trickles down his face as he admires her beauty.

She gasps for air. Tears escape the corners of her eyes as her orgasm approaches. She had hoped to prolong the moment, but she proves no match for her loins. A warm, tingling sensation builds.

He withdraws himself as she convulses and the hot liquid squirts from her body. She loses control as he reenters her. She can hardly stand it. Her muscles contract and her clitoris throbs.

He forces their faces together.

"I love you."

"I—I love you too, Bax."

His kisses her while burying himself as deep as he can go. Just when she thinks he's going to pull out, his hot spurting wetness connects with her walls. His orgasm seems to go on and on. He groans, thrusts, and shivers until he's emptied his entire load. He still doesn't exit. They lay in each other's arms. He rests his head against her breasts, with her legs wrapped around his waist, and her arms around his body.

Tonight, she's truly lost her virginity, because tonight, she's finally made love.

Zia. For all the praise Dwight had retracted in his moments of rage, has proven herself to be the Queen he had always hoped she was. She'd stood over him and took fearless control, without belittling the emotion he'd laid on the table. Though he can be quite a convincing actor at times, he refrained as much as possible this time.

He can't bring himself to ask any subhuman to marry him after Margaret's wastefulness ate through his core. So, he thought that purchasing the most expensive diamond ring he could find and placing it in plain view would relieve him of the demeaning act. Zia did not bite, but he is undeterred.

He was initially attracted to her distinct vigor and combative nature. He had once thought those were common traits in African women. After experiencing several dozen, he learned that many African-*American* women were submissive to white men of means. That always disgusted him, and he killed them all without an afterthought. They were not fit to reproduce. Tonight, Zia revealed herself to be worthy to rule an empire and birth many a nation.

Years ago, Dwight also had discovered East African Mitochondrial Eve as he was researching ways to continue the human species without the existence of the subhuman. Scientists were deep into the development of the male uterus, but that just didn't appeal to him. It was only logical that certain women be spared for the purposes of reproduction. This way, the female population could easily be controlled.

To his extreme delight, Zia came into his sights. He recalls the evening when he'd questioned her about her eye color, hoping she was not of European descent. When she'd made it clear she was a black woman with a rare eye condition, her pride and strength only captivated him further.

Holding her in his arms tonight, he smiles inside of the darkness because his original plan has effectively changed course. Had Zia not shown him she was capable, he would have ended her life after he killed Guzman and continued his search.

Once he witnessed her fight an armed man and escape him, he knew there was something more to her. Zia is the one he never thought existed. She has to be Mitochondrial Eve, reincarnated because the contrary made no sense to him.

But now, she must be trained to obey her one true master.

Chapter
SEVENTEEN

FLOATING INTO FARGO Tower, Zia decides to keep her recent escapade with Baxter a secret. She wouldn't call it a secret so much as just not anyone else's business, but she won't share the details with anyone except her therapist. Although she's fairly certain about her feelings for him, a professional opinion always shines a different light. That light usually helps her think deeper than just emotionally.

She is, without a doubt, torn between the two men. Baxter placing the engagement ring where she would discover it as a gift, isn't a marriage proposal. Therefore, she did not take it. Unless he explicitly asks, she will not assume.

Jenn is on the phone, as usual, so Zia waves and skips right into her office. When she flings the door open, she halts. The room is completely empty. Only the stock desk, sofa, and file cabinets remain. Her personal effects are missing. She turns right back around and approaches a smiling Jenn.

"Jenn, what's going on? All of my stuff is missing from my office."

Jenn hurriedly disconnects her call.

"Oh, I thought Jazz would've told you."

"Told me what?"

Her heart nearly beats out of her chest as she wonders if Spark has discovered her affair with Baxter. If Spark knows, then Bryce knows.

"You've been moved to Sector 5," Jenn announces as she fiddles with the notes on her desk. "Uhhh, 5-L."

5-L is where the senior agent offices are. Zia gasps at the realization.

"Uhhh?" Zia manages.

Jenn smiles and points her in the right direction. She pushes the frosted glass door open when it dawns on her who's missing from the scene.

"Is Jazz here yet?"

"No, I don't think she's coming. She would've been here already."

Zia immediately calls her. She doesn't answer, so she leaves her a voicemail. With so much going on in Zia's life, she hasn't even asked Jazz how she's been lately. She couldn't blame her if she decided to take a break from the friendship.

Zia loves and appreciates her so much. She certainly needs to act like it more often. Next, she phones Bryce. He doesn't answer either, so she leaves him a voicemail telling him about the promotion.

Just around the corner from their main entrance, she encounters a door that's labeled: *Private Entry Only*. She taps her badge against the sensor and places her palm on the thermal scanner. The door unlocks. She follows the signs towards Sector 5, passing different doors with various names on them along the way.

She reaches the end of the hallway where there are two offices on either side. Both are set back from the hallway, with separate entrances. The one on her left has a blank name plate. The one on her right has her name on the door.

With her mouth agape, she inches forward. She runs her fingers across the engraved lettering on the locked door. She unlocks it with her badge and enters. The adequately sized office faces Wilshire Boulevard. She can even see the mountains. Spark has finally removed the lid from her coffin. Light streams inside, brightening the entire space.

On her desk is a huge cellophane wrapped gift basket with a card attached. It's from Spark's Corporate Offices, welcoming her to Sector 5. All her personal effects have been placed along the shelves where she can easily see them. The office is equipped with its own coffee machine, laser printer, oak bookshelves, multiple file cabinets, leather sofa, and what looks to be a restroom in the corner.

There's a hefty stack of mail waiting for her on the desk, and the largest leather chair she's ever seen is calling her name. She bounces into it and spins around in circles. Her mind starts questioning why Spark gives their senior agents these large offices when coming to work is strictly discretionary. She quickly dismisses the possibilities because she's made it to senior status.

As a senior agent, she'll no longer receive a base salary, but she also no longer requires it. She opens her laptop and taps the power button when her desk phone rings.

"This is Zia."

"Ms. Lennox, you have a call from Larson Francis on line one."

"Take a message. Actually, send all my calls to voicemail until further notice."

"Yes, ma'am."

No sooner than she hangs ups, the phone rings a second time.

"Ms. Lennox, you have an urgent call on line two."

"Who is it?"

"He wouldn't say. He just said that it was urgent."

Believing it could only be Baxter, a smile spreads across her face.

"Okay, I'll take it." She clicks the button. "Hello."

"Hello, Ms. Lennox. My name is Detective Johnathan Barnes from NYPD homicide. Do you have a minute?"

Her smile evaporates.

"Actually, no. You'll have to speak with my attorney. His name is—"

"I know his name. I really just need to ask you a few questions about—"

"No, I can't. I'm sorry. You'll need to contact my attorney of record."

"Ms. Lennox, if you'll just give me a few moments of your time, I can clarify…"

"…I'm sorry, but no. Goodbye detective."

After disconnecting the call, she notifies the switchboard not to accept any further calls unless they're from Bryce.

Back to work. She needs the day to catch up on things. She'll call Larson back after lunch. She grabs the stack of mail and thumbs through it. Her OS has loaded, so she shifts her focus to emails, beginning with Spark's.

Her slush has been sufficiently dwindled in her absence. There are three new inbox folders labeled as Prime Queries, Partials, and Fulls. Spark must've assigned her a permanent dedicated human filter, or two. She excitedly pumps her fist in the air.

She then logs into her personal email. There's one from Baxter with the manuscript of the final installment of the Kelp series attached. She sends him a quick thank you note, then clicks to print. There's a knock at the door that she'd meant to leave open. Just as she pushes away from her desk, an impeccably dressed brunette woman enters.

"Hello, Ms. Lennox. My name is Bridgette and I'm the Administrative Assistant for Sector 5. I apologize for not introducing myself sooner, but I've been swamped."

She chuckles as they shake hands. Although Bridgette seems nice, Zia misses Jazz terribly.

"Mondays are always the worst. Well, I didn't mean to disturb you. I just came to deliver this message. The caller said it was urgent I deliver it to you."

She hands Zia the slip of paper and exits.

Johnathan Barnes. 212-555-0197. We should talk.

She crumples the message slip and stuffs it into her back pocket, annoyed by his persistence. She plans to notify Tom Silverstein later.

She returns to her inbox. There are two emails from Kevin Phillips. The first one asks if she's certain that the name she'd provided him was correct. The next one contains a message with an attachment.

I wasn't sure which Dwight Fairfield. But on a hunch, I limited my search to the state of New York since the Baxter Leopold search was New York. Attached, are my findings. Any questions, call. Do not reply.

She clicks on the attachment. Daring not print the pages, she views them on screen. There are various addresses, different names of possible neighbors, relatives and acquaintances. Her scrolling abruptly ceases when an enlarged image of a New York State Driver License with Baxter's face and Dwight Fairfield's name appears on her screen.

Dwight Ian Fairfield
DOB 11/12/1973

Her eyes bulge from their sockets and her jaw hits the desk. She doesn't stop there. She continues scrolling. There's a New York City Clerk marriage document showing that he's married. She carefully reads the accompanying documents clarifying that Dwight Fairfield was widowed by the death of Margaret Fairfield.

She moves on to the various newspaper clippings and articles on Dwight Fairfield. Forbes, Time, Business Week, etc. The lying sneaky son of bitch is also majority shareholder of Paradigm—the largest conglomerate in the United States. Zia wonders why no images of him appeared in the Garble search results, then she realizes that Paradigm is majority shareholder of Garble.

She reads a few sentences here and there from the many articles. None of the photos are recent. They're all rather old. She reads the captioned names underneath a few of them. There are several of him alone, with his wife, and then also with his daughter. She angrily scrolls past and then stops. Something pulls her back. The little girl looked familiar.

She returns to the family photos, looks closer into the little girl's eyes, and then reads the caption.

She gasps.

"No way! No FREAKING way in the world am I seeing what I'm seeing!"

But it's true. It's there, in black and white. She slams her laptop closed, grabs her purse, and all but runs down to the parking garage.

Zia speeds down the boulevards and highways with heartache pulsating through her. She swerves madly into the driveway—tires screeching to a halt. She sees a face peer through the window just as she stomps up the walkway.

Jazz opens the door with confusion oozing from her eyes. Zia never thought she'd be confronting her best friend in the foyer of her home on the subject of betrayal. She was so blinded by her own that she didn't see this one coming.

"Zee, what's wrong? Is your mother..."

"Why didn't you tell me Jazz?"

"What are you talking about? Tell you what?"

"Why didn't you tell me that you were Baxter's daughter?"

"You're kidding, right?"

"Come on, Jazz. Don't deny it. That hurts even more. You've been keeping tabs on me this whole time! I'm sure there's a reason why you're not at work today right?"

"Look, I don't know where you're getting your misinformation from, but don't accuse me of lying when you're the queen of that shit," she rebuts while angrily poking her finger.

Zia reasons that guilty people are normally defensive, unless they're truly sorry. Besides, if Jazz wasn't tracking her movements at Spark, then who was?

"That's a low blow. I trusted you with my secrets and you were keeping your own from me."

"I stayed home today because I didn't wanna be in Sector 2 without *you*! I know who my own damn father is, and his name isn't Baxter!"

She turns her back, huffs and walks into the living room, with Zia on her heels.

"No? Well, how about Dwight? Ring any bells?"

Jazz whips around and her mouth drops open.

"How do you—I haven't spoken to my father in years. How do you know him?"

She grabs Zia by her upper arms. Her eyes bulge out of their sockets as if she's seen a ghost.

"Zia, answer me. How do you know him?"

Zia snatches away from her.

"As if you don't already know. Baxter Leopold is Dwight Fairfield's pseudonym. Or his catfish alias, as I see it."

Jazz expels the oxygen from her lungs and leans over.

"Zia, you listen to me and listen carefully. My father is extremely dangerous. I never knew that he created a fake identity using the name of Baxter. I would've told you that from day one. You don't have to believe me. Nobody else ever did."

"What do you mean by that?"

"The last time I spoke to my father was a year after my mother died. She was involved in a freak car accident. I didn't think anything of it at first but then…"

"Then what?" Zia implores, with a mouth as dry as the Sahara Desert.

"Then my father started acting really strange and creepy. He would walk around the house singing and spend hours online in chat rooms. He never cried. He was never sad. He changed. Or I should say, he came out of hiding."

"You mean he's gay?"

"I mean, he's an evil psychopath and I just wasn't paying close enough attention until my mother died, leaving the two of us alone together."

She paces across the floor in a daze as she travels down memory lane.

"After my father started revealing his true nature, I decided to investigate the car accident. I discovered that it was no accident. Someone had tampered with her brakes. I knew better than to ask him because he'd just lie with a straight face. I know for a fact that he did it because two things happened. One, my mother just had her car serviced a few days prior. She didn't tell my Dad things like that because he didn't care to know."

"Two, my mother was home the day of her accident. She was sick and too weak to travel. Dad was supposed to stay home to take care of her, but he claimed there was an emergency at the office. I was at my internship when she called, asking me if I could pick up Dad's prescription from the pharmacy. I told her I wouldn't make it in time. She told me that he made a huge deal about needing it right away. I didn't understand the urgency, why he couldn't just get it himself, or at least send one of his corporate slaves to get it. Long story short, her brakes failed and…"

Tears stream down her cheeks and she sniffles.

"Not too long afterwards, I found a little notepad next to his computer with scribblings on it. He was jotting down weird phrases like 'they shouldn't exist' and 'the extinction of the subhuman is imminent'. He claimed that those were ideas for a book he was planning to write, but I didn't believe him. My gut told me to get the hell out of there, so I moved all the way across the country..."

"...from New York to California," Zia concludes for her, lowering her head.

She wraps her arms around Jazz.

"Yeah."

"I'm so, so sorry Jazz."

Click, click, click. Zia's mind connects the dots. Everything has just come full circle for her. Subhuman is a term that Kelp regularly used to reference his female victims in the books, starting with the first sequel. The books that oddly resemble actual murders taking place in New York.

Baxter intentionally failed to mention Paradigm because Zia would've put the pieces together long ago. Baxter said he controlled Vex. Vex is a subsidiary of Paradigm. Rebecca Horton was a Paradigm employee. Paradigm owns Spark. She works for Spark. He planned this from the start.

Baxter is entirely too powerful. Too much power is dangerous because those who possess it tend to be above suspicion.

"Zia, listen to me. I know him. He's highly intelligent. If he has *any* indication that you're on to him, freak accidents will start—"

They simultaneously gasp.

"Mom! He tried to kill my Mom already! Shit, shit, shit!!"

Zia paces back and forth as she mumbles expletives.

"Holy shit. Holy fuck. Holy fucking shit. What have I gotten myself into?"

"Calm down. Just calm down so I can think."

"I can't calm down, Jazz. I'm scared to death!"

"Okay, okay. If nothing else, he's predictable. Repetitive. He once told me that repetition is the cure for human error."

"What does that mean, Jazz?"

"It means we need to do our homework. We need access to the case files on the NYC serial murders."

"Why? How will that help?"

"Think, Zee! Whatever he's done to those women, he's planning to do to you! THINK!"

Zia nods her head, accepting that Jazz is right. If they can find out what was going on in those victims' lives leading up to their deaths, they just might be able to get ahead of this.

"I don't know how we'll get our hands on those files, but there's always a way," Jazz optimistically declares.

Zia recalls being attacked in the Bronx and how Baxter just happened to show up at the right moment. The phone call earlier today from that detective comes to mind.

"Maybe this might help," Zia suggests while handing Jazz the message slip from her back pocket.

"A detective named Johnathan Barnes from NYPD homicide called me today."

"Ole Uncle Johnny? Of course!"

"You know him?"

"He and my father have been best friends since grade school. I remember sharing my suspicions about the accident with him. He told me I was driving myself crazy. I bet he'll believe me now."

She grabs her jacket and purse.

"Come on. We're going to New York."

"What? Why the hell would we tap dance on the lion's tongue?"

"Fight back or die, Zee. The files aren't going to come to us. We have to go get 'em. Besides, Uncle Johnny apparently wants some information from you. Time to negotiate."

Chapter
EIGHTEEN

JAZZ AND ZIA stand amidst the LAX hustle and bustle, waiting to board their flight. Of course, the tickets were disgustingly expensive, but Zia's nerves are too splintered to care. She's shaking her knee nervously while Jazz is as cool as an arctic glacier.

As a clever ruse, Zia told Bryce there was an emergency meeting with Reaping that she and Jazz had to attend. A brick of disgust tanked in the pit of her stomach when she forced herself to accept that she's lied to him for the sake of a two-faced lying sack of sick.

She had truly thought that she was in love with Baxter after this last time. He's one hell of an actor because he had cried real tears for her. He'd looked her dead in her eyes while he was inside of her and told her that he loved her.

Her mind is frantic over how many times she likely came close to being killed while she was in New York. She suddenly recalls all the many times Baxter's facial expressions were blank and his eyes vacant. The choking incident where he'd nearly killed her and seemed to enjoy it. The time they met with Tom Silverstein and Tom had no clue why she had referred to Dwight as Bax. All the red flags have been there. She was simply blinded.

"I hope we don't get all the way to New York and this detective tries to play us for fools."

Jazz pats Zia's quivering knee.

"I wouldn't worry about that."

"Why?"

"Because I've known Uncle Johnny for a very long time."

"Well I haven't. What if he lets Baxter—I mean, your father—in on the fact that we know? He'd kill us, and we'd have no way to protect ourselves."

"Shhhh, keep your voice down. Uncle Johnny isn't stupid. Besides, he knows I'd never allow him to use us as bait. I've never been stupid, Zee."

Jazz most definitely has never come across as stupid. Come to think of it, she always seemed rather versed on various things, including legal. Zia had filled her in on the Bronx incident and the subsequent romantic encounter. Jazz has never lied to her, so she'd decided to tell her.

Baxter, on the other hand, has lied to everyone. Every single day she'd looked into Jazz's face and never thought anything of the resemblance. She has her mother's green eye color, but she has her father's nose and chin.

Now it makes sense why Jazz never cared about money and didn't blink an eye when that $50 million-dollar check was handed to them. She's the daughter of a billionaire. She must work at Spark for a very good reason and Zia wonders what that reason could be.

After leaving JFK, the ladies check into a hotel of Jazz' choosing. Zia paces back and forth inside of the room. She still can't believe they traveled where she knows there's a serial killer on the loose, who just happens to be obsessed with her for some reason. Of all the women in the world, she'd found her way into the arms of a murderer.

"Zee, sit down. You're driving me crazy."

Zia sits on the bed.

"Jazz, why do you work at Spark? I mean, come on. Your father owns—freaking everything!"

"Incorrect. Technically, Weingart does."

"No, I checked. Paradigm is the largest—"

"That's just for show. Weingart has deeper roots, better client relations, and money they don't brag about."

"But still."

"Zee, you don't take news very well, so do you really wanna know?"

"Yes, Jazmine. I really do."

"I own Spark. It was part of my inheritance."

A grin spreads across Zia's face at the revelation.

"You witch!"

Zia dives on her, tickling her ribs.

"All this time you're my boss and you let me stress over stupid stuff?"

"I wanted to tell you, but that would've put me under a spotlight I just didn't want anymore. I left that world behind when I moved to California."

Zia understands and doesn't judge her friend.

"Oh my God. You didn't even need your $10 million dollar cut of the Kelp deal."

"What? Bitch betta have my money."

They erupt in roaring laughter.

"Well, why Sector 2? Why not bourgeois Sector 5?"

"Because I don't like uppity rich folks. Especially, newly rich ones. Money changes people in disgusting ways. Makayla, for example."

"No, people are already disgusting. The presence of money just serves as a springboard."

"You're right about that."

"Wow, so you're my boss huh? Well, guess what? I QUIT!"

They burst into laughter, then there's a knock on the door. They snap upright. Jazz places her arm across Zia's chest and pulls out her cell phone.

"I told him to call when he was outside the door, so I'll know it's him," she whispers.

Her cell phone lights up and she answers. Zia hears a faint but familiar voice.

"I'm here."

She unlocks the door and in walks Johnathan Barnes, carrying files. No visible badge. He's dressed in dark denim, white Nikes, and a blue Yankees t-shirt. He doesn't look like a cop.

"Good to see you, kid," he greets Jazz.

His voice is rumbling deep and there's a very faint British undertone present, though the New York accent overpowers it.

She hugs him.

"Uncle Johnny, this is Zia."

"It's a pleasure to meet you, Ms. Lennox."

"I'm really sorry about before. I just—I thought you were calling about the…"

"I understand. Trust me."

Jazz offers him a seat and he leans against the desk with one leg up.

"Now Jazzie, you're family but this is serious business. No laughing matter. Women are dying out here. I'm not giving up these files unless your friend here gives me something I can use."

"I understand. Zia has much more to lose than anyone here. She's in the greatest danger and she needs an arrest to happen swiftly."

"I can't arrest anybody without probable cause."

"I know how it works," Jazz reminds him.

Detective Barnes then focuses on Zia.

"What do you have for me, little lady?"

Zia tilts her head to the right, preparing to give Detective Barnes a crash course in Ziaology.

"Here's what I know; you've known this man your entire life and you have absolutely zero evidence on him. That means he's been lying and killing right up under your nose for decades without being caught. Apparently, he's smarter than all of us. I will not give you information you can use while maintaining discretion to withhold those files from us. My ASS is on the line here. I'm the one who has to pretend to still be in love with a murderer, so he won't be suspicious of me. I won't play games with you, so don't bullshit me."

"Zia!"

"No, Jazmine. No one in the world has greater access to him than I do."

"You're absolutely right about that," Barnes concurs. "Now let me tell you what I believe; Dwight has likely been killing since we were teens. Girls would mysteriously go missing after we moved to the States. Something in his eyes—he just couldn't hide it all the time. I'd catch glimpses of the evil, but he was like my brother. I loved him. Still do. That kept me in denial for too long. Many lives have been lost because of my denial. I could've saved Margaret, but I just refused to believe he was capable. My gut tells me he's got something to do with the recent murders and you're likely next."

Solving this case is personal for Barnes.

"Uncle Johnny, allow us to view the files overnight and I promise to give you a piece of information tomorrow morning that'll be a sufficient lead in this case. No one wants him caught more than I do. He killed my mother."

Zia wonders how her friend plans on keeping that promise.

"How I see it, there's no harm in allowing you to view these files. I'm doing this as a favor. Don't make me regret it. I'll be back tomorrow at 10am sharp."

"Thanks, Uncle Johnny."

"See you girls tomorrow."

Jazz locks the door behind him.

"Jazz, why the *hell* did you promise him that? I don't know if I have anything he can use."

"I just had an epiphany."

Zia's intrigued.

"If we're using these files to get an edge, perhaps the answers Uncle Johnny's seeking have been right up under his nose this entire time."

She walks over and unzips her suitcase. She pulls out the Kelp books and stacks them on the desk next to the case files.

"Uh Jazz, I hate to break it to you, but I'm sure everyone in the country has read these books already."

"No Zee, he hasn't. You know how I know?"

"How?"

"He's never mentioned the name Baxter Leopold once. NYPD's finest clearly hasn't made the connection between the author and the corporate executive."

"How is that possible?"

"Because law enforcement is trained to think inside of a box. Whatever is the easiest lead to process, is the one they follow."

"Well, how do you explain him contacting me then?"

"That's easy. Luck," she shrugs. "He got lucky when your name came up alongside my father's in the Bronx incident."

"Hmm."

"Think about it, Zee. You cut him off when he tried to question you because you thought along the same lines. You thought he was calling to ask you about the Bronx attack when he was really calling to ask you about your relationship with my father. If you hadn't cut him off, he would've squeezed a few bits of information from you, and likely would've tipped off my father in the process."

Yes, and that likely would've hastened her demise.

"How exactly are these books going to lead him to an arrest though? That's the part I'm missing."

Jazz sighs.

"Zee, these case files contain information that *we* don't have. These books are like case files of information for Uncle Johnny because he hasn't read them yet. They're indirect statements or admissions from my father. Like a diary, of sorts. Remember when you mentioned how the books seemed eerily similar to the actual murders?"

"Yeah."

"Well, after you told me my father was Baxter, a light bulb went off in my head."

Zia understands now. Baxter didn't have access to the police files, as she had once assumed. He knew certain details about the murders because he committed them. If Detective Barnes can find one simple slip up in the books, that might be enough for an arrest.

"You're brilliant. Do you know that?"

"I am aware of this."

"Oh, and Jazz, I'm sorry I've been selfish lately. I could've been a much better friend to you. I promise I will be from now on."

Jazz hugs and squeezes her friend.

They immediately start combing through the files. Anxious fingers turn pages throughout hours upon hours of excavation. The photographs are gruesome and unbearable. When Zia reaches Rebecca's file, she reads slowly and carefully.

When she'd seen Rebecca on the news, it was a photo the media had likely chosen because she was smiling or something. Whatever the reason, Zia always assumed that Rebecca was white. This case file contains more realistic photographs. Rebecca was biracial. Her mother is black, and her father is white.

She continues analyzing the file until the hours escape her.

"I'm starving. Let's go get food," Jazz whines while patting Zia on the bottom.

"I don't have much of an appetite."

"You haven't eaten. You need your energy. We both do. Come on."

"I…I'm kinda scared to go out. Can't we order in?"

"New York is a very big place and I've hired us a driver. No taxis for us."

Reluctantly, Zia scooches off the bed. Jazz isn't the type to accept 'no' answers anyway. Like father, like daughter.

Zia zips her hoodie and throws on a pair of dark sunglasses.

"Zee, seriously?"

Zia dramatically throws her hands up in the air.

"Hell yes, seriously! This isn't just an obsessed ex we're talking about here. Don't make me say the words, Jazz!"

"Alright, alright. Calm down. I'm too hungry to fight with you. Let's go."

They hurry downstairs and into a waiting all black Escalade with tinted windows. They're shuttled to a café that's comfortably nuzzled in a part of Brooklyn Zia's never been. She's just happy to be out of the City. The driver parks where they can easily see him.

They order so many entrees and appetizers the entire table is covered with plates. They enjoy their food while discussing the details of what they've read in the case files thus far. Jazz even pulls out a note pad from her purse. Zia hadn't thought about keeping notes because she was so wrapped up in Rebecca's life. With two cheeks full of food, Jazz speaks in a focused, but relaxed, tone.

"As far as I can see, he seems to be systematically destroying these women."

"Systematically?"

"Well, yes. If you notice, his victims may seem random at first glance. But if you read between the lines and pay more attention to their lifestyles, it's not so random."

"I think I know what you mean."

Zia refrains from speaking the words she wants right away, but she didn't come this far to bite her tongue, nor to be timid. She dips her fries into the tangy lump of ketchup and just blurts out her thoughts before Jazz can elaborate on anything else.

"Jazz, I think your father might be targeting black women."

"I agree, but here's the twist; I don't think he's targeting them in the same way as women of other races."

"Go on."

Zia's definitely titillated by how easily she'd accepted her theory.

"The violence employed on the victims who weren't black was just... violent. The kind we read about in newspapers all the time. But when he killed black women, it seemed, ritual. Almost as if he was looking for something, didn't find it, but he separated certain portions of their bodies to symbolize a deeper meaning. I don't know how to explain it."

Zia continues chewing on her food and on Jazmine's words.

"Remember when I told you, after my Mom died, I found a notepad by his computer?"

"Uh huh."

"Remember what it said?"

"About *they all must die* or something like that?"

"Exactly. I think he hates women. He wants all women dead. Or wanted."

"Well, he hasn't stopped killing so..."

"Zee, I swear if you don't stop with this cutsie crap and start using your brain. I know you're smarter than this, so think!"

She jabs her finger into her temple and then into Zia's forehead.

"You've been in his life for a year. You've survived a whole year. I know there are things you know. You're just blocking it. You're still in denial."

Zia thinks Jazz is right. She's still waiting to wake up from the nightmare.

"You said wanted, past tense. What makes you think that?"

"I think he still wants women dead. I just noticed that his victim pool changed. I think it's possible that he rethought whatever his original plan was and likely realized that humanity will die out without women."

"That's common sense though, Jazz. He never struck me as being dumb. To ever think of completely obliterating the female population is just plain stupid."

"Mmm hmm, but when you're blinded by hatred, what is logical? I think it's very possible that his hatred morphed into a smarter plan. What if he's selecting the few he deems fit to live and killing all the rest?"

There are a trillion women in the world. Zia ponders what kind of plan would be this far reaching. They silently chew, swallow, and think.

"Jazmine."

"Hmm?"

"Name Paradigm's subsidiaries or any company related to Paradigm."

"Hmm, let's see. There's Spark, Vex, TransMedia, Reaping—"

"Reaping? Really?"

"Yep."

That angers Zia, for obvious reasons.

"Umm, Langfordshire, Willow Creek—"

"Langfordshire Pharmaceuticals?"

"Yeah, they—oh my God!!!" she gasps.

A moment of realization rains down on them. Langfordshire (LFS) was recently acquired by Paradigm's executives, but not as a subsidiary. The fat pharm company had recently revolutionized every form of birth control and developed a potent treatment, and vaccine, for breast, cervical, and ovarian cancers.

"Jazz, if we're right, Nanocen (Nan) birth control could kill off the younger female population, and Zenelex (Zen) would take care of the rest! How the hell could we prove something that complex? No one will ever, ever, ever believe it. We'll be branded as conspiracy theorists."

"One thing at a time. We can't focus on tackling that just yet because we haven't exposed my Dad. He's the key to all of this. As long as he's innocent, nothing else we say will matter."

Jazz is right, once again. So right that it pisses Zia off and frightens her. If Baxter has had a plan in place for God knows how long, he's likely so far ahead of them, they can't catch up. Zia's frustrated with the entire situation, but she refuses to give up. She fears she already knows the answer, but it's buried so deep inside of her mind, she won't find it in time.

ANNOYED BY ZIA'S inaction, Dwight sits behind his desk with his lean muscular legs crossed, contemplating a way to expedite total dominance over his slave queen. She didn't take the ring. In fact, she never mentioned the ring at all. He'd reviewed the surveillance videos numerous times, focusing on her reaction when she opened the box.

Perhaps she's unsure because she doesn't know that the rare South African, 51 carat, flawless diamond ring cost $57 million. Sotheby's pennies.

After a successful weekend rendezvous, he expected she'd do away with her torn female emotions. He surmises that as long as Zia has another to turn to, she'll not be dependent upon him, as required for her own safety.

He reasons that she could've, at the very least, taken the ring with her. But she'd left it behind. Not quite a rejection, but also not obedience. Clearly if he placed it before her, she's obligated to accept it.

She'd mentioned no intentions of returning to the city anytime soon and his plans have been prolonged for far too long. He's tried vigorously to impregnate her during sex, but it hasn't come to pass.

His anxious feelings remind him to follow up regarding the patents, distribution, and FDA approvals. He employs the intercom to summon his borderline incompetent foreign assistant.

"Claire, I require LFS updates within the hour. No exceptions."

"Right away, sir. But—the current project?"

"I won't repeat myself."

"Yes, sir."

Claire is a typical fearful waste of space. Once her purpose has been fulfilled, she'll cycle herself into extinction, just like the rest. When he visits his homeland, he's always anxious to return to the States. The female population, though more diverse in London, fancy themselves untouchable. He never leaves without disposing of a few dozen, if possible.

Before the clinical trials for Nan and Zen were completed, he'd captured several dozen subhumans to experiment on in his free time. As they slowly and torturously expired, he ensured that his private scientists could neither prove nor disprove the elements of Nan or Zen contributed to their deaths. Just as the tobacco industry has successfully done for long enough to make their fortune. Weingart, specifically.

Except Dwight isn't staving off proof for a payday. Once they start dropping like flies, no one will be the wiser of the true cause. Cancer isn't going anywhere, nor is reproduction. If they ever figure anything out, it'll be too late. His drugs and plans are safe.

His most pressing issue is getting his personal affairs with Zia on schedule. The existence of a fiancée angers him in such a way that it gives him murderous focus. She had to choose to accept the proposal of a man from an equally powerful rival conglomerate.

He shoves the contents of his desk onto the floor.

Claire rushes into the room.

"Sir, are you alright?"

"Close the fucking door."

The timbre in his British tone is low, growling, and fearfully intimidating. His eyes flare murderously. She slowly backs out of the office with fear oozing from her pores. The scent arouses him.

If a leash wouldn't frighten Zia away, he'd invest in one. His need for her sends him into a lustful rage. It's time her need for him exceed his for her.

He contacts his personal assistant, Violet, to arrange for the delivery of a clean body. He requires forceful release. Only then can he think clearly enough to plan anything. He's identified an open door. It is time to walk through it.

Chapter
NINETEEN

IT'S HUMP DAY and Zia's apprehensive about returning to New York. Baxter requested to see her, and her refusal would've only aroused his suspicion. She, Detective Barnes, and Jazz had decided she's to play it cool until a resolution is found.

Jazz shoved the books at Barnes the next morning. It upset him until she explained herself. He decided he would take a week off from work to read the novels. Zia expects he'll compare them to the case files. She prays he acts swiftly because she doesn't want to be near Baxter any longer than necessary.

With Bryce in Beaufort tending to Weingart business, she has plenty of time and space to fix the mess she's created. Bryce didn't specify exactly what was so important that he needed to go without notice, but she was too grateful to inquire. She just hopes that by the time he returns, Baxter will be in prison forever and their lives will be out of danger.

Lucy all but begged her to come along with Bryce, while Turner remained silent in the background. Her plate is too full to worry about what Turner might be planning, so she'd ignored the undercurrents she felt, knowing Bryce will be exposed to his father's trickery.

Zia finishes up her half day at Spark before heading home. Lately, she's been feeling like she should tell Jazz every little detail of her life. Though honestly, not everything is her business. That's not to say she doesn't love her friend beyond measure. It's just that telling someone every little thing can become annoying.

Besides, Zia can't recall Jazz ever telling her about any man that she dates or has ever dated. Come to think of it, that's rather weird. Zia forces that anomaly to the back of her mind. Her head is already exploding.

She pulls into her garage, happy to be where she feels safest in the world. While deactivating the alarm, she calls her parents to make sure they're okay. Vivien's physical therapy is going great and they're rekindling the spark in their relationship. Satisfied, she commences packing her suitcase for New York and falls asleep mid-fold.

BAXTER'S DRIVER ESCORTS Zia to his condo. As soon as she reaches the door, he yanks it open and grabs her around the waist. He spins her around in circles like he hasn't seen her in forever, when it's only been two weeks. She forces a smile and a kiss. If she's pretended this long, she can do it for the sake of her own life.

She turns on the charm.

"I missed you," she lies while batting her lashes and puckering her full lips.

He sighs and runs his thumb over her mouth.

"I would take you right here, right now, but we're leaving."

"Huh? Where?"

"It's a surprise. Let's go."

Into the chopper they go. They jet off within the hour. He refuses to tell her where they're going, so she sits back and focuses on controlling her temperament, hoping she's not laying it on too thickly.

"There's a bedroom up front. You may want to get some rest. We'll be in the air for a while."

She considers protesting or asking questions but decides better of it.

"I am a bit sleepy."

Her obedience greatly pleases him.

She kisses him before the flight attendant escorts her. She rolls her eyes and climbs into the bed, acknowledging she can't stay awake forever. She needs to be alert and sharp for whatever is coming next.

The descent of the plane wakes her. She rubs her eyes until the bright daylight doesn't sting. Baxter's asleep next to her. There's a knock on the door.

The male attendant enters.

"Please prepare for landing."

Baxter stirs before sitting upright. He groans, stretches, and slips on his shoes. She does the same. They make their way back into the cabin to fasten their seatbelts. She glances down at her phone to gain a sense of the time, but alas, it's no use. Her GPS hasn't caught up to their location.

He smiles and kisses her cheek.

"Just relax."

She sits back and allows him the control he requires.

They land within minutes and de-board at Juan Manuel Gálvez airport. A black limousine awaits them with a driver standing with the door ajar.

"Welcome to Honduras, my Queen," Baxter whispers into her ear.

She shudders at his queen reference. They ride along in silence. When they exit the limo, she takes in the breathtaking surroundings. The beauty is indescribable. It's December and here she is on a sandy beach with crisp emerald palm trees and golden sun. The water is the bluest blue and the breeze hugs her like a childhood friend. He grabs her hand as she gawks.

They enter their private Villa residence and she's taken aback by even more luxurious beauty. The furnishings are exquisite. The spacious hut adorns a shore that's right outside the door.

While their luggage is brought inside, she stands in front of the sliding glass, staring and smiling. She slides the door open to allow the warm air inside.

She can't help but to step out and dig her toes into the sand, wowed, against her better judgment.

"Roatán is one of the most beautiful places in the world. Especially this time of year."

"It's beautiful."

He hugs her from behind as they gaze out at the aqua water together. She's eager to dive in, but she didn't pack any clothing for tropical weather.

"I wish I had known. I would've packed a few bikinis. The water is calling my name."

"Come with me," he implores, taking her by the hand and escorting her upstairs.

He pulls the closet door open inside of the master bedroom and her mouth drops open. There are a dozen rows of swimsuits with the price tags still attached. All the pretty colors of the rainbow twinkle in her eyes.

"Bax, how do you *do* stuff like this?"

"I planned to bring you here as a surprise. I figured you needed a change of scenery."

He smiles, and she sincerely returns the gesture.

"Take your pick. I'm going to grab a shower."

She runs her fingers across every swimsuit hanging in the closet. All of them are in her size. She feels like a kid in a customized candy store. Her mind understands the situation, but her life depends on her sincere actions. She needs to fall into this or he'll discover what she's been up to. If that happens, she's dead.

She settles on a swimsuit and takes a quick shower.

She doesn't bother drying her skin. Instead, she throws on the orange-fuchsia starburst bikini and runs toward the ocean, yelling like a mad woman.

"Woooooooooooooo!"

Her wavy hair bounces as she screams and dives into the lukewarm, turquoise water. She thanks God for this heavenly moment of peace.

She floats on her back with her eyes on Big Blue. She revels in the moment and allows the current to pull her wherever. Baxter watches, but allows her a moment of peace before joining.

They spend the day snorkeling, swimming with dolphins, zip-lining, and other wholesome activities. Viewing him in this light is disturbing because he appears to be so normal. He's smiling, thoughtful, gracious, and all around *good*. It creeps her out.

They dine at an outdoor restaurant on the water, surrounded by crackling bonfires. Tiny golden sparks shoot into the sky. There, they converse with other couples on vacation. Being around other people is the part she enjoys most.

As the night progresses, most of the couples retire to their huts. Zia and Baxter remain, consuming tropical drinks at a rapid pace.

The one interracial couple who's taken to them are South Africans,

Kungawo and Amahle. Kungawo is a white man whose accent clearly indicates he was born and raised in South Africa, despite his ancestry. He's average height, medium build, and quite handsome.

Amahle has a milk chocolate complexion, sultry eyes, high cheek bones, modest voluptuous figure, and a beautiful bright smile. Baxter has been hanging on their every word, especially Amahle's. Some pathetic part of Zia is jealous of her intoxicating smile and exotic accent. Amahle's crown is wrapped proudly atop her head in a lavender print scarf.

Kungawo and Baxter are both enthralled by her every word and movement, so Zia withdraws from the conversation, accepting Amahle as the star of the evening. She reminds herself that she's just faking it to make it until Barnes hauls Baxter to jail. She orders another Guaro and rests her back against the chair. Buzzed, she barely realizes that Amahle is speaking to her.

"Beautiful, Zia. I hope we are not boring you with our conversation."

"Not at all. I enjoy hearing you speak. Your tone is very pleasant. Soothing."

"Why, thank you! What a lovely compliment." Amahle's almond shaped eyes twinkle. She moves away from the men to sit next to Zia. Baxter and Kungawo's eyes follow.

"You are quite an exotic beauty. Were you born in the United States?"

Zia clears her throat, preparing herself for the inevitable question.

"Umm, yes. California."

"I don't mean that the way it sounds. Your facial features are reminiscent of the extinct, and royal, African tribe of Yoruba."

Zia's mildly intrigued and leans forward.

"Oh, I don't know anything about African culture." She smiles in hopes that Amahle will continue.

"Well, Yorubian women were rare gems dating back to the beginning of civilization. Probably mankind as we know it."

Baxter leans forward and Kungawo proudly enlightens them on his wife's knowledge of the subject.

"My Amahle is a teacher. She specializes in ancient cultures and extinct civilizations."

"Oh really?" Baxter's eyes light up in a way that Zia's never seen before. Amahle beams at her husband before continuing.

"Yorubians were believed to have gone extinct because their female companions slowly diluted themselves, as they were drawn, and taken, from their tribes by men from other tribes and nations."

"Diluted how?" Zia inquires.

"Over the centuries, our country Akebu-Lan, became occupied by many people of different races, just as yours. Diversity is unstoppable because human beings will migrate everywhere there is land. Well, those who were not of African descent were mesmerized by the Yorubian woman's physical features—as they were not typical of the majority. Her sharp bone structure, but most notably, her eye color."

Zia dips her head and stops Amahle before she insinuates any further.

"That is very fascinating, but my eyes are not a color. I could not have descended from that tribe. I regret to inform you I am not royalty, but I would love to hear more about this tribe."

"And how could you be so sure of something, you yourself, have admitted you know nothing about?"

"I'm not denying I am of African descent. I proudly am, but the Yorubian tribe thing, I could not be part of."

"I'm quite versed on this, but how are you sure, my dear?"

"Because I have an eye condition. I was not born this way. So, it's impossible."

Amahle glances at her fair-haired, green-eyed husband, and smiles. One would think that she just struck gold. Kungawo lowers his head with a smile on his face. They share a laugh and Zia's eager to be in on the joke. Baxter has become anxious as well.

"What's so funny?" Zia demands.

"Zia, my *pragtige Koningin*, I feel quite certain that we have traveled all this way and stumbled upon an ancient artifact. I mean that most respectfully," Amahle beams while pressing her palms together in a pleading manner.

"What?"

Kungawo claps as his wife exhales. Baxter is so drawn in that if he moves, even infinitesimally, he'll fall off his seat.

Zia, on the other hand, needs to know what Amahle means by ancient artifact.

"How can a living person be an ancient artifact?" Zia probes.

"I have written many texts regarding the Yorubian tribe, focusing on the female population. When so much time passes, facts turn into myth. I, myself, theorized that the Yorubian woman was born with a genetic defect that likely affected her vision. That some hereditary condition contributed to the discoloration of her eyes."

"Zia, your ancestors gave birth to the most powerful and even the richest in all of existence," Amahle explains. "Sub-Saharan African civilizations believe the extinction of the royal tribe of Yoruba contributed to our descent. Europeans desired to possess the Yorubian Goddesses with the fair-colored eyes so much that they even stole them away."

"After so many years, they eventually cycled themselves out of existence, as far as the world knew. But human DNA and genetic markers prevail. Lying dormant, they are passed down for generations until the traits re-manifest and here you sit before us...the only known living descendant of the royal tribe of our ancestors."

They are all so captivated by her words that there is only silence for a moment. Zia wants to drink "the kool-aid", but it's just too farfetched for her. Though flattering, to be sure. An eye condition may be rare, but not rare enough to for Zia to buy into this tale.

Zia shakes her head in disbelief, but with a tender smile on her face. Amahle has certainly entertained her, taken her mind off her situation with Baxter, and earned her rightful place as the star of the evening.

She places her soft warm palm on Zia's forearm. The look in Amahle's eyes has softened. She leans closer and whispers in Zia's ear.

"It is an honor to be in your presence, my Queen." She kisses Zia softly on her cheek before kneeling before her and kissing her hand.

Zia's eyes bulge a bit as her husband follows suit. The sudden turn of events startles Zia.

"Come on you guys, this is very flattering, but quite a bit much," Zia croons.

The look on Baxter's face is priceless. He is truly mesmerized by the moment. He grins widely and suggests they all return to their hut for a night cap. Zia's anxious to lay her body on something soft and comfortable.

Baxter offers more drinks when they make it inside. Everyone accepts. Candles are lit in the living area and he lights the fireplace. Amahle removes her sari and glides across the room as she speaks.

"Is there a radio? I know a great station."

Baxter directs her to a glass box that's so fancy, no one would've guessed it was a radio. She tunes it and ethnic music softly fills the room. Amahle dances seductively, swaying her hips and twirling her body. The others eye her every move. Kungawo is seated on the sofa next to Zia. Baxter leans against the mantel, sipping on a drink with his white collared shirt unbuttoned, and his tanning skin aglow.

Kungawo's arousal bulges inside his Caribbean amber cargo shorts. Zia scoots away from him and leans against the arm of the sofa. Baxter comes to stand next to her, hoping to quench her discomfort.

Amahle continues her exotic dance by grinding her modestly sized bottom against her husband's erection. He groans and unravels her African head scarf. Her ample dark brown tresses fall gloriously over her shoulders.

Zia is entranced by her beauty but decides she's a little too drunk for this scene and decides to retire. When she leans forward, Amahle tosses her a wink and reaches for her. Zia stoically gazes at her hand hanging ambivalently in the air. Amahle pouts, puckers her lips, and smiles before dancing over to Baxter. She pulls him to the center of the room where they dance. She undulates while he hangs on to her hips. Soon, they're kissing each other.

"Come and join us my Queen," Amahle pleads.

Zia's bolted to the sofa, stunned by the turn of events.

"Do not be afraid of her. She is the most generous and loving creature in all of existence," Kungawo suggests in a low and husky voice. He seductively winks his eye at Zia before joining them.

They all dance as Zia watches. Baxter and Kungawo's hands gradually join as they move to the beat of the music. They flirt with each other as Amahle caresses their shoulders.

When the two men share a kiss, Zia's chin drops to the floor. She suspiciously scrutinizes the drink in her hand, believing she's been drugged. She slams the glass down on the end table, astounded to discover Baxter's bisexuality.

Amahle dances Zia's way and attempts to peel her from the sofa. When she doesn't budge, she sits beside her.

"Are you bothered, my Queen?"

"Stop calling me that and yes, I think I am."

"You appear to be quite young. I am just 31 this month," she says, distracting Zia with conversation.

Zia turns to gaze into Amahle's youthful face, believing she couldn't be any older than 21.

"When we spoke of your eyes, your exasperation was swift and sharp. This melanin, though absent in your iris, will make for your very best friend as time passes. It will keep you young for decades."

Zia's heard of that myth, but perhaps that's why her own mother still looks 35, though she's almost 60. Zia shakes her head, attempting to sober herself up.

Amahle's hand is on her knee, caressing her. Before Zia can fully protest, Amahle's lips connects with hers. She pushes Amahle backwards.

"Amahle, this is not natural. It doesn't feel right."

"How would you know? You have felt nothing yet."

Zia looks up to see Baxter's eyes trained on her. She's so scared that her eyes well up and tears spill over. He instantly kneels before her.

"Zia, don't be afraid. I'm here. I would never let anything bad happen to you."

That comforts Zia a little bit. No sooner than she feels comforted, he slips his hand between her thighs and thrusts his fingers into her vagina. She gasps. He leans forward, forcing her back into the sofa. Eyeing her intently, he advances.

"Don't you want to please me?"

She's unable to respond. She simply gazes into his eyes and remembers her mission. His jaw clenches. She's afraid to tell him no, so she nods yes.

"Don't be afraid."

That's one emotion she's unable to avoid. He smiles sadistically while withdrawing his fingers. She recalls having seen that look on his face before the night he'd nearly choked her to death. He licks his fingers and points them in Amahle's direction. She kneels beside him and opens her mouth. Zia gasps again as she licks his fingers so seductively that he groans.

Feeling left out, Kungawo joins them by the sofa. He positions himself behind his wife, caresses her bottom, and then unties the straps of her bikini bottom. The fabric falls to the floor. Zia eyes him incredulously. Baxter and Amahle's eyes are on Zia as Kungawo shoves his entire face into Amahle's bottom.

She groans and grabs Zia's hand. Baxter attempts to relax her with liquor. She gulps it down, sincerely hoping she'll pass out and wake to a new day.

Kungawo removes his shirt, unties his shorts, and enters his wife from behind. His thrusts push Amahle's face closer and closer to Zia's. Zia leans away from her until Baxter caresses the back of their heads, guiding their lips together. He kisses Amahle and Zia. He overflows of lust for Amahle and love for Zia.

Baxter takes Zia by the hand and lifts her from the sofa. He swiftly undresses her, kneels again, and shoves his entire face into her vagina. Kungawos' eyes drip with desire as he glares at Zia's naked body.

Amahle smiles as Baxter undresses. The flickering light from the fireplace dance on their skin. Amahle's eyes twinkle in much delight as Baxter reveals his massive manhood. He grins at her before plunging into Zia. When she cries out, Amahle grabs her hand.

Zia slightly turns her head, Baxter snatches it back. He won't allow her attention to be diverted while he's inside of her. He's jealous and demanding, even in a room full of strangers who are having sex right in front of them.

He has Zia's knees pinned against the cushions, restricting her movements, and intensifying the sex. Unable to control his depth, she digs her nails forcefully into his skin, breaking it. He growls before releasing.

She sits up before he can take her again. He pulls Amahle up by her arms.

"Bax?" Zia hopes that he doesn't intend to have unprotected sex with this stranger after he's just made love to her.

He sighs and snatches the end table drawer open, producing a condom. Amahle anxiously rips it open and slides it on him. He lifts her into the air and she wraps her legs around his waist. He's inside of her with one thrust.

Zia doesn't know what else to do but watch. Amahle's having the time of her life while Kungawo hungers for satisfaction. He approaches Zia with his erection pointing at her face. She recoils. He kneels and leans close to her face.

"You are the Royal Queen. I think deep down, you've always known it. The way you walk and speak. You know." He touches Zia's face while grazing her lips, praying that she will allow him inside.

"Look at you. So beautiful."

He carefully kisses her while grabbing the nape of her neck.

"I cannot believe I have been chosen to make love with the Queen of mankind."

Although she knows this queen stuff is pure crap, it flatters her beyond belief. Especially coming from his mouth. His sexy voice and accent arouse her against her will. She's now completely convinced she's been drugged because she refuses to believe that she would allow this situation to happen if she were sober.

Kungawo attempts to maneuver his way between her legs, but she scoots back and pins her knees together. He leans even closer and produces a condom.

"You will remain clean throughout."

Zia covers her eyes and shakes her head. Some part of her desires him. The intoxicated part, surely, but she doesn't want to do this.

Hopeful, he slips the latex barrier on. Her legs remained closed, so he changes his approach.

"Look into my eyes as I speak. Only if or when you want me, I will come inside. Not a moment before. You rule us all. You control us all."

After a few moments of quivering, she glances over at Baxter. Her knees slowly and grudgingly part ways.

Across the room, Dwight steps into the light, retiring Baxter. He is absolutely convinced that God chose him and Zia. He's received confirmation in various forms. After their last excursion, he harbored sneaky suspicions that Zia might be on to him, but when she eagerly returned to his arms, he dismissed them.

They could have been anywhere in the world. Yet, they wound up in the company of a South African expert of ancient African civilizations who validated Zia's deity without anyone asking or hinting towards the subject.

As Amahle's semi-sweet vagina devours every inch of him, he loses interest in her heat, as she was Baxter's conquest. Not his own. He refuses to remove his eyes from his Queen, Zia. She's apprehensive and without protection on the sofa.

Kungawo is inches from entering her. As his slithering body squirms her legs apart, Dwight decides no one else will have that pleasure but him. He rejects Amahle and dashes over to the sofa, grabbing a frightened Zia into his arms, and placing her near the fireplace.

Behind him, the sounds of Amahle and Kungawo having sex slowly fade into another dimension. He snatches the used condom from his penis and discards it in the fire. He nearly desecrated his own Queen—the only living descendant of the Royal Yorubian Eve. This act would've proved him unworthy and that is unacceptable. He'd much rather eat a bullet.

While delicately caressing Zia's face, he apologizes with kisses. He does something he never thought he would or could. He *sincerely* begs her forgiveness, as she is no longer a subhuman, but the mother of his new world.

"Zia, will you please forgive me?"

A single tear escapes his left eye.

She touches his face and nods. He holds her inside his arms and instructs the visitors to leave. They bow on their way out.

Once they're gone, Zia makes love to him several times, several ways, until he passes out from exhaustion.

Chapter
TWENTY

As Baxter sleeps soundly, Zia tip-toes into the restroom, and gently closes the door. Once inside, she exhales while leaning over the sink, and splashes cold water on her face. She flinches from as her swollen vagina throbs torturously. With no time to be a wounded soldier, she regroups to complete the mission. This is it, the moment of truth. If she's going to find any evidence, the time is now. She grabs a fresh pair of panties from the drawer and slips them on.

Next, she retrieves the miniature flash drive from the empty lipstick tube Detective Barnes provided her, sticks it into her underwear, turns off the light, and returns to the bedroom. Thankfully, Baxter is still sound asleep and snoring loudly.

She creeps around the hut. Her only light is the dying fireplace and candles melted down to the end of their wicks. She wastes no time locating Baxter's laptop. She frowns because it isn't the same one she'd seen on his desk the morning after the Bronx attack, but as far as she knows, he has a dozen, and there's no time to split hairs now. This is her only chance.

She looks around and listens for the sound of snoring. Feeling certain he's still asleep, she carefully unfolds the personal PC. When it wakes from hibernation, she's met with password protection.

For a moment there, she'd thought that a murderer wouldn't take precautions to protect his deadly secrets. She starts typing various words and numbers, trying to guess the password, all without success. She pauses and thinks deeper. She tries words like subhuman, Jazmine, and Margaret. None work. She then tries her own name. That doesn't work. With nothing left to lose, she types 'QueenZia'.

Access Granted!

She quickly inserts the flash drive and locates the files. Her eyes nervously dart around the dimly lit room, expecting Baxter's hands to appear around her throat at any moment. She copies all the files from the hard drive and bites her nails during the process.

After the copy has been made, she closes all open files and puts the PC back into hibernation. She sticks the flash drive into her underwear and creeps back into the bathroom. She then conceals it inside of the lipstick tube, flushes the toilet, and jumps back into bed with Baxter.

They wake the next morning and resume their vacation activities before returning to the freezing cold reality of New York City.

WHEN ZIA RETURNS to California, Bryce is at work. She jumps into the shower, takes a quick nap, and wakes to cook dinner. Nothing in this world, not even Baxter's imprisonment, can relieve her of her burden to confess what she's done. She emails Detective Barnes then starts chopping veggies.

Pacing back and forth in front of the kitchen stove, she accepts the reality closing in around her and decides that it's time to tell Bryce. He never deserved to be lied to. She allowed herself to be used and misled, but aside from that, she simply cheated all on her own, and there's no way around it.

Once the olive oil has heated inside of the pan, she tosses the vegetables in. The crackling, sizzling sound fills the silent condo.

She surmises that their relationship will likely end, and she'll never see him again. She'll never wake up to his breath on the back of her neck, his arms protectively around her, his laughter at the breakfast table, or his beautiful loving spirit. She mourns the loss of him already.

Whatever Baxter was to her, he is no more.

"I'm home!" Bryce announces when he walks through the door.

He hugs her from behind while she sautés veggies.

"Mmm, that smells delicious. What's for dinner?"

"Meatloaf, veggies, and mashed potatoes. As close as I can get you to a southern dinner."

He roars, kisses her on the cheek, and smacks her bottom.

"Babe, I like food. Doesn't have to be southern."

"I just figured I'd give it a go. Oh, and I'm baking fresh bread too."

"Mmm, I knew I smelled it when I came in the door. Nothing like the scent of fresh baked bread. Mmm, mmm."

"Go get washed up."

"Yes, ma'am!"

His smile is all the sun in her sky. She bites down on her bottom lip, afraid. She can't believe she's about to shatter the light in his eyes. Meatloaf won't soften the blow, but she doesn't know how else to set the mood.

Her stomach dances.

It's time to face the music.

CHICKENING OUT OVER dinner just confirmed her cowardice. She's determined not to allow another day to pass without confessing her sins to the love of her life. She picks up the phone and dials.

"Babe, can you come home a bit early? I need to talk to you about something."

"Uh sure. Is everything okay? Why can't you just tell me now?"

"I need you to come home."

"Alright, let me wrap up a few meetings and rearrange my schedule. I should be home in an hour."

"Okay, see you then."

She's taken the first step. There's no going back now. She sighs and paces.

When he walks through the door ninety minutes later, she throws her arms around him, selfishly reveling in one last moment of perfection before shattering it.

"Babe, are you alright?"

"We need to talk."

"Okay." He slowly removes his satchel, neck tie, and jacket.

She leads him to the sofa where they sit.

"Bryce, I…I have something I need to tell you."

She lowers her head like the coward she believes herself to be. He nudges her face upward.

"Zia, what's wrong? Is your mother okay?"

"Oh, she's fine."

She only realizes she's crying once the cooled tears splatter against her collar bone.

He grabs her hands and moves closer.

"Whatever it is, you can tell me."

She clears her throat and shakes her head. In a tremulous voice, she raises the guillotine on their love.

"Oh Bryce, I've done something awful." Her lips tremble as she gazes into his eager eyes.

His considerable lashes flap when he blinks, choking her heart in their vice.

"Bryce, I…"

"Stop," he sighs.

"Not this time. You need to…"

"…no, I don't." He places his fingers on her lips to quiet her.

Unsure of why he won't allow her to speak, she lovingly removes his fingers, dedicated to seeing this through.

"Bryce, please listen. I…"

"…I know."

"What? No. No, you don't."

His eyes drop with his sigh before he glares at her.

"I knew it when it you slipped up and called him Bax. It wasn't that you shortened his name. It was the tone of your voice when you spoke of him. It was too…comfortable. Once I knew, I had to decide. I took the time to think about it. I thought about it until I could think of nothing else."

Her eyes bulge from their sockets.

"I'm not throwing you away. When Grandma Tess was on her death-bed, she told me that if we spend our lives rushing through the hard parts because we're anxious for the good ones, we'll waste half of our lives by always desiring the time that we feel we lost. She said that's why we're never ready to go. If I have the good fortune of growing old, it's going to be with you."

Unable to believe her ears, she remains frozen.

"What you did is *not* okay. You broke my heart. I was crushed for everyday that passed and you didn't tell me. But when you called me home early, I actually felt relieved because I knew you would."

"But why? Why did you believe in me? Why didn't you say something sooner? Be angry? Throw me out? Curse me or something! I deserve it. All this time I thought you just didn't desire me that way, so it might not have mattered to you."

"Zia, you're still clueless, after all of this time."

He cups her face and gazes intently into her eyes. The color of his irises darkens a shade.

"Here's what you need to know. Every single day and night, I've wanted to be inside of you. I've wanted to take you and have you in every possible way. I've fantasized about rough sex, tender sex, kinky sex. You name it, I've thought of it. It drives me insane. Even right this moment, I want to be inside of you."

He slips his fingers between her legs and caresses her clitoris through the silk crotch of her panties. He yanks her head back and leans over her while grazing her jaw line with his lips. He takes the palm of her hand and places it on his bulging erection. Her breath escapes.

"Do you feel that?"

"Yes."

"I could take you right now."

"Then why don't you?"

He leans back, and they release each other.

"Because we only live once. We only have so many chances to get something right. Being as young as you are, you have a very limited concept of time. I was raised a certain way. But as I became a man, I decided for myself that this was the right way for me. Do you care to hear about the many women I've bedded before I met you? How I allowed my lust desires to control and eventually destroy something that could've been meaningful? Huh? Is that what you wanna hear?"

"No, I…"

"No. Exactly. So, if you're going to tell me you did this because you thought I didn't desire you, then we might just be a lost cause."

"No! I did what I did because I was weak, naïve, and stupid…and I'm sorry. I'm so, so sorry. I know that—"

"You've shown me you can mess up, as humans inevitably will. Now show me that you can be better. Zia, you are my future. I forgive you. But if you ever lie to me, cheat on me, or give me reason to *think* you've done either of those things, we are through. Completely."

He saunters off into the bedroom. Within seconds, the shower water is on. She's frozen. She confessed, or at least she thinks she did. She finally fessed up to her sins only to discover that Bryce had forgiven her while still immersed in them. She wonders what kind of human being is capable of that.

She was so wrapped up with the devil that she didn't even notice that he knew. Of course, he knew. True love can't harbor secrets for long. She cannot wait to become his wife. She completely undresses and joins him.

When she opens the shower door, his eyes linger on her naked body. She doesn't plan to tempt him when he's made a decision that she now wholeheartedly respects. She has other plans. She hugs him from behind. He doesn't turn around, so she stands in front of him. The water soaks her before splashing onto him. She throws her arms around his neck and kisses him passionately and deeply until his erection slides right through her box gap. He groans. She maintains eye contact with him as she kneels.

His chest rises and falls.

"Zia…"

Before he can utter another word, her mouth is around his shaft. He hunches his shoulders and tries to pull away. She gazes up at him, opens her mouth wider, and swallows as many inches as she can. He pounds the shower wall with his fist.

He trembles and backs up once again. She throws her entire head at him and very nearly chokes herself in the process. He whimpers and pleads with her.

He glares down with tortured eyes. She maneuvers her head back and forth. Saliva oozes down her chin, onto her breasts. He leans into the feeling, grabbing her head, and touching her face. She moans while dribbling all over him.

"I love you," he breathlessly whispers.

She allows his crest to tickle the back of her throat. He warns her of his impending load and tries to withdraw, but she denies him.

He convulses and growls in a tone she's never heard from him before. He bites his bottom lip while adoring her face with his eyes and fingers. He lifts her from her knees, wraps his arms around her, and attempts to apologize.

"Don't."

She smiles and leans into his warmth.

They towel each other dry and jump in bed. He holds her tighter than he ever has. They lay in complete silence with his heartbeat in her ear and Bugs content in the corner.

Here they are, surviving what most couples perceive as a deal breaker. Their survival may be attributed to the fact that neither of them made a deal in the first place. She simply fell in love, messed up, and is blessed enough to have someone willing to fight for her and with her.

"Let's go on a mini vacation," he suggests, interrupting her thoughts.

"Where to?"

"It doesn't really matter. As long as we're together and no one else is involved."

Music to her ears. She grins inside of the dimness.

"Let's go."

DWIGHT WAITS IMPATIENTLY inside of his immaculately designed Villa at West Bay Lagoon in Doha. He sits in front of the spacious bay window, taking the lush scenery for granted. His guest is late. He glances over his right shoulder at the charcoal Darcy chaise lounge and envisions Zia's nude body draped over it. The fantasy provokes his smile.

The doorbell interrupts his thoughts. In walks the only person in the world who holds the power to move his plans along.

"You're late."

"I apologize for my tardiness, but I had a pressing engagement to tend to."

"More pressing than this one?"

"Actually, yes."

Dwight doesn't like anyone or anything being of more importance than him or his plans for mankind.

"Try not to be upset. You'll understand momentarily."

They sit and converse for hours before his guest departs.

Intrigued by the proposed plans, he grows anxious for progress. Now, all Dwight must do is sit back and allow someone else to do their part for a change—remaining prepared at all times to kill whomever stands in his way.

Chapter

TWENTY-ONE

Z IA RECEIVES AN email from Detective Barnes asking her to be patient and cease the incessant emails. Sure, she'll do exactly what he hadn't when he'd called her dozens of times when he was in need of information.

She smacks her lips in anger while sitting on the living room sofa, mid-morning, reminiscing. Her and Bryce's five-day Nevada getaway was just what the doctor ordered. Though it was only a temporary reprieve, they recognized that nothing hurtful magically goes away. They'd agreed that they were both in it until the end.

She had occasionally caught glimpses of his sorrow during the flight, but by the time the plane touched down at McCarran International Airport in Las Vegas, he had rebounded. No matter how skilled he was at hiding it, Zia saw she'd truly hurt him.

She'd be a narcissist if she felt no guilt. As much as she wants to move on, she can't allow herself to just be over it. She doesn't know how long it'll linger, but for now, it is well deserved. She had the fun, but Bryce is paying the price for it.

Jazz tells her that she's too hard on herself because several weeks have passed, but remorse is just the beginning of her atonement. What most adults know is that there's nothing worse than a cheater who rushes the victim to hurry up and get over it, so she thinks about it relentlessly. All hours of the day and night, she thinks of it. Nightmares, night sweats, cold sweats, and insomnia. Partly because she's afraid of a murderer stewing in anger across country at her abrupt departure and partly because there's no escaping the devastation she's caused.

Showing up for work became taxing, so after a few attempts, she decided to work from home. Though if she continues to stay home, she'll torture herself to the point where she won't be any good to Bryce. She won't allow it. That's not a part of the healing process. Productive behavior is. At least that's what her therapist tells her.

She contemplates between going to Spark and having an impromptu session with her therapist. She's quickly grows tired of thinking about it and decides on Spark. Besides, she and Bryce have a joint session scheduled for tomorrow. She reasons that she may as well save her ears and lungs for then.

She sets the alarm and grabs her keys.

"Be good Bugs."

He lifts his brow but turns his head away.

"Still mad at me huh? Yeah, so am I."

She opens the door and inadvertently kicks something on her way out. She looks down at a white, eight-by-ten envelope. She picks it up and examines it. There's no return address. She backs up and resets the alarm, locks the door, drops her keys in the bowl, and rips the envelope open.

A black flash drive falls out first, followed by documents. Her eyes zero in on photographs. She gasps.

"No, no, no. It can be."

There are dozens of pictures of her and Baxter in the throes of passion. Their faces are so clear, it's undeniable. She slams them down.

"Oh God."

This explains his eerie silence. She snatches the flash drive and rushes into the bedroom. In her haste, she trips and falls along the way, banging her knee. Bugs barks and jumps around her. She cries, not because she hurt herself, but because she's afraid that she already knows what she's about to see.

She hurriedly opens her laptop and shoves the flash drive into the USB slot. It takes longer than she can stand for the system to boot.

"Come on!"

Her breathing is so loud it sounds like a fan is spinning on the highest setting. Bugs jumps onto the bed, barks, and presses his paws against the laptop keys. He's ride or die, even when he's mad at her.

Finally, the system is fully loaded. She enters her password and sighs before clicking the file folder titled '*Mine*'.

She clicks the video file. Her face cracks and she doesn't hold back her emotions. She sobs as she watches herself on screen, with her legs spread, breasts exposed, begging Baxter not to stop. The scenes are clipped and pasted from their various sexual escapades.

Every erotic thing a person could imagine is in the videos. She's screaming, scratching him, biting him, pulling him into her, and telling him that she belongs to him.

She can never allow Bryce to see this. She slams the laptop closed. Her chest sinks into itself, like a black hole, sucking her heart down into an abyss. Bugs jumps onto her lap, whimpers, and licks her face. She holds him and cries into his fur with her shoulders shaking.

"It just won't go away."

She grabs the flash drive and dashes into the kitchen. She ransacks the drawers and cabinets in search of a hammer or something similar. She grabs a pot and pounds the flash drive with it, but it remains unscathed. Undeterred, she grabs the lighter fluid and places the drive into of the pot. She runs back to the sofa, grab the pictures, and dumps them into the pot also. She drenches it all with lighter fluid, lights a match, and drops it inside. Bugs barks and jumps until she picks him up.

She cradles him inside of her arms and watches the flames until they simmer. The fire alarm sounds, so she bashes it to pieces. She then runs water inside of the pot only to see that the flash drive isn't melted enough.

She sets it aside and dumps the ashy flakes from the photos down the garbage disposal. She grabs the drive and her purse before dashing out of the door. She speeds away in her car with focused thoughts.

She needs acid, a wood chipper, or something that will obliterate the flash drive from existence. She has no clue where to find such things. Then she remembers she has money. People with money silently buy things to help cover their tracks. Baxter's backstabbing, trifling ways taught her that much.

"Siri, find me a wood chipper for rent."

Her erratic driving causes other drives to blare their horns at her, so she slows down a bit. The options Siri provide aren't immediately available, so she calls Jazz, believing she'll know what to do.

"Zee?"

"Jazmine," she cries like a little kid.

"Zee, what's going on?"

"He sent pictures, Jazz…and videos!"

"Calm down. Where are you?"

"I'm driving to you."

"Zee, pull over right now and stop."

"I need to destroy this—"

"Zee, pull over! Your brakes might have been tampered with. Just pull over and I'll come meet you, okay?"

She pulls into a shopping plaza, parks, and rests her head against the steering wheel while waiting for Jazz. Recalling her mother's accident and Margaret's, she's naïve not to have anticipated this. She pounds her head against the horn repeatedly. Bryce seeing these videos will be like pouring salt on an open wound.

Jazz arrives in a black Lincoln Town car. She yanks Zia from the driver's seat, locks her car, and shoves her into the back seat.

"Don't say anything. Not one word until I tell you. Understand?"

Zia nods and leans back, feeling defeated. She glances down at the battered flash drive in the palm of her quivering hand.

After they've been on the road for a while, Zia's tempted to ask where they're going, but Jazz had specifically instructed her not to speak. For once in Zia's life, she decides to obey. She texts Bryce to let him know that she's with Jazz. She doesn't say where because she doesn't know. Surprisingly, he doesn't give her a hard time. He just wants her to be home by the time he gets there.

They arrive in a wooded area with a freestanding cabin tucked amidst trees. Jazz exits first.

"Two hours," she instructs the driver.

He speeds away, back down the road outlined by tire tracks. She grabs

Zia's wrist and guides her into the mysterious house. Once inside, Jazz disappears. The lights turn on in her absence. Zia sits down on the sofa next to the black fireplace.

"I'll light that in a minute," Jazz informs her.

Zia nods once again while Jazz removes her sweater and purse, tossing them both atop the circular oak dinette table.

"Oh, right. We can talk now."

"Jazmine, what is this place?"

She kneels in front of the fireplace and shoves wooden logs into the pit. After it's lit, she makes her way into the kitchen and speaks from there.

"This is my peace of mind. Silver Lake. Off the books."

The scent of fresh brewing coffee swirls into Zia's nostrils.

"If you prefer cocoa, I can make some."

"Coffee is fine."

She joins Zia on the sofa with two ceramic mugs, filled with piping hot coffee. After years of working together, Jazz knows how she takes hers. The hazelnut flavor dances on Zia's tongue, calming her nerves a bit.

"I brought you here because this is the only place I know for a fact hasn't been bugged," she enlightens Zia while crossing her long beautiful legs.

"Do you actually think my condo is bugged?"

"Highly possible. Show me the flash drive."

Zia opens her hand and pries it from her imprinted skin.

"What the hell happened to it?"

"I tried to destroy it."

Jazz places her mug on the coffee table and retrieves a laptop from between the loveseat cushions. Zia hopes she doesn't plan on watching the video, but she shoves the drive into the slot.

Zia covers the screen with her hand.

"Jazz, don't. I don't want you to see it."

"Are we best friends or just friends?"

"You're my best friend and you know that."

"Then stop being afraid of what I'll think. We're mature women. We need to act like it. I need to see what's on here. There might be a message."

Zia hadn't thought that far into it.

"Have you opened all of the files?"

"I clicked on the '*Mine*' file."

"There are multiple…see," she points at the three folders marked *Mine*, *Yours* and *Ours*.

"Why didn't I see them before?"

"Each file is located inside of the other. It forces you to open them in a specific order. So, after you clicked on the '*Mine*' file, you would have the option of clicking on the '*Yours*' file and so on."

Intrigued, Zia scoots closer. She clicks on the '*Mine*' file, containing the graphic video. Zia turns away, disgusted, and ashamed. Jazz only watches for a few seconds before skipping to the end of it.

"No message at the end of the video, soooooo…"

She clicks on the next file. There are copies of Zia's contracts with Reaping, a list of various Spark clientele, bank records, the details of her promotion, etc. She gets the implied message so far. The last thing inside of the '*Yours*' file is a singular photograph of Bryce dressed in a suit and smiling ear to ear.

"Have you ever seen this picture before?"

"It's an old college photo."

The Ivy League patch on his left breast pocket soothes Zia a bit. At least it doesn't seem that Baxter has been recently following Bryce around. She now wonders what the implied meaning of the photo is.

Jazz clicks on the '*Ours*' file.

Several research documents open containing East African studies dating back to ancient times and various drawings of widely unrecognizable African Queens. No Nefertiti or similar well-known images. Only information on less-known extinct civilizations, Mitochondrial Eve, photographs of men in white lab coats holding vial tubes of specimens, and Extinction Level Event data. Then there are photographs of Zia.

The first are at the Fire Pages event. The others are of her at the other conferences she's attended over the years. Some are before the Fire Pages event and she wonders how long he's been watching her. Jazz closes the laptop and exhales.

"I get it. Do you?"

"It's a warning. Blackmail."

"I think it's more than that, Jazz. I think he's built a plan for his new world around me. He must think I'm capable of what this ancient Eve Queen was theorized to be capable of."

"So, he plans to kill off the female population, saving you, so he can start fresh," Jazz concludes. "He wants to be in complete control of any existent women."

"Clearly, he plans to build a whole new civilization where women are enslaved for the purposes of reproduction," Zia sighs. "I get the craziness of that idea and it's never going to happen. I'm more concerned with what he's willing to do to try and see it through."

"Zee, we know he's willing to kill. We know that much."

"I can't let it happen to Bryce. I just can't. I'll kill him first, Jazmine. I will kill your father before I let him harm Bryce."

Jazz squeezes Zia's hand.

"If anyone deserves to die, he does. He killed my mother."

"Jazmine, I'm so sorry. I don't even know how to express how sorry I am."

"I'm sorry too, but for my mom."

They embrace.

"Before he embarrasses me, I'll resign at Spark. I'll go clean out my desk tomorrow."

"Do it tonight, babe. Don't give him reason to think you're not meeting his demands."

"Right. I can't lie to Bryce, so I'm going to tell him as soon as I get back."

"Don't drive that car until it's been inspected."

"Then how will I get around?"

"You're rich now, remember?"

"Right," Zia grumbles.

Her mind still hasn't caught up to that. She glares at the flash drive protruding from the laptop. Jazz follows her gaze.

"There's another reason I brought you out here. Come on."

She takes Zia by the hand and they walk outside, casually through the creased auburn trees, past the glittery refreshing lake.

"Here," she stops.

Zia swings her head around. Before her lies a hunk of metal on wheels, with a protruding horn, similar to a miniature steel elephant. Jazz fiddles with it until it roars to life.

"What is it?"

"It's a wood chipper. Here," she says as she hands Zia the flash drive.

Zia stares at it. Unsavory images flash in her mind. She blinks them away.

"Go ahead. Toss it in there."

Zia inches near the opening and tosses the drive inside. It barely makes any excess noise. She turns the motor off and points in the direction of the pile of debris. Atop the wooden chunks, lies black and silver bits.

"No one will ever be able to put Humpty Dumpty back together again."

She smiles and rubs her friend's shoulder. Neither of them says it, but they know that Baxter has copies of everything he sent.

"Thank you, Jazz."

"Come on, let's get back."

Chapter
TWENTY-TWO

ZIA TOLD BRYCE about the package and he assured her he'd look into it. She trusts him enough to wait; though, impatiently. She has nothing better to do with her massive amounts of free time but think, so she thinks and rethinks about the case files, the novels, Baxter's words, the flash drive she'd made a copy of and stashed inside a coffee mug at her office, and Kevin's findings. All of it connects in some way. Or perhaps, many ways.

She double checks the new security system Bryce had installed. She can't wait until they move out of the condo and into their new home. They'd selected property right on the Malibu coast and it's being rehabbed right this moment.

Since Bugs is with her parents until they move, she's alone every day, gazing around at the mounting boxes. She hasn't told Jazz, or anyone, for that matter, that she and Bryce had eloped while they were in Vegas. She even had her IUD removed when they returned, at Bryce's behest.

Her and Bryce's parents deserve a proper ceremony and they plan to eventually give them one, along with a grandchild, in the future. Right now, they're still healing over her betrayal. She sighs while placing her hands on her hips.

Jazz had warned her to resign at Spark ASAP, but she'd put it off until today. She's leaving in a bit to collect her belongings. As she grabs her purse and keys, a tiny lightbulb goes off in her head. That one photo of Bryce on the blackmail flash drive, in the *'Yours'* file. She couldn't figure out why it was there, until now. She tosses her keys back inside the bowl and frantically searches for her cell phone.

She dials Bryce. He doesn't answer. She redials ten more times, but all calls go straight to voicemail. She then calls B&F. The receptionist informs her that Bryce left work hours ago. She becomes frantic. She searches the names of all the hospitals in the area. Los Angeles is a huge place, so the only logical place to start is the Wilshire area.

She goes down the list, eliminating one at a time, asking for Bryce Fink or John Doe. Then it dawns on her that his medical records might still be under his father's last name. She systematically calls them all back, asking instead for Bryce Whittle. Still no luck. She calls Jazz and she doesn't answer either.

She asks her parents if they've heard from him and they hadn't. Next, she asks his parents and they hadn't heard from him either. She doesn't know who else to call, so she dials Detective Barnes. No answer. She calls his precinct and they tell her that he's out of town on business. She wonders where the hell everyone has gone all of a sudden.

She paces back and forth for a moment before rushing out of the house. She decides to drive to Jazmine's on the way to Fargo Tower. After she starts the engine and prepares to reverse, she receives a text from Bryce.

"Hey babe. I had to take an emergency flight to Beaufort for business. Phone will be on airplane mode. I'll be home tonight. Love you."

It explains away her calls going to voicemail, but if he can text, he can call. She shelves her mounting paranoia, believing he's probably exerting Weingart's power and influence to investigate the blackmail package she'd told him about.

She decides to go ahead and pick up her things from Spark. She's already given them her letter of resignation. She reverses out of the driveway.

She makes her planned stop at Jazz'. She can't tell if she's home because her garage door is closed and there are no lights are on inside. She rings the doorbell several times, but no one answers. She drives away, hoping she's at Spark.

Zia stands inside of the luxurious office she hadn't had the chance to get comfortable in. She won't miss Sector 5, but she will miss her old coffin of an office in Sector 2. That's where she dreamed, hustled, and made things happen. Her life has changed so much since that first day she walked through those frosted glass doors, bubbling over with high hopes and outlandish ideas. She consoles herself by remembering that she'd made her dreams come true, but Jazz isn't here to see her off, and that makes her a little sad.

She does away with the sentimental memories, places the cardboard box on top of the desk, and begins packing. She tosses her MacBook, framed photos, coffee mug, and various documents inside. She pulls out the drawers and empties them.

Next, she tackles the bookshelf. Having kept most of the books at home, the ones there are mostly vanity copies, except the Kelp books. She tosses the rest into the pile before snatching open the file cabinets. She doesn't care to take most of it. Spark will dispose of it after they've completed their audit. She does, however, pack Baxter and Larson's contracts.

She then sits in the leather chair and gazes around the room, floor to ceiling, double checking, and thinking. When she spins the chair around, she notices that the printer output tray is full. She reaches over and picks up the final manuscript in the Kelp series she'd completely forgotten about. It's titled *Eve*.

She has until the end of the day to be out of the building and they won't deactivate her security access until tomorrow morning due to system delays, so she decides that she may as well read and dispose of it now. Besides the contract, she refuses to bring anything with Baxter's name into her and Bryce's home.

She sits back in the comfy leather sofa and turns the first page with anxious fingers. She slips off her shoes and kicks her feet up on the arm rest.

As the plot twists and thickens, her heart pounds. It's like reading a diary. Eve is clearly Zia and Kelp is madly in love with her, but that's just what he's convinced his crazy psychopathic mind of. He's incapable of love because he's a killer! She zips and speeds through the steamy story, anxious for the ending.

As with any closing book in a series, it explores Kelp's past, explaining how he became the dark demon he is. He initially grew up in rural Australia. He wasn't sexually or physically abused. He was simply a confused child who grew angry and resentful because he was jealous of his sister. He was bullied because he was highly intelligent. His childhood friend, Jason, always came to his defense.

Once they moved to the United States, Kelp slowly shed any mental personality traits belonging to Julius and adapted a new identity. He began referring to himself as Richard. Jason laughed it off, but never knew the most scandalous secret of all. Richard was in love with Jason.

They grew up with Jason never being the wiser of Kelp's dual thoughts and actions. Jason turned a blind eye when Kelp's mother and sister died under mysterious circumstances and even when their neighborhood female friends and classmates went missing. Kelp/Richard never made a move on Jason, but he hated every girlfriend Jason ever had.

As Kelp grew into a man, he became dedicated to the extinction of the subhuman race. Kelp spared Jason's life only because he couldn't bear to permanently bid his first love goodbye. His heart still had minuscule soft fragments at that point. He went off to college and Jason joined law enforcement.

Over the years, Kelp became a successful billionaire and Jason moved up the ranks at his job. With every life Kelp ended, a fragment went with it, one piece at a time until he felt no more. With his transition complete, he shifted his focus to solidifying his plan.

Utilizing his massive wealth and power, he concocted a fool-proof plan of annihilation. He'd compiled the data and wrote dozens of textbooks to be circulated among the survivors, explaining why the subhuman must remain limited and controlled at all times.

He was ready to implement, but there was just one problem. He knew that he required one, and only one, to rebirth the limited female population. After coming into the Mitochondrial Eve data, he knew that it was nothing but divine intervention; confirmation that his plan was that of the one true Creator.

Soon after he began his quest, he eliminated hundreds upon hundreds of women of African descent. Women from the United Kingdom, Iraq, Iran, India, Brazil, Haiti, Morocco, Africa, Qatar, Jamaica, and of course, the United States. Middle Eastern women were trained to be far too subservient to rule alongside a King. British women were beyond lesson. African-American women viewed him as a devil. Until, Eve.

Kelp first sees her face on a bulletin board advertisement. Her exotic physical features initially deter him—presuming she's of partial European descent. He conducts countless web inquiries, discovering as much as he can about her. Her likes, dislikes, passions, and dreams. Most gathered from social media sites.

His open door to meet her comes when she lectures interns at his annual corporate Upward Bound program. He disguises himself as an intern and they develop an intense relationship.

Zia swallows as she reads, but her throat is as gritty as a sandbox. She grabs a bottle of water from the mini fridge with her eyes glued to the pages. She takes a sip and continues reading.

Though Kelp meets her first, she allows herself to become infatuated by another at her job. Kelp reasons that it's because of their close proximity to one another. Kelp lives at a greater distance. This doesn't deter him. With the passage of time, Kelp's relationship with Eve matures and he becomes convinced she's the *one*.

However, her distinct European features give him pause and he decides that he must know her origin. One night as she sleeps, he swabs the inside of her cheek with a DNA applicator and delivers it to his medical lab in Qatar. Once the results come back 99% Sub-Saharan African, he ceases his search and becomes attached to Eve.

Meanwhile, Eve is in love with her coworker Brandon across the country. This creates a love triangle between the three of them. Eve is torn between Brandon's wholesome goodness and Kelp's fiery passion. Eventually, Eve chooses Brandon and ceases communication with Kelp. This sends him into a murderous rage.

When Eve visits for a business meeting, he seizes the opportunity to win her back. Though, not honorably. He cleverly stages an attack and then rushes in to save her. As planned, she runs back into his arms and they resume their relationship.

Kelp then systematically eliminates all viable threats to Eve's enslavement, beginning with her family and friends. He blackmails her, exposes her, and she loses her job. He sends Brandon a package containing videos and photographs of Kelp and Eve having torrid sex—hoping that Brandon would break her heart and she would choose Kelp by default.

Unfortunately, Brandon forgives Eve and their relationship progresses. Learning of Eve's plan to marry Brandon, Kelp decides to kill them both and choose a second best to carry out his plan. He takes a private jet across country. He eliminates Brandon first. He then slips into Eve's place of work, and—Zia gasps!

It's like reading her own life story. Jason is Detective Barnes, Brandon is Bryce, and Julius Kelp is Richard…as Baxter is Dwight Fairfield's alter ego. She needs to get home and reach out to Detective Barnes. She'd sent him the flash drive some time ago. He should've made an arrest already. Now she has to sit around wondering and waiting for a mad man to come and murder her and Bryce.

She doesn't have to wonder how Baxter could get into Fargo Tower because she's certain he still owns some portion of the company in some way. If not that, then he has an old contact of some sort. She wastes no more time wondering, she jumps up, anxious to get the hell out of there and never come back.

She slips on her shoes and tosses the manuscript into the garbage— saving only the last few pages of the ending. She attempts to call Detective Barnes, but her phone is dead. She picks up the desk phone, but she doesn't have a line out anymore. Her extension has been deleted.

She finally glances up at the nightfall, grabs her box, and heads out. It's quiet and the building is empty. She peeks at her watch. It's past ten. She hastens her stride, but the box slows her down a bit. She presses the button to summon the elevator.

Ding.

The door opens.

"I've been calling you."

She freezes and her heart leaps from her chest. She turns to her right and there he is, wearing all black. Most notably, black gloves.

She trembles, and her words come out shakier than she'd like.

"I…I've been busy with trying to get everything in order."

"Zia, don't do that. Don't lie to me. You've been avoiding me. Why?"

She nearly swallows her tongue as she chokes over the words.

"I couldn't just leave. As you can see, I just quit my job and I…"

"You were what? Going to move to New York with me?"

"Eventually, once I closed all of these open chapters." She chuckles nervously as he casually approaches.

He reaches out to touch her and she inadvertently flinches.

"You're afraid of me."

"Of course not."

"Here, let me help you with that."

Baxter removes the box from her grasp and presses the elevator button again. The door opens immediately. He holds it ajar and she enters. They descend in silence. She nervously glares at the black gloves on his hands.

Winter doesn't explain them away because this is Los Angeles, not New York. She knew this day might come. While they descend, she prays, asking for forgiveness before the end comes.

The elevator opens. She exits first.

Chapter
TWENTY-THREE

ZIA STRUGGLES TO open her eyes. It's either very dark or she's lost her vision. Her fingers tingle and she's lying on her left side. She can't move her legs. Her wrists and legs are stuck. There's a cotton cloth in her mouth that's making it very hard for her to breathe.

As her vision slowly comes into focus, she scans the area. They're in Fargo Tower's utility room. She knows because the supplies are branded.

Baxter is sitting in the corner. Their eyes connect. He walks over.

"Zia," he coos in a gentle tone while caressing her hair. "I'm not going to hurt you. The only reason I bound and gagged you was because I knew you wouldn't hear me out otherwise."

She's convinced that whatever comes out of his mouth will be a lie. She chokes on the cloth as it inches closer to the back of her throat.

He removes it and she gasps for air.

"Zia, don't scream. Be smart. I'm going to untie you, but you must hear me out. That is my only condition. Do you agree to my terms?"

"Yes."

"I saw the pages of my manuscript inside of your box. I'm sure you must think the very worst of me. So, I'll start by being completely honest with you. I have taken the lives of several women."

Since he began with a truth, she's interested in where he could possibly go from there.

"I once believed that *all* women were a threat to mankind. That all women shared a predisposed genetic defect causing them to be wicked. I believed the world should be cleansed of that evil, in its entirety. With no exceptions. That was my personal belief. But God came to me. Showed me that woman, like man, though horribly misguided, were his creation and worthy of preservation. Just not all of them."

"He showed me the Earth required a fresh start. Just as the flood had cleansed the Earth before, it was time for another. He guided me to the beginning. If all women weren't meant to perish, then the one remaining to repopulate society must have the ability to produce all of the different genetic variations of us."

"Mitochondrial Eve. Ancient Yorubian Mitochondrial Eve. The one that science has proven time and again, possessed the ability to birth men and women of all races. Without her, the world would remain plagued, because it couldn't be restarted. When God sent you to me, it was His answer. There are many portions of my plan you may not like. But as a Queen, you must learn to accept casualties of war. That many must fall for the survival of the human species."

She gulps.

"You're the key, Zia. Don't you see that? I would never harm you or allow any harm to come to you. If you die, we all die. You're our Genesis."

He truly believes all of what he says. Zia refuses. He's a confessed murderer, but if she makes light of his carefully laid plans, she has no doubt he'll kill her too. She decides to play along.

"If I am Queen…"

"You are."

"Then why am I a slave? A Queen cannot be both." She shoves her bound wrists at him.

He rushes over and unshackles her. She massages the sore spots. He lovingly massages her ankles.

"You are not a slave. Don't ever refer to yourself as a lowly thing. But I am your King. As such, you must obey my commands."

She'd deciphered as much from his speech.

"But King and Queen rule together. You've made plans without me. Plans I still know nothing about." She continues thinking on her feet to keep him calm.

"I'll show you everything. If something absolutely must be changed, then we change it together. But one thing cannot change."

"What's that?"

"These vile subhumans cannot continue to breed more evil into this world. It must be cleansed. There must be a fresh start. That is God's will."

"Then, as Queen, no one is more capable of selecting who shall survive The Cleanse."

"Oh yes, of course."

She feels much like an actress auditioning for a role, but her goal is to get out of the utility room.

"I need to use the restroom," she states.

His facial expression twists into a darker and more suspicious one.

"I haven't emptied my bladder since this afternoon. If I hold it any longer, I'll develop a urinary tract infection."

He swiftly moves out of her way.

"No, no. Your temple is far too important. Go ahead."

She dismounts the counter with his hands around her waist, guiding her safely to the floor. As she places her hand on the door knob, he reminds her of just how serious he is.

"Zia, I'm trusting you. Don't try anything crazy. You're too important to me."

She understands the implication.

"I'll be right back, my King."

His entire face brightens, and he relaxes his posture. He also knows the vacant building is secured, and her security access has been revoked.

She walks down the hallway until she reaches the restroom. She forgot she needs her badge to unlock the door. She tries her luck and twists the knob anyway. To her surprise, it opens. He must've deactivated the system.

She turns on the faucet, leans over the sink, and starts hyperventilating.

Without warning, there's a hand over her mouth.

"Shhhhh."

She looks into the mirror and sighs at Jazz. They back into the stall and lock it.

"Jazz? I've been calling you all day," she whispers.

"I've been in touch with Uncle Johnny. He was supposed to have my dad in custody already. I naturally assumed he'd show up here. Then I remembered your hard-headed ass didn't resign and clean out your desk when I told you to."

They whisper as low as possible.

"He's completely lost his mind. I can't go back in there. We've gotta get out of here."

"We're going to try to sneak out through the garage. The front door is rigged."

"He has my keys," Zia informs her.

"I have my car."

"Okay."

"Follow me. We should be fine if we don't make any noise. Let's go."

Zia removes her loud heels before they creep out of the restroom. They look east, west, and south before heading north. Just as they reach the staircase entrance, a rattling noise startles. Baxter flies out of the utility room.

Detective Barnes is pushing on the revolving door, expecting it to be unlocked like a moron. Now they're trapped between a locked entrance and a seething murderer.

"Zia? I trusted you. What are you doing with Jazmine?" he demands with pleading eyes.

He is truly hurt by her betrayal. She lowers her head.

"Dad, just let us go."

"Jazmine, this doesn't concern you. Just let her go and we'll leave."

They slowly inch backwards until Zia's palm clutches the handle leading to the staircase.

Baxter inches forward with something in his hand. They can't make out what it is. Detective Barnes shatters the glass and enters while shouting instructions at Baxter. His gun drawn.

"Freeze, Dwight! You're under arrest for the murder of Rebecca Horton. Put your hands up, man. Please, don't make me shoot you. I don't want to shoot you, Dwight."

Dwight emerges, stealing the light from Baxter. No longer feeling a soft spot for his childhood love, Dwight accepts the task at hand. Without warning, a shot rings out. Detective Barnes falls backward, flat against the hard-white tile. His left leg breaks from the shallow fall. His head tilts Zia and Jazmine's way. There's a tiny red spot on his cheek, near the bridge of his nose that drips onto the linoleum.

Jazmine rushes to his side and sobs over him.

"Uncle Johnny, no, no."

Dwight is now only a few feet from them. When he holds out his hand, Baxter reemerges. So much sincerity oozes from his eyes, that if Zia didn't know he was a killer, she would believe him.

"Come with me, my Queen, please. You're not safe here."

"But, you just killed him. He didn't need to die."

"He would've stopped us. Dwight had no choice."

Zia hesitates, crying, and trembling.

"Zia, please! We don't have any more time. You don't know the whole story of what's going on here. Come with me!"

She swallows her nerves and takes a small step towards him. When she does, there's another gunshot. Baxter falls sideways. His gun skids across the floor. Jazz walks closer and stands directly over him.

"You killed my mother, you sick son of a bitch."

She shoots him two more times in the head, then drops the gun.

Zia slumps to the floor, blanketed in shock. Red and white flashing lights appear at some point. Law enforcement personnel file into the building, though she doesn't fully register what's transpiring. Her thoughts explode into a fiery ball of suspicion that swirls around the best friend she thought she'd known so well.

Unable to process even one more conspiracy at the moment, she closes her eyes, eager to awake from what she prays is a nightmare.

One
YEAR LATER...

IT'S BEEN A year since the nightmare that was Dwight Fairfield came to an end. A long but rewarding year. Jazz sold Spark. Neither Zia, Jazz, nor Bryce wanted to be associated with that place ever again. Bryce and Zia held a proper wedding ceremony in Oahu, Hawaii. It was quite beautiful.

Bryce received his full inheritance, as did Jazz. The two conglomerates finally joined forces, ending decades of business rivalry. LFS' drugs were thoroughly inspected and cleared. After Bryce and Zia discovered they were pregnant, Bryce moved Turner into a CEO position at one of Weingart's subsidiaries to placate him and stave off any vengeful plans he might've formed after losing hold of Weingart. To everyone's surprise, Turner's attitude flourished afterwards.

Zia, Bryce, and Jazmine decided that the wisest thing for them to do was to start all over with something completely separate from their family corporations. Fairfield Fink Literary Law Firm was born. Or FFL, for short. They purchased an office building in a prime Santa Monica location. Having secured dozens of clients already, they expect to turn a profit within the first year. They're all excited about the future.

Zia waddles around the lobby, ensuring that every furnishing is perfectly in its place before the grand opening. Her loving and protective guard buddy, Bugs, is on her heels at every turn. Being five months pregnant has shifted her center of gravity quite a bit and her lower back is killing her. She drops a pen on the floor. She attempts to retrieve it, but quickly gives up. She doesn't think she'll ever get used to the slow disappearance of her feet.

Jazz is busy directing the assistants. She's quite tenacious when it comes to business details. That's what makes them ideal partners. Bryce kisses Zia and rubs her belly.

"How's my son doing?"

"Uh, well gee babe, I'm fine. Thanks for asking."

He chuckles.

"The love of my life is being stubborn right now, forfeiting her priority privileges. Can you please sit down somewhere? Jazmine and I can handle it from here."

"I'll call it quits in a bit. I just need to do one last walkthrough."

"I'm going to hold you to that," he teases.

He kisses her belly and smacks her bottom before rejoining Jazmine and the others. Seeing them work together warms Zia's heart. Her husband and her best friend working as a team and getting along is what she had hoped for when she'd first fallen in love.

Memories of Baxter appear as she stares stoically at Jazmine, but they quickly fade. She's not sure how long she'll experience the echoes, but she prays she has it in check before the baby is born. Something tells her that Baxter will always be a part of her, no matter how horrible he was.

She begins her walkthrough. Starting from the back offices, she works her way forward, twisting knobs, and scanning each room from ceiling to floor. She smiles at each assistant that she passes. She exits the building, checks the mail, and decides to get a view of the front on her way back.

Jazz and Bryce are hanging the grand opening banner.

The warm Fall breeze tousles her curly mane, filling her ruffled chestnut dress with air. She watches them in awe, overflowing with appreciation. After all that they've endured, they did it together, as a team. She's never been so proud.

She fiddles with the keys attached to the rainbow-colored coil on her left wrist while wobbling approximately thirty feet across the parking lot, to the mailbox. Her steps pull memories of the day she'd returned from the Fire Pages event and had walked into Spark with the confidence her life would change that day. It did.

With her back to FFL, she unlocks the box and removes the paper contents. Bills, ads, and notices. Near the bottom of the stack is a semi-rigid white envelope addressed to Zia Lennox—not Fink. There's no return address. She doesn't bother opening anything, she just walks back to the front door, preferring to live in the moment.

Bryce jogs over and kisses his sentimental wife. His eyes speak only of the love in his heart. He tenderly wraps his arm around her, then bends over to talk to the baby.

"You see that? One day that'll be all yours."

"Don't scare him, babe. Now he may never want to come out."

They share a laugh and a multitude of kisses. She clutches the unopened mail in her left hand. Bryce laces his fingers through her right, the same way he did the first time he told her he loved her. Together, they gaze upon the perfect new empire they've built from the ashes of their imperfect love.